Sugar Daddy?

By B J Gallimore

As told by
Debbie Wilson

Grosvenor House
Publishing Limited

All rights reserved
Copyright © B J Gallimore, 2024

The right of B J Gallimore to be identified as the author of this work has been asserted in accordance with Section 78 of the Copyright, Designs and Patents Act 1988

The book cover is copyright to B J Gallimore

This book is published by
Grosvenor House Publishing Ltd
Link House
140 The Broadway, Tolworth, Surrey, KT6 7HT.
www.grosvenorhousepublishing.co.uk

This book is sold subject to the conditions that it shall not, by way of trade or otherwise, be lent, resold, hired out or otherwise circulated without the author's or publisher's prior consent in any form of binding or cover other than that in which it is published and without a similar condition including this condition being imposed on the subsequent purchaser.

This book is a work of fiction. Any resemblance to people or events, past or present, is purely coincidental.

A CIP record for this book
is available from the British Library

ISBN 978-1-80381-884-9
eBook ISBN 978-1-80381-968-6

Debbie Wilson is not the real author. Debbie is a fictitious character that has no resemblance to anyone, living or dead, with that name. This applies to all the other characters in *Sugar Daddy?* All names, places, and events are totally fictitious.

Sugar Daddy?

Hi. I'm Debbie Wilson.

You know what? In the summer I, like, met the man of my dreams; Stevie.

He might be as old as my mum, but, like, oh my God, he is just sex on legs!

Fit. Handsome. And drop dead sexy.

Join me as I tell the story of how we met and, like, fell in love and the roller coaster of the most exciting couple of weeks of my life.

Chapter One

God, I'm sexy.

Me. Debbie Wilson, age twenty, size sixteen and, like, dead sexy.

It's Friday night and, finished work for the weekend, I'm out to let my hair down. With any luck it'll be letting my knickers down later. Checking myself in the ladies' loo mirror, the image coming back is looking good. Sexy good. I check my hair, my mascara, and just a touch-up of lippy then pout at myself in the mirror, practising a kiss. *Or is that practising a blow job?* I run my hands down my sides to straighten my dress; nice and short tonight. I plump up my boobs like you would a pillow before laying down your head, and I'm, like, that's a cleavage to die for!

I might not be a perfect ten like Haze and Jules – in fact, Haze is probably an eight – who are out there in the bar getting the first drinks of the night in; the first of many to come. But some guy is gonna, like, hit the jackpot tonight. Because, God, I'm sexy.

I'm not really sure why they chose to start the night off in this place. It's not, like, the best drinking hotspot in town. It's called The Jungle because it used to be called The Cherry Orchard and got nicknamed The Jungle by the regulars. It's now called The Cherry Tree – an attempt to do away with the nickname. But, like, old habits die hard. So I'm told. Like, before my time.

Putting my lipstick back in my handbag, I make my way into the bar, but Hazel and Julie are nowhere to be seen.

They're not at the bar getting drinks in, and I'm gagging for one now. I check round the corner to see if they're sitting round there. No. I look through the pub, but I can't find them anywhere. It's busy, I can see lots of men here. But I've looked everywhere, and they don't smoke so it's not like they're gonna be outside. I'll take a look anyway.

I walk straight out the front door, look round to the left, and round the corner of the pub. No, not there. Then, turning on my heel to look down the street and, like, CRASH! straight into this guy. I bash into him so hard, like a rugby tackle, that I nearly knock him over, only saving him from falling into the road by quickly grabbing his fleece jacket and yanking him back. But his weight makes me stumble, and we're both, like, trying to stop ourselves from falling over, his arms wrapping around me. He's strong and manages to steady us both.

'Whoa!' he calls out. 'Crikey. I know my horoscope said a dark beauty would fall into my arms, but that's not what I expected,' he says when we're balanced, and he loosens his hold on me.

'Sorry, sorry,' I reply, all embarrassed and not looking him in the eye, although I'm still holding onto him. 'I was just, like, looking for my friends. I seem to have lost them.'

He went, 'Your friends? What, two skinny girls, all short skirts and long legs, high heels?' I just nod, still looking around and not at him. 'Well, when I say high heels, they were carrying their shoes in their hands, running down the road laughing and hiding round the corner,' he says, pointing down the road with his thumb over his shoulder. 'They'll be long gone by now. I suggest you choose your friends a little more carefully if that's them.'

Running off down the road laughing? I'm, like, pretty cut up by that; he can't be serious. But hang on. Did he say 'dark beauty'? I finally look up at him for reassurance and do a double take and, oh my God, like, wow, he's handsome! Ok, a bit older than me, late thirties, no more than forty, but he's dead fit, and I'm looking straight at some high-class eye candy. I'm like, wow! I could pull his face down to meet mine and snog him right now. Suddenly I'm, like, all of a quiver and become a bit flustered and start babbling.

'They, they wouldn't leave me, not on my own, like. They're my besties, we're always out together at the weekend. Are you sure it was them? I can't believe it...' I almost start to cry, and he puts a consoling arm around me. I can feel the goose bumps appearing on my skin.

'Calm down, you'll be alright. Just go and look for them.'

'On my own?' I ask incredulously. *Are you having a laugh?*

'Well, where would you normally be going, anyway?' he asks. 'Just go there.'

'Yeah.'

'Can I have my jacket back now, please?' he says, gently taking the lapel of his fleece from my hand.

'Sorry.' I finally let go of him. But letting him go is not what I want. He begins to move away. 'No. Wait!' I practically snatch at his coat again. 'Don't leave me.' That was a bit pleading. 'Er... er...'

He raises his eyebrows at me. 'I'd love to stand around and chat all night but, er, what do you expect me to do? I'm not some knight in shining armour or private detective.'

'Just stay with me. Like, I dunno. Help me to look for them or something.' I look up at him, all puppy-eyed. I said some boy was gonna hit the jackpot and I'll be letting my knickers down, and here is this guy... like, sex on legs, a real hottie. I arch my back to make my cleavage more prominent, but he don't seem to have noticed it yet.

'Right. Ok. So let's see,' he says, mulling it over. 'You actually want me to escort you around the bars around town looking for "your friends",' he says, air quoting, 'and then what?'

'Yeah.'

'Yeah, what?'

'Take me around the bars and look for Haze and Jules.'

'Oh. They have names, these friends of yours? Look, I'm not saying those girls I saw are your friends, and I'm not exactly dressed for a night on the town, even if I wanted to. Jeans. Trainers, you know?' he says, pointing at his feet. 'I could go home and change, if that's what you'd like. But then I'll come back and you're nowhere to be seen. You must think I was born yesterday.'

'I'll come with you,' I quickly suggest – perhaps a little too quickly.

'Erm…' *He's not losing his bottle now, is he?* No, perhaps he's married. *You stupid idiot, Debbie.* Of course he's married. Got no ring on his finger, though; I'd already made a point of looking. But he does have what looks like a wedding ring on his right hand. And if he is married, why is he out on his own?

'No. Ok. Of course, I understand. You're not no knight in shining armour. I'll let you go. Sorry for giving the wrong impression.' No. He hasn't noticed my cleavage.

He begins to walk off, but as I watch him walk away, I'm like, *come on, Debbie, don't let him slip through your fingers so easily.* I run after him and take his arm.

'If you won't let me come with you, then I'll be waiting.'

'No you won't,' he says matter of factly as we continue walking, and he bleeps open a car with his fob. I let go of his arm and move to the passenger door and open it. He looks at me across the car roof and I give him a sweet smile and get in the car. He gets in and closes the door, but I've still got mine open. 'You don't know me from Adam, and you want me to drive you to my home—'

'Adam who?'

He shakes his head. 'Have you got a mobile? Call your friends. Find out where they are, and I'll take you.' He begins to drive off before I've even closed the door.

I make a call, let it ring a few times, and cut the call. 'She's not answering,' I say.

'Well, call the other one.'

'Haze never brings her mobile. She don't carry a handbag.'

Silence.

I start up the conversation again. 'Debbie,' I offer my hand.

He stops at the junction and, before pulling onto the road, he turns to me. 'Steven. Steven Taylor,' and he shakes my hand. I'd rather have a kiss.

'Well... If this is what you want to do. Look, here's my mobile phone,' he says, passing it to me. 'I can't make any guarantees about my trust, but take it as insurance.'

I take it gingerly, not really sure how to take what he's saying. Yes, I'm brave to be putting myself in this position, yet somehow, I feel ok in Steven's presence. I've been with many a boy at the drop of a hat – or the drop of my knickers – for a one-night stand, so this isn't much different.

'So, how come you want to go out with a bloke old enough to be your dad?'

'I ain't got a dad.' I say with a bit of disdain in my voice. Perhaps too much, but...

'What d'ya mean, ain't got a dad? Everyone's got a dad; it's how it all works. Boy meets girl and everything...'

'I don't mean I ain't got a dad. It's, like, he's just a waste of space. Did the dirty on me mum and left us. Don't hear from him at all. Subject ends,' I tell Steven very abruptly.

'Ok.' A pause. 'Then I'm old enough to be your mum.'

'She's forty-six,' I tell him.

'There you are then. She's younger than me.'

Bit more silence. As he's concentrating on driving, I'm thinking about what he's just said. *Older than Mum?* I'd thought forty at a push, but I daren't ask.

'So, where're you off to on your own, like, not dressed up and somewhere to go?' I ask, re-breaking the ice.

'I've been to the cinema. I was just on my way home.'

'What you been to see?' I ask conversationally.

'James Bond. I'm not much into going to the pictures. Films are all too violent or too much sex these days, but I like a bit of Bond. Contradiction or what? But I remember my grandad took me to see my first James Bond, *On Her Majesty's Secret Service.* You know, the one with George Lazenby. Didn't really get it; too young, I suppose. I was about seven or eight, but I enjoyed the chases and stuff. And that was it. Hooked. But it's all a bit unbelievable, you know. They get an actor in his late thirties at least, and ok, he's handsome and got chiselled looks.'

I'm looking at him as he chunters on. *Have you looked in the mirror lately?*

'Then they get some young, barely-half-his-age actress to be the Bond girl. Not the real world, is it?' he adds.

I'm listening intently as it seems to be his specialist subject and he's keen to talk about it. But 'On Her Majesty's what'? *No Time To Die*, *SPECTRE,* or *Skyfall*, even *Casino Royale* at a push, but George who-zenby?

'What about non-violent films, like a rom-com for instance?' *Is that an attempt to prompt a date?* 'I like a good chick flick.'

'Well, yeah. But being on my own, it's not the first thing that's gonna catch my eye. But I suppose in the right situation I might go and see something. I do like things that can make me laugh. Never say never.'

On his own? Sounds promising.

He slows the car and pulls up, switching off the engine. Releasing his seatbelt, he slightly leans toward me and points out of the passenger door window. 'Here we are.'

I undo my belt and climb out of the car then allow him to lead me along the path to his door. *Nice place*, I'm thinking, but somehow I can't say it as I'm a little trepidatious about going in. There has been plenty a time that I've been with a boy on a whim for a one-night stand but, like, usually it's them coming back to my place, not theirs. Yes, I do trust him, but why? I've, like, only just met him, and ok I have been with boys before on instinct, but this is different. He's old enough to be my mum, for one thing.

But what if he's like only got one thing on his mind? Well, isn't that the case with me? He doesn't seem to be taking any notice that I've gone quiet, but just politely invites me in.

'Come in, make yourself comfortable. Would you like a drink? I don't have much, but I've got some beer in the fridge, a limited choice of spirits, vodka, gin, or you can have a cup of tea if you like.'

'Can I have a vodka? With some Coke, please.'

'No problem.' He goes out to the kitchen as I take a seat on the sofa and make myself comfortable. I cross my legs, a bit of thigh on show. He brings me my drink which I take gratefully. Even got ice in it. I don't think he's noticed my legs.

'I won't be a couple of minutes. Just a quick change and I'll be with you. Call a taxi; there's a number on my mobile under T in the directory. See you in a minute.'

I ask him his address and call the taxi. That done, I begin my drink and take a look around the room. I take a look at some CDs on a shelf by his hi-fi. *I mean, CDs?* Queen. The Who. Elton John. Yeah, old enough to be my mum. The fact that his favoured music is all on CD shows his age.

There are some pictures on the walls, one of him in sportswear holding a trophy of some sort. That probably explains why he looks so good for his age. There's one of what I assume is a family group with his siblings all in sportswear and then, turning around… oh my God. It's him, a bit younger but, like, in a wedding photo with, obviously, his wife. *He IS married!* I nearly spill my drink. *Oh no, what have I done?* It's not even, like, going off with a man who's not single – done that before. But, like, I'm in his house. His missus might walk in any second and…

I put down my drink and make my way to the stairs and call up to him. 'Steven?' No reply. So I begin to climb the stairs and call him again. 'Stevie?'

He pops his head around the bedroom door. 'Yes, Debbie. What's up? Did you call the taxi? Is it here?'

I look him straight in the eye. 'Are you married?'

'No…' he replies. He seems about to say something else, but before he gets to say anymore, I ask him about the photo.

'There's a wedding photo with you in it downstairs.'

'Yes, that's me and my beautiful wife on our wedding day, but sadly I'm now widowed. Couple of years now. It's not always easy to deal with, but life goes on, as they say.'

Whoops. Debbie 'feet first' Wilson stumbles in again. 'I'm sorry, I didn't realise,' I mutter, looking down at the floor.

'Of course not. And I'm sorry to you, too. I should've told you instead of leaving you in my living room without warning or explanation. I mean, it's not like I am married, but you just came with me. You're actually the first girl I've invited into my home for a very long time. Not practised enough, sorry.'

'Is that your wedding ring?' I ask, pointing at the ring on his right hand.

He nods. 'I can't not wear it, but I am officially single, so I put it on this finger instead,' he says, holding up his hand. 'Never say never.'

'Is that your catchphrase?'

'What?'

'Never say never?'

He just grins and shrugs his shoulders.

I look down at him sitting on the edge of his bed and smile. I sit down next to him; he doesn't seem to mind. I'm getting the opinion that since his loss there have been no women in his life, and that I am probably the first one to, like, try and connect with him.

Looking at him gives me even more reason to smile. Some nice dark trousers and a dark shirt, even a tie, loosely tied. His hair is gelled and tousled, and, like, I just want to run my fingers through it, mmm. And he's just putting on his shoes, the trainers ditched for the night. What a transformation from the guy I... er, bumped into earlier. I really am, like, getting attracted to him. There is a cool and calm nature about him, his senior years extolling experience and maturity.

Not like some of the boys I end up with, all so dumb and immature, swearing and shouting in a football hooligan manner, drinking far more than they can handle but thinking that they can, believing they're the bee's knees in bed. And they all want a blow job, but when it's, like, their turn to go down – not happening. They've shot their bolt and it's, like, game over. Don't get me wrong, I love giving head. I'm, like, the world cock-sucking champion, but once they get their wish, they can hardly raise a proper hard-on because of, like, so much drink, and they promise they won't come in my mouth. Yeah, I take it on the chin when they say that. If they do – and, like, spitters are quitters – I always make sure there's some left on my lips and give them a good snog. So they literally get a taste of their own medicine, because once they're done they ain't good for nothing.

As we walk back downstairs, Steven hears his phone chime. 'Is that my mobile going off? It's probably the taxi.'

I check his phone, still in my handbag, and the taxi is waiting outside. As we leave the house and he locks up behind us, he turns to me and says, 'By the way. It's Steven, not Stevie.'

Chapter Two

The taxi pulls up right outside the Talk of the Town, and Stevie pays the driver before turning to me, saying, 'Wait there, I'll come round and help you out.' He climbs out of the car, walks round to my side, opens the door, and offers me his hand. *I'm like, wow! He's a gentleman, too.* Never, in all my dates, has a man done that.

I take his hand, and once on my feet I take his arm in both of mine and hug it close to me, looking up at him with a massive grin across my face. If anyone I know sees me tonight, *I'll* be the talk of the town.

We walk into the bar, where bouncers on the door greet us. 'Evening, sir, madam,' they say. *Crikey, I've never been called madam before. I'm liking this.*

It's a little later than normal, so the bar is quite full and rocking to the sounds and lights of the disco. People are on the dance floor, the place is in full swing, and I feel like a celebrity coming in from the red carpet. I've known Stevie just about two hours now, and we're on a first date and it's fantastic, overwhelming.

He asks what I would like to drink, and he gets me my usual tipple, my favourite alcopop with a straw. They say you get pissed quicker drinking through a straw, but with Stevie that's not really my intention. I want to enjoy this night. I've been with many boys, but not boyfriends as such. I've never really been taken out, this is all so new to me, and I'm loving every minute.

He has a beer, and we stand talking for a while. 'Is there anyone here that you know? What about Sharon and Tracy?'

'Who're Sharon and Tracy?'

'You know, your so-called friends. The fat slags, running off from you.'

I laugh at his description of Haze and Jules. 'Fat slags?'

'You must have heard of them from that comic? Sharon and Tracy, the fat slags.'

'Yeah, I know. Haze and Jules, Hazel and Julie. But you were, like, calling them skinny earlier,' I remind him.

'Skinny. Fat. Still slags to me for dumping you like they did. Ok, slags is a bit of a, er, degrading word, but, you know… Why do think they ran out on you? I get the impression that you go out with them regularly, so what happened tonight?' He's inquisitive but then shakes his head and waves his hand under his chin in a cutting motion. 'Do you wanna dance?' he asks, nodding in the direction of the dance floor.

'Yes, come on.' Putting down our drinks, I take his hand and almost drag him to the dance floor. I thought he'd, like, never ask. We dance at a slight distance apart at first, but then I take his hands in mine and pull him closer, and he immediately embraces me. We dance in hold for quite a while – I'm not really sure for how long, but I just enjoy the moment.

I then look up to him, all puppy eyes again, our faces close together, and we kiss. Even I didn't expect that, especially as the kiss becomes lingering. I feel his tongue just brush across my top lip, and I tingle from head to toe. The feeling is exquisite. *Who is this man? What is this magical spell he's casting upon me?* My very own James Bond. And I'm his Bond girl. *Oh, James.*

We break the kiss and I look up at him with what must be a twinkle in my eye; he certainly has one in his as he smiles down at me. 'Where did that come from? Do it again,' I say, and he does. *Oh my God.*

When the second kiss breaks I, like, need either a bed or a drink. I could make love to him here and now on the dance floor. Unfortunately, the only option is to go back to my drink. I must be grinning from ear to ear, because for just that second I have completely forgotten anything that has happened, what brought us two together and that he has really taken to me, too, and I feel all hot and sexy and happy. This man is, like, older than my mum – I don't know by how much – but he's all mine, and I want him.

'So, how old are you, Stevie?' I suppose I really need to know, though it's irrelevant right now. But he retaliates first.

'What about you? How old are you? We've already established that I'm old enough to be your mum. It is important, really, because remember we're only out to have fun and find the fat slags. I apologize for that affectionate reaction. I don't know what came over me. Instinct, I suppose, all in the moment. I can't even blame the drink when I haven't even finished my first one yet.'

What? 'Oh my God, don't apologize. I loved it. And I'm twenty,' comes my reply, 'and I'm a size sixteen. I was an eighteen till about four weeks ago, so I'm losing it.'

'And? Is that relevant? I asked your age not your dress size. Sounds to me like you're very conscious of your size and weight, but it makes no odds to me. You're an attractive woman, so be confident with yourself. Marilyn Munroe was a size sixteen.'

'Yeah,' I say with irony in my voice, 'an American sixteen. But my size doesn't matter to you, yet my age does. How come that's the more important matter?' I'm actually thinking about what he just said about only out to have fun and look for Haze and Jules.

'Well, if I'm old enough to be your mum, then you're young enough to be my daughter.'

'Yeah, but I can't shag my dad.' My instant reply brings a smile to his face and I'm like, I've cracked him with that one.

'You said you didn't have a dad.'

'You know what I mean.'

'I'm forty-seven. Does it still make no difference to you? That's twenty seven years between us, more than double your age.' He says it matter-of-factly.

'No.' My reply is also matter-of-fact. 'I'm, like, having a wonderful time, and it's the company that's the important thing.'

'Of course it is. And that's why your dress size is of no consequence. Half a woman's beauty is her personality, and you're also very pretty to boot.'

'Flattery will get you everywhere.' I smile at him suggestively and stroke his face. He smiles at my touch.

'Steven,' he says.

*

The night progresses and we find ourselves in Bar 8T; it's a retro bar with the disco playing mostly eighties music, hence the 8T. This is probably more up Stevie's street, but there are plenty of my age group in there, and we all know the words to the songs.

Some friends I know come into the bar and I rush up to greet them with a big hug. 'Amy, Marie, this is Stevie,' I make the introductions. 'Stevie, meet two of my better friends, Amy and Marie.'

He smiles and shakes both their hands. 'It's Steven,' he says, then looks at me as if to reiterate the point.

'Better friends?' asks Marie.

'It's a long story. I was, like, out with Haze and Jules and lost them,' I explain.

'They ran out on her earlier on. And then we bumped into each other, literally, and here we are.' Stevie seems keen to give his voice an airing and his opinion. I'm surprised he didn't use the fat slags tag.

'We saw them earlier in the Talk of the Town,' says Amy. 'Seemed to be getting tanked up with the boys sniffing round.' She rolls her eyes as she speaks. *Yeah, sounds like them.*

'We were in there ourselves earlier but didn't see them,' Stevie points out. 'We were perhaps too busy enjoying ourselves to notice.'

I blush a little at that, thinking about our 'first kiss', but I'm sure we would have seen them if they were there, too.

'It's a shame they weren't there, because I would like to meet them. I wanna know why they upset my Debs,' he continues.

'It's Debbie,' I tell him. But he did say '*my* Debs'.

'*Touché.*' He inclines his head to me as he speaks. 'Sorry, force of habit.' Then turning to Amy and Marie, he says, 'Come on, girls, I'll buy you a drink as well.'

'We're on Jagermeisters,' they say, almost in unison, almost in melody.

'Jagermeisters all round then.' He leaves us as he heads off to the bar, and we sit down at a table.

Once he's out of earshot, Amy is quick to ask, 'So, who's Stevie? Steven. Whatever. Is he your uncle or someone?'

'No, we're on our first date.'

'Debbie Wilson. A date? Oh wow!' Marie exclaims. 'But he's a bit old, ain't he? Dishy, yes. But—'

'He's not that old—'

'He's, like, old enough to be your dad,' points out Amy.

'No. He's old enough to be my mum,' I tell them, and we all laugh.

'But seriously, where'd you meet him? How long have you known him?' Amy asks.

'I met him outside the Jungle, would you believe, about eight-thirty,' I start to explain the events of the evening.

'Eight-thirty?' asks Marie, looking at her watch. 'What, tonight?'

'Yeah. I went in there with Haze and Jules, and they did a runner while I was in the ladies. Went out looking for them and bumped into Stevie. Like, love at first sight and all that.'

'You be careful. If he's that much older, he's only after one thing,' Marie points out.

'I hope so. Anyway, I've already been in his bedroom, and I've come out unscathed.'

'His bedroom? I mean, like, you know, fast mover!' Amy is impressed.

Just then Stevie comes back with the drinks – three Jagermeisters, and another beer for himself.

'There you are, ladies,' he says, handing out the drinks. 'Forgive me for not joining in with the Jagermeisters, but I'm a beer man. Pint of, in a glass. Not like you youngsters.'

Ouch! That hurt. I'm just trying to convince my friends that everything is ok, and he drops a bomb. A Jager-bomb.

'So, what have you been saying about me? My ears were burning terrible over there. Something good, I hope,' he asks, breaking a silence which obviously showed we had been talking about him.

Amy is first to respond. 'Debbie was saying you met at the Jungle. What's a nice guy like you doing in there, dare I ask?'

Stevie looks at me questioningly as if to say 'you didn't say I was in there, did you?'

'It's a gay bar,' he says. 'I'm sitting here with three gorgeous girls, but earlier I was in a gay bar? I don't think so. I was just walking by. It was Debbie that had been in there.'

Oh, cheers, Stevie. Thanks. I give him an ironic smile. 'He was in jeans and trainers, so we went back to his house so he could change. Scrubs up well, don't he?'

'Oh, so that's how you got into his bedroom,' Marie says, going in feet first, but you can see she's fishing.

There must be an obvious grin on my face as Stevie says, 'Debbie! First you tell them I'm in a gay bar, and then the next thing you're in my bedroom.'

'Don't worry your pretty little head, darling,' says Marie, and I scowl at her for the forwardness. Then she goes and winks at him. 'Your reputation's safe with us.'

*

Later, we're all four of us up on the dance floor together, and Stevie seems to be really enjoying himself with three girls all young enough to be his daughters. He's in his element, but this is, I suppose, his kind of music, Whitney Houston and everything. It's almost as if he is a regular lady killer, got good looks and a trim figure, flaunting it because he's still got it.

He's quite a mover on the dance floor for an old guy. *Oops. Did I really think that?* But it's me he's pulled tonight, and I make a physical reminder of it by pulling him close and re-enacting our brief bit of passion from earlier on. I then put my lips near his ear. 'Shall we move on?' I ask.

'Yeah, sure. What about these two?' he indicates Amy and Marie.

'I mean just us two. We can go to BJ's.' It's another bar that has a nickname. It's really called AJ's bar, but everyone knows it as BJ's. Can't think why. 'We can finish off the night there; they do cocktails. And I'm sure that's where we'll find Haze and Jules.'

'If that's what you want. The night is still young, and the world is your oyster.'

'I thought your intention was to meet them to wind them up.'

'To show them that the error of their ways led us to meet. I don't wanna sound too egotistic, but I don't necessarily wanna meet them, not tonight. The initial idea was to find them for you so you can carry on as normal. But I don't wanna spoil a good night, and I might not be very polite to them. But I'm happy with BJ's.'

'Good.' We break off from dancing and turn to Amy and Marie. 'We're gonna move on to BJ's.'

'Ok,' says Marie and turns to Stevie and kisses him on the cheek. 'Been lovely to meet you. Hope it's not too long before we do again.'

I look at her and, taking his arm and hugging it to me, I say, 'Yes, but he's all mine,' with a big smile on my face.

Amy comes forward to kiss him too, and while he's not looking, Marie gives me a very exaggerated theatrical wink and a thumbs up.

We make our way to the door, and I realise there's a big glass panel reflecting like a mirror. *Did Stevie see Marie's wink in the reflection? Whoops.* And I notice by looking at our reflection that he has a broad grin. Yes, he must have seen it. I look up at him and smile back.

Outside in the street, it's a cool evening and busy with people all walking in and out of the various bars and restaurants. It's almost midnight, and the town is alive with activity, everyone having a good time. And I am one of them. I really am having a wonderful time with my new man.

'Are you enjoying yourself?' I ask him.

'I'm having a lovely time. Not something I do on a regular basis. It's quite a twist of fate that we've gotten together. How about you?'

'The time of my life.' I say it with real enthusiasm, taking hold of his hand. 'What did you think of Amy and Marie?'

'Nice girls. Marie's a bit of a laugh, and I like her bright orange hair.'

'She's always dying it bright colours...'

'She carries it off well,' he says. 'I liked it.'

'Did you not think them sexy?'

'Why on earth do you ask such a question?'

'That skirt Amy was wearing was well short, and yet you hardly seemed to notice,' I point out.

'Well, I suppose so. She looked better from behind. Better still from behind me.' His sense of humour is, like, I dunno. 'I don't really look at young girls quite like that. Ok, an attractive girl is attractive whatever her age, and I suppose I can look. Just because I'm on a diet don't mean I can't look at the menu, but they're just not the type of girl that I could date.'

Boom! He's just dropped another bomb. Amy and Marie are, like, my age group, but he wouldn't date them, and yet here he is dating me. Isn't he? I consider asking him if he thinks I'm sexy, but think better of it. This man holds a magical spell over me, and I don't want the bubble to burst.

We get to BJ's – it's not far down the road from Bar 8T – and we walk straight in. Normally, there's a bit of a queue to get in, but tonight there's no problem. But once inside we find the place heaving with people. And it's rocking.

We make for the bar, and he buys us drinks. He has a short this time; a clear drink – vodka, gin, I dunno. He buys me another Jagermeister. That's my fourth tonight, as well as a few alcopops from earlier, and he's treated me to every single one. I haven't spent a penny. I'm not quite used to this, and I wonder if he's rich or something.

With it being so busy, we have to stand whilst we have our drinks. Someone comes up to us; must be a friend of Stevie's. 'Hello, mate,' says the newcomer. He's about Stevie's age and shakes his hand.

They chat for a brief moment, but I'm taking no interest, still looking round the bar to see if there's anyone I know, like Haze and Jules. Stevie's taken my hand again, and the slight tug on it tells me he's introducing me.

'This is Debbie. Debbie, meet Andy, we went to different schools together,' jokes Stevie.

'Hello,' I say sheepishly.

Andy smiles at me and says, 'Nice to meet you. You're a Debbie, too?' He's studying me with that look in his eye, the way older men do, all wishful thinking and egotistical, looking at my breasts, not my face. *Yeah, 'nice to meet my cleavage' more like. Get lost, grandad.*

It then dawns on me that Stevie is that age, too, but he hasn't looked at me in that manner, nor did he with Amy and Marie.

'Hold my drink, Stevie, just popping to the ladies.' I make my excuse to leave them to finish their conversation, and then he can concentrate on me again. I don't think he's gonna run out on me while I'm in there. I bet Andy is all inquisitive about me.

I can picture the scene…

*

'You sly old fox. How did you manage to pull a young bit of totty like that?' asks Andy, watching Debbie all the way to the ladies.

'I still got it, mate.' Stevie is all smiles, boasting.

'So, where did she crop up from?'

'She bumped into me, literally… It's the only way I'm gonna be meeting women these days at my age.'

'Yeah, you must be old enough to be her dad,' Andy points out. 'There must have been some magic spell you cast upon her.'

'Fate just brought us together. One of those chance meetings, and the rest is history,' Steven says.

'You old shark you, getting to shag a bird barely out of school uniform. Cradle snatcher. You should know better.'

'She's not that young, give me some credit,' Steven claims. 'And we're not shagging; we're just good friends.'

Andy has a wry smile. '"Just good friends?" Not that old chestnut. She's twenty if she's a day.'

'Yes, she is actually. That's why there's no shagging.'

'If she hadn't called you Stevie, I would've thought she was your daughter or something. She obviously looks up to you like a sugar daddy. She's besotted with you; I can see it in her eyes. That little twinkle…' Andy pinches his thumb and forefinger together to emphasise 'twinkle'.

'No. Like I said, just good friends, having fun.'

*

Another check in the mirror and a bit more lippy, then I leave the loo to rejoin Stevie. His mate is still with him, but on seeing me he gives Stevie one of those theatrical winks that Marie did to me earlier, pats him on the shoulder, and goes his own way.

'My turn to ask. My ears were burning in there, so what's he got to say?' I'm looking for some good answers. Not so much what Andy had to say – I can guess that – but Stevie's response.

'I said that we met by chance and we're having a great night out together,' he replies. 'He did comment on our difference in age, but he was complimentary to you.'

'I'll bet. Complimentary about my cleavage, more like. Couldn't keep his eyes off it. Didn't look at my face.'

'If you don't like men looking, why do you dress like it?' Stevie asks. I just harrumph. 'It's like when girls wear short skirts and then spend all day pulling at the hem. When you dress like that, it's for everyone to see, not just the boys you want to.'

I'm like, *why ain't you looking then?* But I decide to move on. 'So, what was he on about, saying I'm a Debbie, too?'

He pauses for a second before answering, then takes a deep breath he went, 'My wife was called Debbie. Debs. My Debs.'

Again! He's done it again; he keeps building me up then lets me down with a solid thump.

'Andy's not a close friend,' he continues, 'but he knew Debs and knows that she passed away. It's just a coincidence you share the same name. I'll try not to call you Debs again. Sorry.'

'Don't be sorry. A lot of people call me Debs,' I point out, though I'm thinking he's more sorry to his wife. 'You never said anything when I introduced myself.'

'No. But then we'd only just met, and it's not like it's a rare name, is it? There's more Debbies out there, I'm sure.'

'It's the best name,' I say with pride.

'I agree,' he says. But I think his pride is, like, about his wife. I finish my drink, and he takes my glass.

'Let's have another dance before we have any more, shall we? I like dancing with you. You put up with my clumsy moves.'

'You're not clumsy,' I tell him as we take to the dance floor. Then, tongue in cheek, I add, 'Much.'

'I heard that,' he says. 'Come here,' and he pulls me tight to him. That's more like it. I can feel him and smell him, his scent, his aftershave. I breathe it in and it's intoxicating. I'm like, mmm.

He leans in close to my ear. Just as I think he's about to bite it, and I'm all of a quiver in anticipation, he whispers to me, 'Don't look round just yet, but I think your two friends have just come in… if it's them girls from earlier.' I look up at him and he holds my face gently, but firmly enough to stop me turning to look. 'I might be wrong because I probably wouldn't recognise them. But two skinny girls have spotted us, and their chins are on their chests.'

In a dancing move, holding very tight to Stevie, I manoeuvre to be able to see who he's talking about. And sure enough, it's Haze and Jules. Fantastic! This is our chance. I wiggle my hips and begin to bend my knees and, looking into Stevie's eyes all the way, I slowly lower my body down in front of him until I'm crouched with my face right in front of his groin. There's only the material of his trousers separating his penis and my face, and I glance round to see Haze and Jules still watching.

I close my smiling eyes and breathe as though I'm sucking him, having the blow job of a lifetime for both of us. After a few seconds I open my eyes to see Haze and Jules still with the look of astonishment on their faces, and I wink at them and feign wiping away semen from the corner of my mouth with my middle finger before standing up again. There's a smile on my face, but when I'm back on my feet Stevie doesn't look impressed.

'Well done, Debbie, I think that's shown them,' he says in a sarcastic way. 'Don't forget, it's only pretend. We're just two acquaintances, and I'm escorting you.'

Only pretend? No, Stevie, this is for real. I'm just enjoying the moment too much to comment. We'll see later. My juices are flowing, my nipples erect, and I am feeling, like, exquisite tingling sensations all down below. This is all so crazy 'cause, like, I've never felt like this before. It's a completely new experience rushing through my veins, pumping my blood, making my heart pound. My head is light, and not just from the drink.

I'm having the time of my life, and I'm not pretending. Like, this is really happening. I've had many boys, and they're all loud and boisterous, but Stevie is the man of my dreams, and I'm gonna call him that: Stevie, my Stevie. He's kind, he's calm, and he dances too. I normally dance with the girls, don't dance with many boys; they just want to shout and get drunk. Stevie is everything they're not, and I'm melting to his charm.

So, he's older than me. *Like, so what?* And as I hold him tight to me, all heaving bosom and passion, I just want to rip off his clothes – now. He's so close I can feel the beginning of a hard-on, and I'm tempted to go down in front of him again. But I think better of it, because it would be far too tempting to actually pull down his zip and take him in my mouth. I'm salivating at the thought.

We stay on the dance floor for what seems like ages. I'm just intoxicated with his warm feel against my body in rhythm to the music, until he stops for the need to go to the gents. I do hope it's because he needs a wee and not, like, you know. No sooner has he left me than Haze and Jules are over like a shot.

'Who the hell is that?' asks Jules. 'And what're you doing going down on him like that?'

'I wasn't going down, that is for later. I was only pretending.' Of course, that's what Stevie meant by just pretending.

'We could see that, stupid. I wouldn't expect you to do it in the middle of a packed dance floor,' Jules again.

'It wouldn't stop you,' I remark. Jules blushes. She knows it's true; she probably has.

'So, come on then. Where did you pick him up?' Haze wants to know. 'And how old is he? Gotta be, like, forty.'

'And like sex on legs! He's my knight in shining armour, my very own James Bond coming to my rescue when you two bitches dumped me.' I'm feeling quite proud of myself, on the offensive, and these two are dumbfounded. And jealous, too, I bet. 'Where're your dates tonight? 'Spose you've had all the strays and ferals sniffing round, plying you with drink and then leaving them with no more than lipstick on their cheek. Or their cock.'

'We were only having a laugh, 'specially leaving you at the Jungle with all those gay boys,' says Jules, trying to placate me. 'We actually went back there to find you. Thought you'd be safe. But no,' she is getting aggressive, 'you turn up here pretending to have sex with some old grandad. We've been texting you and calling you all night, because we were, like, worried, 'specially when you didn't reply.'

Oh my God, I haven't looked at my mobile all night. I've been far too engrossed in enjoying myself, and it never even crossed my mind to text them. I made that call when Stevie first suggested it, and didn't bother trying again. I had more important things on my mind. I look at my mobile to see half a dozen missed calls and loads of texts.

Looking up at the girls, I reassert myself. 'Well, it won't be pretending later, and you two are just jealous. Go on, deny it. He's a hunk, and that's all there is to it.'

'We're not saying he's not a hunk or anything, but you only just met him tonight and, like, you're all over him like a rash. You don't know what he's like. Could be a sex attacker or something,' warns Jules.

'Well, he's had his chances if he is. But that's no different to all the other boys you wander off with.'

'But those boys are our age group, not some old boy looking for a quick bit of young to shag.' Jules is incredulous.

'I'm ok, he's ok. And stop saying he's an old boy. If it was Brad Pitt or somebody, you would be all over him, and he's just the same age,' I point out.

'Well, that's fair enough,' says Haze, 'but you could've let us know.'

'Bollocks!' I am incensed. 'Didn't fucking think about me like that earlier.'

I am saved by the bell as Stevie comes back from the gents and gestures to me to meet him at the bar to get another drink. I need one, right now, before I really blow my top.

I meet Stevie at the bar. 'Those two are in-fucking-credible.'

'I thought my ears were burning again, but I'm keeping clear of them because I still don't think highly of them about earlier. What did they say about it? Only having a laugh, I suppose.'

'They've been calling and texting all night. Said they were worried.'

'Didn't sound that way when Amy and Marie were telling us they'd seen them,' Stevie reminds me. 'Do you want a cocktail?'

'Yes, please. I'll have sex…' I pause, and Stevie takes up the line.

'…on the beach.'

'But we're miles from the seaside,' I say.

He orders drinks with the barmaid. She's a pretty little thing, barely dressed, lots of midriff on show and only strappy shoulders, but Stevie takes no notice.

'Oh,' I say, rummaging in my handbag. 'Let me pay this time. You've bought all the drinks all night…'

'Ok.' *He didn't think twice there.*

We sip at our drinks as we watch the fat slags flirting with some boys. Typical. *Crikey, even I'm, like, calling them the fat slags now.*

Then we see Jules dancing with one of the boys, and she crouches down in front of him just like I did to Stevie. And, oh my God, she's actually giving him a blow job! She's undone his trousers and taken out his cock right there on the dance floor. And she knows we can see her. The whole bar can, especially as the other boys in the crowd are cheering, attracting attention. She looks at us, still with his cock in her mouth.

Then, leaving him to put his erect cock back into his pants, she feigns wiping away semen from the corner of her mouth with her middle finger. Or was there really semen there? The 'lucky' boy is now a hero to all his friends, all chanting his name in football crowd style, going mental. 'Darren! Darren! Darren!'

I look at Stevie and he looks back down at me as if holding his breath. Then he lets it out in a laugh, and I start laughing, too.

Chapter Three

The night goes on and we dance a while, drink some more, and dance some more. It's getting late, and everything is winding down as we smooch through a couple of slow ballads. We begin to make our way out, and I look back: no sign of the fat... er, Haze and Jules. We walk hand-in-hand to the taxi rank and queue along with all the other revellers making their way home, all organised by the 'bouncers' to keep everyone in order.

'It's been a wonderful night, Debbie, thank you so much for some great company and a good old laugh,' Stevie says to me as we wait in line. 'Was it a good night for you?'

'It has been fantastic, it really has. Like, I'm so glad I bumped into you. And I'm glad I didn't knock you over or things could've been completely different.' I smile at him, my best puppy eyes again. 'But the night doesn't have to end here.'

We get to the front of the queue, and as we wait for the next car to pull up, Stevie takes me completely by surprise. 'To save you having a taxi all on your own, I will come with you back to your place then carry on home after dropping you off.'

'B-but I thought I might come back with you,' I almost plead.

'Oh. There a problem at home?'

'No. I just thought...'

'You can't come back to my house, I've only got one bed,' he says.

'Yeah.' *You don't get it, do you?*

'I can't do that. I'm sorry if you thought that I might, but I just can't. It's been a really great night. I haven't been out like this in ages. But beyond that, I can't go any further.'

'What's wrong, Stevie? Is it me? Don't you fancy me? All that close dancing and snogging must have meant something, surely?'

'It's because I'm old enough to be your mum, that's the reason,' explains Stevie. 'It has been fun, all the kissing and dancing. But...'

The next taxi pulls up. 'Why do you keep saying that?' I ask as we get in.

'Where do you live?' he asks, so that he can tell the driver.

'But—' I begin.

'I need to tell the driver.'

'Stevie—' Again I'm cut short.

'Come on, love, I ain't got all night,' says the driver.

I look down at my hands, knitting my fingers. 'It's 118 Calverton Drive.'

The driver pulls away, and Stevie tells him to take us there, drop me off, and then take him on to his house.

Ok. So, I've had a great night out, but it ends here. I regain my composure and accept it. There's no point in, like, getting angry or upset or anything. And not in front of the taxi driver. Stevie's been great fun and a gentleman, but perhaps an easy shag wasn't his aim.

'I'll go back home to Mum then.'

'You live with your mum?'

'Hmm. Why do you keep saying you're old enough to be her?' I ask again, getting back to the subject before we got in the car.

'Because when I said I was old enough to be your dad, you said drop the subject.'

'No.' I smile; it's back! 'I mean saying, like, that you're that old?'

'Ah, yes, well, that's why I can't go any further tonight. I'm just too old for you, and you're too young for me. The age gap is a problem for me, and I will have to just drop you off safely and live with some memories of a good night out.' Stevie does seem a little troubled, but I don't think he's ready to tell me everything.

I delve. 'Are you impotent?'

'No.'

'Are you celibate?'

'No.'

'Are you, er… we met outside a gay bar?'

'No.'

'So what then?' I need to know why this man has lavished me all night but doesn't want to come to bed with me for a night of sexual athletics, when it's there on a silver platter for him.

'I'm just old,' he sighs. 'There's a generation of difference between us, physically and mentally. And there are other issues, too, like I'm a widower. I, I just can't…'

'But you keep saying "never say never". Surely there's gonna be a time you meet someone new.' He must be troubled somewhere deep in his mind, or deep in his heart, and I respect that. If he can't tell me now, I'll find out in the future.

I'm not gonna ask to see him again, as he might say no. But I'll just meet him again, like, unannounced. I'm quite disappointed but I'm not cruel. He's been wonderful to me tonight, so I'll respect him now.

All too soon we are at my house. There are lights on. Mum is not still up, surely? It's, like, 3am.

SUGAR DADDY?

The car pulls up and I turn to him. 'Thanks, Stevie, it's been fantastic,' and I lean over, and we have a long embrace. No kiss, just a cuddle. Chubby girls cuddle better.

I open the door and climb out. Before I close the door, I look back and blow him a kiss. And although he smiles, I can see a sadness in his eyes, probably reflecting my own.

I walk up to the front door and let myself in, and it's not till I've almost closed the door that I see the car pull away. *Was he just making sure I was in safe, or was he just watching me till the very last second?* It's hard to decide which I'd prefer it to be.

*

Mum is up; I'm quite amazed. 'Hi, Mum,' I say when I find her sitting in the kitchen in her pyjamas, having a cup of tea.

'Hello, sweetheart. I couldn't sleep.' We hug and kiss. 'Have you had a nice time tonight? There's another cup in the pot.'

I help myself to some tea, and move to the fridge to get the milk. 'I've had a wonderful time. I met a man, and he was, like, a real gent. We spent the night cruising the clubs and dancing, it was fantastic. A magical time.'

Mum takes the cup from her mouth. 'A gent? Wow, that's not your usual standard.'

'Mum!' I'm almost shocked.

'It's usually some waif and stray, one night of lust and that's it. So, where is this gent, didn't you invite him in?'

'His name's Stevie and he's wonderful. I'm gonna see him again.' It's true, because I intend to, even though it's not arranged.

'And when are you going to bring him to meet me?' asks Mum.

Ah, I hadn't thought of that. How can I let her know he's older than her?

I sit down at the kitchen table and drink my tea, looking at my mum. She's beautiful, and I love her. She had a shit time with my dad, who was hardly at home, out drinking and womanising, like, all the time. Makes me think of some of the boys I meet. Before Stevie came along; but then he's a mature man. That was the problem with my dad. He never grew up from being a young drinker and bird-chaser. It made me think of that Darren in BJ's tonight that got his cock sucked by Jules.

He met my mum, had his twenty minutes of fun, got her pregnant with me and, like, went off, continuing to be a single man leaving her at home, like, literally holding the baby. Me. She was the one who brought me up; he was a complete waste of space. He was never there in my early school years, not at any school plays I was in, or sports, or nothing. As I got older, it wasn't him that taught me to ride a bike, it wasn't him that took me for my first swim. No, it was Mum. She was there for me all along.

Him? Just out like a single man, picking up women and getting blow jobs on the dance floor. And the day I left school and entered the big wide world, that was when I needed the biggest support, but Mum caught him with his trousers down with one of his whores in the middle of the afternoon. And that was when they finally split up. She kicked him out of the house without his trousers on, along with the totally naked tart, then threw his clothes out of the bedroom window into the street in broad daylight.

I never had a dad; no father figure to look up to; no being a daddy's girl. I didn't even know the word 'dad' till I was about five when other kids at school were using the word. And like when it came to me having boyfriends for the first time, no dad check to see if they were 'suitable'. It's probably one reason why I've never had a proper boyfriend, certainly not in a sexual relationship. But like, I've met Stevie now, and my heart is all a-flutter. *Oh, Stevie. Why do you have to be older?*

'I've only met Stevie tonight but I'm keen to see him again, he's so lovely,' I say in response to her question. 'I suppose you'll meet him soon enough.' I'm lying through my back teeth here. Well, maybe one day if it gets serious. Never say never.

'I thought you were out with Hazel and Julie tonight,' says Mum. 'Nice girls, them two. I like them. I remember when you were at school and always out together.'

'They, er, we were, like, separated at one point, and just by luck I bumped into this guy, and it was Stevie. We chatted, and he basically took me out on the town before bringing me home safely.'

'Sounds like he's the sort to play it steady, not just rushing in for a night of passion and then home before it gets light.'

'We just had a good laugh, but it was like we'd been dating for years.' I'm practically daydreaming. 'I don't know what it was. Is there such a thing as love at first sight?'

'Oh, Debbie, you're using the L word.'

'Maybe not love as such, I dunno, but like, we hit it off straight away. There was a certain chemistry there. Do you know what I mean?'

'Could he be the one? Do I need to buy a hat?'

'Don't get too far ahead of yourself, Mum. But never say never.' *Oh. Did I just say that?* 'I think he'll be worth it.' His age might be a bit of a stumbling block, but I really want more of this man before I give up on him. And I don't mean just in the bedroom either.

'Just follow your heart, sweetheart. There's always a pot of gold at the end of the rainbow. But if you want rainbows, you gotta have rain.'

I smile at my mum; I love her so much. 'We've had enough rain in our lives, Mum. Perhaps the sun is coming out now.'

I take off my clothes, get into bed, and turn off the light. I can't see much in the dark, but I'm lying on my back with my eyes wide open. I wish Stevie was here beside me. Or better still, on top. I hold my boobs and finger the nipples, imagining it's Stevie. Mmm. I close my eyes and wonder what he's doing.

I can picture the scene…

*

Steven walks into his house and makes his way straight upstairs and into the bathroom to brush his teeth. Whatever the situation, wherever he is, it's his ritual of last thing before bed. He looks at his reflection in the mirror and gives a heavy sigh.

'After all this time, I meet someone, and she's twenty years old,' he says aloud to his reflection. 'And she's called Debbie. I should've just walked away.'

He thinks to himself, *It was a good night, not done that in years. Drank far too much but at least I'm not pissed. Was she out for a quick shag?* She's a nice girl and I enjoyed being with her, dancing and holding her close. Even the kissing. But I couldn't go further, just couldn't.

He gets into bed and turns to a photograph by his bedside. 'Goodnight, Debs. Love ya,' he says, and switches off the light.

Chapter Four

I walk up to the door of 17 Morley Street the next morning and ring the bell. As I see the figure approach to answer the call through the frosted glass, my heart skips a beat. *I'm like, am I doing the right thing?* The door opens, and Stevie is back in his jeans and trainers, a little stubble on his face; obviously not shaved this morning. Before any words are spoken, I hold out his mobile phone for him.

'Debbie. Come in, lovely to see you again. Thanks,' taking the mobile from me, 'was gonna give it till about lunch time and call it to see if you'd answer.'

'I wanted to bring it to you personally.' I was actually hoping that he'd kiss me or hug me, but no. 'I, er, took the liberty of taking the number and also put mine into yours.'

'You're welcome. Would you like a cup of tea, coffee?' he asks, leading me to the living room.

'Tea, please.'

'Certainly. Make yourself comfortable, sweetheart, I'll put the kettle on.' He heads for the kitchen. *He called me 'sweetheart'; I like it.*

I follow him to the kitchen. 'About last night,' I begin.

'Yes?'

'It was fantastic, thank you.' I smile and hug him. He hugs back briefly with one arm whilst switching on the kettle.

'How do you take your tea?' He's all formal again.

'With biscuits, usually.' He smiles and I smile back. 'White, no sugar.' Then the thought hits me: *He's my sugar daddy.* 'Can we do it again? I mean, like, go out?'

'Yes, that would be nice. But last night, much as it was fun, it's not really my scene. Yet I bet that's you every weekend, out with the fat slags, short skirt, loads of Jagermeister and alcopop, and maybe a snog with some lucky lad.' *Good guess.*

'What's your scene, then?' I enquire.

'Theatre, cinema, as you know. A nice meal. What could be better than a nice juicy steak with a lovely glass of Merlot? Or an Italian veal cutlet washed down with a bottle of Pinot Grigio, or a jalfrezi and an ice-cold Indian lager?'

He's lost me there; he's stopped speaking English. *What on earth is 'pee no gree jo'? But if it means a date with him...* 'Yes, it sounds lovely.'

'Ok then. How about tonight?' he asks, and I smile. I'm, like, yes please. 'Or have you got plans? Out with the fat, er, Hazel and er, whassername?'

'Jules; Julie,' I correct him, then myself.

'So, tonight? Is it me or them?'

'No contest.' I can't believe we're planning to go out to dinner. I've never done that with a boy before. Like, not with anyone.

'So, what do you fancy? Any of them I suggested, or something else, something you especially like?'

'Whatever's your favourite is fine by me. We did my scene last night; it's, like, your turn tonight.'

'I'll tell you what, I'll surprise you. Is there anything you specifically don't want, or can I choose anything?'

'No, anything will be fine. I can't wait,' I say with enthusiasm.

'Good, good.' He pours our tea, and we go back to the living room and sit together on the sofa. 'How did you get here this morning?'

'I came on the bus.'

'Ok, I'll take you back home later, or wherever you want to go. What do you normally do with yourself on a Saturday morning?' asks Stevie, sipping at his tea. It's too hot for me so I put it down on the coffee table.

'Most Saturday mornings I'm in bed till like, lunch time, or at least sitting about in my pyjamas...'

'How come you're up today then?'

'I woke up thinking of you. I still had your mobile and, like, decided to come and see you. How are you feeling after last night?' I'm getting comfortable with him on the sofa, and I move closer to him, tossing my head to shake my hair back.

'I'm not hungover, so that's good. I don't normally drink that much, but it was going down so well.'

No! I don't mean like that. 'I was thinking more about having been out with me, what are your feelings? There must be something there because we're already arranging tonight.'

'Yes. I'm, er, happy for us to be friends, for us to go out like last night and again tonight. But we must remember our age gap is a hindrance, or at least that's how I feel.' *He doesn't want me as a girlfriend, just as a companion.* 'You're a lovely girl, and I enjoyed going out with you immensely and I'm looking forward to tonight. I haven't taken a young lady out to dinner since... er...'

So, that's it, is it? He wants to be friends but no more than going out. I'm not sure if that's what I want. My feelings for him are quite deep despite having only met just over twelve hours ago. He's kind, gentle, and handsome. Yes, handsome. Twenty-seven years? Pah.

'Yeah, ok. I understand and I'm happy with that. I mean, like, you know, going out with you.' I can work on the rest later, because I feel there's something there, some spark, and I intend it to catch fire.

'Good, thank you.' And he kisses me. On my forehead.

I'd rather have it on my lips, a proper good old snog with, like, his tongue brushing my upper lip like he did last night. The memory of it sends a tingle down my spine, and I realise I'm biting my lower lip. But I don't think Stevie has noticed.

'What about the rest of today? What did you say you do on Saturdays?'

'Some weekends I might go shopping with Haze and Jules for, like, shoes and stuff, but they're not flavour of the month right now. So, no plans today. How about you?' Maybe we can have a day date, too.

'Come with me, I want to show you something.' He leads me outside and to his garage. Inside there's something covered in tarpaulin or something, and he pulls it back to reveal a Harley Davidson motorcycle. Not just any old motorbike, this is a sexy beast of a machine. I'm like, wow!

'My pride and joy. An FX Springer Softail. Goes like a dream. Fancy going for a ride?' He smiles. This is his style, and it thrills me.

'You mean you wanna, like, take me out on that?' I ask, pointing at the bike. 'Wow! Yes, please.' My eyes are wide with excitement, and I'm actually stroking the bike.

'It's a lovely July morning, so we can burn up a bit of tarmac, get the wind in our fur.' He's so enthusiastic. 'We'll have to get you kitted up. Short dresses are not for motorbiking. The heels, I like, but… Let's see if I've got a leather jacket for you, or do you have one?'

'No. Well, probably not for biking, no.'

'Come on, let's have a look.' We head back off into the house, and he takes a leather jacket out of the cupboard under the stairs. 'Try that on.'

As I try it on, I'm wondering if it belonged to his wife, which is an unnerving thought. But he reassures me by telling me, 'It will zip up in a man's style.' So I'm guessing it's one of his. I'm a bit fingers and thumbs as a result, but the jacket fits a treat.

'There you go. Size sixteen you said?' he says.

'Yep. Chubby girls cuddle better,' I tell him, and he smiles. 'More to grab onto; more to squeeze; more to kiss; more to feel; and more to love. Much more.' I really emphasise the words 'kiss', 'feel', and 'love', running my hands down the front of the jacket over my bust at the word 'feel'.

'That makes me a size sixteen, too.' I have to laugh at that. He smiles again. 'Now try on a helmet. I'm sorry, but this one was Debs'.' Oh, now I am unnerved slightly, but I try the helmet all the same. It fits. 'Ok?'

I nod and suddenly grab for the helmet, its weight catching me by surprise.

Stevie smiles. 'Right, I suppose we better go back to your place and get you some clothes. A pair of jeans?'

'Yeah, ok, I got some nice jeans.' But I'm thinking about Mum. *Will she be at home?*

*

We drive to my house, and Stevie pulls up outside. 'Wait there. I won't be a couple of secs,' I tell him, and jump out of the car before he has the chance to say anything and run up to the house. Mum's not in. *Phew!* I'm not ready for either of them to meet yet.

I go to my bedroom and dig out some jeans and a suitable top, along with some suitable shoes. They're not quite high heels but small-heeled boots, perfect for motor biking. And if Stevie likes me in heels, then heels it is.

I get back into the car carrying my clothes, still dressed as I was. 'I thought you were gonna get changed,' he says.

'I'll change back at your house,' I reply. 'Didn't want you sitting in the car too long.'

'I could have come in.'

'I did think about it,' I say, lying, 'but I thought a quick in and out and, like, back to yours.'

Back at Stevie's house, we're in his living room and he sits down on the sofa. 'Ok, Debbie, if you wanna get changed, we'll make a move. We can go for a ride and have some lunch.'

Without any prompting, I pull the straps of my dress off my shoulders and let it drop to the floor, standing in front of Stevie in just bra and knickers. And heels. And not just any bra and knickers; top-of-the-range undies. In red. *God, I'm sexy.*

He instantly turns his head away but says nothing, looking out of the window. I kick off my heels and pull on my jeans then move into his view again, still in just my bra. 'Is that ok?' I ask, running my hands over my jeans, especially over my bum.

'Yes, fine, but I meant go to the bedroom or something to get changed,' he says, still averting his eyes.

'I'm not embarrassed. Are you?'

'No. But there's a time and place.'

'Oh, you're so funny,' I say, as I bend down to kiss him on the cheek. Mmm, the feel of his stubble on my lips tingles and sends a shiver down my back.

He smiles back at me; he's looking now. But I just don't get it. *Why does he, like, not just take no notice but deliberately looks away?* I mean, there's, like, being polite, but he's too over the top with it. Our age gap aside, there's nothing wrong at all in us putting all discretion aside. We're a team now, a couple.

I finish dressing, and when it comes to my shoes, I hold one pair in each hand. 'Heels?' I ask, holding them up, and then lowering the heels and raising the others, 'or sensible shoes.' They're still heels but, like, ankle boots.

'Mmm. As much as I like the heels, I think we should go for the sensible ones as this is your first time.' *You see? He likes heels. What's wrong with everything else?*

We go back out to the garage and we put on our leather jackets. He goes to a cupboard on the wall and takes out some equipment. 'Here, put these in,' he hands me some earphones, 'then put on your helmet.'

As I do so, he puts his earphones in and dons his own helmet. He then takes the small microphone on my earphone cable and fits it to the inside of my helmet, and does the same to his. 'So we can talk whilst we're riding,' he explains, his voice clear in my ears. 'Can you hear me ok?' I nod. 'Don't nod, I can't hear a nod. Just speak normally.'

'Sorry. Is that better?'

'Perfect. Ok, let's go.'

He wheels the Harley Davidson out of the garage and fires up the engine. There is a bit of a roar at first, then a gentle purr as the engine idles whilst he closes the garage door. *Wow, he really is gonna take me out on it.* He has something big and throbbing between his legs, and I'm gonna feel it deep between mine! Oh, I'm being silly but, like, the innuendo is rampaging through my head. I'm just so excited.

He climbs on the bike and tells me to get on the back, his voice soft and clear in my head. 'Put your feet on the stirrups,' he says. pointing down. I do as he says. 'Ok?'

I do it again; I nod. 'Yes.' It's all I can think of to say.

He puts the bike into first gear and we slowly pull away. Just at this walking pace I'm excited, then the speed picks up and he goes up through the gears.

'Everything ok at the back?' he asks.

'It's wonderful,' I reply. It really is; I've never been on a motorcycle before, let alone a sexy beast like this; let alone *with* a sexy beast like Stevie.

We ride on at a steady pace through the town and then we reach the outskirts. 'Steven to Debbie, do you copy, over?' He's being silly now as his voice comes through the earphones.

'Loud and clear, Captain.' There must be a smirk on my face as I reply.

'Hold on tight.'

'What to?' I ask.

'Me.'

'I thought you'd never ask,' I say, putting my arms tight around him. And then he opens up the throttle and we're off. *Wow! Oh my God, wow again. This is amazing.*

'Fifty miles an hour,' says his voice in my ear. 'Faster?'

'Yes, please.' And he picks up a bit more speed.

'Sixty. Faster?'

'Go, baby,' I urge, and we're going faster and faster. We ride through the countryside on open roads for at least half an hour. The countryside flashes by, the trees, the fields, the cows and sheep. Overtaking cars and leaning over around bends. Fantastic! I have no idea where we are, as we slow into a small village with a number of shops and a small market. Stevie brings the Harley to a stop in a parking area for motorbikes, and we dismount and remove our helmets.

'How was it for you, baby?' he asks.

'Fantastic!' And I hug him, just like I hugged him on the bike. He hugs me back, so that's a bonus.

'You probably won't need to hug me quite so much when we go on. Your seat does have a nice backrest, so you can sit up a bit more. I only said hang onto me as it was your first time, but now you're used to the increase of speed you should be a little more ready,' he says. 'But hugging's ok,' he adds as if to say, 'I like it'. So, I hug him again. 'I meant when we're on the bike,' he says, and I can imagine his eyes rolling. 'Now, are you ready for a bit of lunch, or would you like to have a look in the shops?'

'I could do with a drink. The excitement has given me a thirst,' I say, looking round the shops for a drinking hole of some sort. Preferably a pub.

'There's a lovely little tea room just along here.' He points with his helmet and takes my hand to lead me to it. 'A nice cup of tea and a bite to eat, yeah?'

'Can't beat a nice cup of tea,' I enthuse. *Oh well, so much for a pub.* We walk to the tea room – Tea Pots – and go inside and take off our jackets. They're fine on the bike but heavy and warm for walking around on a warm summer's day. We sit at a small table, and I look round the room. It's lovely and quaint. 'I've never been in a place like this before.'

'Where did you expect me to take you? To some greasy bikers' café?' asks Stevie, taking the menu from the table centre. 'What would you like? Sandwich, toastie, jacket potato, piece of cake?'

'Dunno. What're you having?' I ask, taking a look at the menu.

The waitress comes over; a small figure of a girl. *Quite cute*, I think, *in her mini apron.* But Stevie? Nothing. Doesn't notice a thing. She must be a schoolgirl or something just doing a Saturday job. She went 'Are you ready to order?'

'I am,' says Stevie. 'I'll have a toasted ham and cheese sandwich, please. Debbie?'

I look up from the menu at Stevie, and then at the waitress, and smile. She beams back at me, and I wonder if she can tell we're not father and daughter. 'I'll have the same, please.'

'And a pot of tea for two,' says Stevie, putting the menu back.

'Thank you,' says the waitress, writing it all down on her little pad, then she walks off. As she walks away, I see that behind her mini apron she has a tight short skirt on, emphasising a cute little bum. Quite sexy. I look at Stevie, but like, still nothing, he appears to have taken no notice.

I reach across the table and take Stevie's hand in both of mine, giving him my best smile. 'Thanks, Stevie...'

'Steven.'

'...for bringing me here. It's lovely. You make me feel special, showing me things that I've never even thought about before. Motorbikes and, like, tea rooms,' I wave an arm around, gesturing the café, 'and I'm really looking forward to tonight.' I beam with excitement and enthusiasm.

'Yes, I'm looking forward to tonight, too. I've got a place in mind, and I booked a table whilst you were in your house getting your jeans. It's great having you as a friend, and I'm sure we'll be able to enjoy each other's company. My life is pretty boring really, being on my own, but you've brought a little excitement to it, even if we've only known each other a day.'

'Boyfriends come and go; usually they *come* and *then* they go, but that's the way I like it. I've never been on a proper date, I don't think. And already you're opening up a whole new world to me.'

'Good, I'm happy, but you're still so young, you've got years ahead of you. Go out there and enjoy life. If going out with Sharon and Tracy is what you do, you carry on.' He doesn't sound as if he really classes himself as a boyfriend, or me as a girlfriend, and possibly never will. It's definitely the age gap that's on his mind.

So, I ask him, 'Is our age difference a problem, Stevie?'

'To a degree, yes. A friend can be any age, and I want you to be mine. But anything beyond that... it won't work. Because, what then? Heartbreak and heartache. Been there, seen it, done it, got the t-shirt. Your friends are your age, and you do your age group things. And it's the same for me. You and I can have some fun,' I nod and smile, 'but when the party's over, it's back to our own little worlds.'

'I'm not worried that there's such a big age gap between us. There's plenty of couples like us. If you was a big celebrity, well, there's loads of them out there with, like, young charms on their arm. I can have a sugar daddy if I want.'

Stevie actually smiles at that. 'And I can have a... what's the female version of a toy boy?'

'Exactly,' I say, hopefully with some conviction in my voice.

The waitress brings our tea and sandwiches, and it puts a pause in the conversation. I again look at her bum. I'm almost willing Stevie to look, too, but he doesn't. *Why?* Yes, ok, she's like, a few years younger than me even, and he's already made his point about my age, but, like, she does have a cute bum and her skirt is quite tight over it. *Oh, stop it, Debbie!*

When she's left us to eat, I continue where I left off, still determined to make Stevie know he's captured my heart and mind. 'You wanna drop everything before it's even been picked up? We met by chance. Let's grab the bull by the horns and, like you say, have fun.'

'We have tonight to look forward to.' Stevie pours some tea and starts to eat his sandwich. 'But like that song goes, we don't have to take our clothes off to have fun.'

'What song?' I ask, but my mobile then starts to buzz and breaks the mood. 'Excuse me.' I look at it and see a message from Amy:

How did it go last nite? x x

'Who's it from, dare I ask?' says Stevie, while I'm already writing my reply.

Fantastic! Wow he's such a hottie ;-) x x

A little white lie, I know, but, like, I dunno, it's true, even if we didn't take our clothes off.

'It's Amy. You know? From last night.'

'I remember. What's she say?'

'Just asking if everything was ok. I told her we had a great time, and I might see you again.'

The mobile goes again.

He looked a tasty dish all right even if he is old x x

He's not old! Mature x x

'Put the mobile down, Debbie, please. There you are, see, that's all your generation know: text messaging, and Facebook and everything with your dextrous thumbs.'

'Sorry,' I say, putting the mobile away, feeling another buzz as it goes off. I'll look at it later. *Facebook? I never thought, and they'll all be expecting something.* 'I don't do Facebook,' I lie, but it's to keep him at arm's length.

'Anyway, I'm not a celebrity, I'm just a simple man. I do a simple, moderately paid job. I'm not rich or anything, wanting young charms to show off. I'm just a widower who's a little lonely and enjoying the company I have as much as I can.'

That's another of his bombshells; that he's a lonely man. Understandable, being widowed.

'But I'm here now. I'm not trying to be your charm. I'm not a quick shag girl.' That's probably a lie. 'I can give love, too.' That was a bit tongue in cheek. Probably.

'Less than twenty-four hours on and you're using the word "love",' he says.

'You know what I mean,' I snap at him. I take a deep breath to calm down, but he's frustrating me a bit. 'It's just that you're the first guy I've met that, like, I dunno, sort of deserves it. You've been so good to me, I wanna repay you… with love. Kindness, then, if you like. I'm your girlfriend now.' I can feel my mobile going mad. There's gonna be dozens of messages when I get the chance to look.

'Yes, of course, I'm being unfair. Sorry. We've got tonight. Maybe we can talk things over.' He seems a bit more obliging now. Perhaps it was me snapping at him that made him understand how I feel.

I like him. He gives me that warm, reassuring tingle that I've never had with a boy before. I don't know if it's love because I've never been in love. But Stevie… I consider what we're saying, and it makes me think. I never had a father figure to look up to, and I suppose when I discovered boys, discovered sex, it was, like, just no thought about them. It was all about me, me, me, and my lust. But here I am now with, like, not just someone that will hopefully satisfy my lust but also someone mature to look up to in a man. My daddy figure. My sugar daddy figure.

'I said I do just a simple job, but what do you do?'

'I work in an office,' I tell him.

'Yeah. And? Lots of people work in offices.'

'I'm in accounts.'

'An accountant? Brilliant,' he compliments.

'No. I just work on the ledgers, liaising with customers and stuff. I'm a statistics analyst. Number cruncher. Boring, really.'

'Yeah, but surely there's room for improvement. What business does your employer do?'

'They're in construction. We build industrial units and stuff.'

'Well, you're not just gonna be some little clerk for the rest of your days, are you? With all those older men.'

I'm, like, current company, yes please. There was that one time....

*

We were having a little gathering after work in the office for old Trevor who was retiring. There was no drink except tea, coffee, and that, but it was a jolly little do with prawn sandwiches and everything. I'd only been at the company a couple of months, whereas Trevor had been there centuries. He was, like, part of the furniture, a nice old boy, quick witted and always with a smile, though I reckon that was more to do with winding down to this day in the short time I knew him.

I went up to Trevor to wish him well and kiss him on the cheek, then when I turned away there was Alex, from R&D, I think, right up close behind me. And as we bumped into each other, he spilled his drink down the front of my dress. Fortunately, it was only squash and not hot coffee or something, but I was wet all the same. It made me jump back with a yelp, but once I saw who it was, I wasn't so bothered. He was, like, quite a bit older than me – I was still only eighteen – yet he was quite good looking, and I had noticed how he, like, regularly cast an eye my way and we'd smile. I reckon that's why he was so close to me there. So, when he apologised to me, he said, 'I'll get that cleaned for you.'

I was, like, thinking on my feet. 'You'll have to get it off me first,' I said with a glint in my eye as an invitation.

'I was thinking that.' Yes, he wanted to get my dress off, looking at my wet bust.

'You could start off by buying me a proper drink first,' I said, waving my plastic tea cup. 'I've had enough tea for one day and could do with something better. I'm not bothered about staying too long here, are you?'

'No, no. I was looking for an excuse to sneak away,' he said, warming to it nicely. But I was surprised by his next line. 'I know the manager of the hotel just down the road,' he said, pointing out the window. 'We could go there, and I'll buy you one whilst we get you cleaned up.'

I was surprised but delighted. *A hotel? And he knows the manager.* I could, like, see a room being taken later.

We said our goodbyes – separately – to Trevor and the party, and made our way out of the office building. It was only a short walk to the hotel, where we went to the bar and he ordered cocktails. 'You wanna try a Long Island Iced Tea?' he suggested. 'They're lovely.'

So, we sat chatting and sipping our cocktails for a while then he, like, looked at my dress and went, 'It looks to be drying out, but it's stained now. Let's see what I can do to keep my promise.'

He got up, went to the bar, and ordered another round of drinks. That's when his friend, the manager, came in. I knew straight away it was him by the way they greeted each other, and as the barmaid prepared our drinks, I could see them talking but couldn't hear them. So, I did what all eighteen-year-olds do and got out my mobile phone, scrolling through but not really looking at much, then promptly put it down when Alex came back with our Long Island Iced Teas. He was dead right, they were lovely.

Alex sat down and told me, 'I've had a word with Vlad,' pointing to where the hotel manager had been, 'and he's let us use a room where you can pop your dress off and he'll get it cleaned in the laundry room straight away. Take an hour tops.' He handed me a room key – you know, one of them contactless credit card-type ones.

'Ok,' I said with a proper Debbie smile – like a proper 'come into my office' smile – twiddling the room key in my fingers. I stood up and said, 'Come on, we'll take our cocktails with us.'

But at this point he hesitated, and I was, like, he's not up for it. Maybe he was just, like, genuine about getting my dress cleaned rather than a desire to get it off.

'Er...' he stammered. Well, he was a good twenty years more than me, and clearly married. Wedding ring and that. 'Yeah, sure. Of course.'

He got up with me and we made our way to the lifts. I considered cornering him in the lift, but just as the doors were closing, someone put their hand in and the doors opened again and they stepped in, so we were not alone.

When we got to the room, Alex gestured to the bathroom and said, 'Take your dress off in there. There'll be a robe for you to wear while you wait, and I'll take it to the laundry room.'

'I need you to help me out of it,' I said, turning my back to him to unzip me. He unclipped the fastener and brought the zip down a couple of inches and stopped. 'All the way, Alex. All the way,' I said brightly.

He did so, right down to my bum, and I turned round, grabbed him round the neck with both arms, and snogged his gob off. I ran my fingers through his hair at the back of his head, his arms around my waist. Then I backed off, slipped off my dress, quickly followed by my bra, put my arms around his neck again and looked deeply into his eyes with a smile, my eyes flickering. 'Let's not let a good hotel bed go to waste.'

I guided him to the bed and basically pushed him down on his back and got over him, undoing his tie and shirt. He began to join in and groped hungrily at my boobs as I arched my back and murmured in delight at the warm caress of his hands. I just love my boobs being squeezed and caressed.

I took off his top clothes and threw them on the floor then, like, started to undo his trousers. I pulled them down, and then his pants and his cock sprang up like a jack-in-the-box to greet me. Oh, yes please!

We spent the best part of the evening shagging away, cock and cocktails all night, before leaving the hotel and making our own ways home. It's funny, but I never did get my dress cleaned.

*

'There must be things you can learn, maybe a bit of further education, a ladder to climb,' Stevie tells me. 'I mean, you're only twenty, so you've another forty years or more to go yet. I'm forty-seven. I'm not reaching for the stars, but I'm happy in my work. Ok, still another twenty years to go, ish, but you've got so much potential in front of you, by the time you get to my age you could be a high flyer.'

'I do a bit of further education on Thursday evenings. That's why Friday is so important for me to get away from it all. And the weekend. To let my hair down.' I keep the 'let my knickers down, too' to myself here, though.

'We all feel that way…' he begins.

'But I go to work on Thursday morning and it's, like, in your face right up 'til five o'clock on Friday.'

'There is some scope there, though. Does your employer fund the education?'

'Yes.'

'There you go. They must be very positive about your career. They ain't gonna pay for you to get qualifications just to stay a junior all your days. I sometimes wish I'd listened at school; I could be a high flyer by now. I could've had a young girl like you as my secretary, with your glasses on the tip of your nose and your stocking tops on display.' I think he was being a bit tongue in cheek there. 'You could take down my particulars.'

'I intend to,' I say innocently. *What a shame I don't wear glasses, and I've got jeans on.* I could just picture him sitting at a desk and seeing the bottom of a pair of heels under the desk front.

Stevie tops up our cups and empties the teapot. 'Lovely cup of tea; the best drink in the world.' I beg to differ, especially on a Friday or Saturday night. 'Do you work with any of the women I was fortunate and unfortunate to acquaint with last night?'

'No, there's only one other girl about my age; some are a little older, and then mostly guys. Haze and Jules are friends from school days, as well as Amy and Marie. We've been clubbing since before we even left school. There was no dad in my case to be standing there saying things like, "You're not going out dressed like that, young lady." I don't know about the others, but what you saw for the most part last night I've been doing since I was, like, fifteen.'

'You seem proud of it.'

I shrug my shoulders. 'It's all I know.' I'm not embarrassed about it, but he makes me feel so.

'How old were you when you lost your virginity?' He's digging deep.

'Fifteen.' I deadpan. 'He was a little older than me, actually.'

*

SUGAR DADDY?

When it happened, my first time, I wanted it to be proper. You know, like, on a bed and not round the bushes or something. I was well ready to open my account from about fourteen. I had a good bust by then, and all the boys at school were, like, pleased to see me. I was well brazen, undoing more buttons than was allowed, always being told by the women teachers to do them up, and always wearing a dark bra under my white school blouse so it was more noticeable. I'd even worn stockings and suspenders to school a couple of times. Thankfully the teachers never saw them, but some of the boys did.

Actually, there were, like, three of us that wore them. Me, Jules, and another girl called Mandy, who I lost contact with after school 'cause she don't do social media. When we went round the proverbial bike sheds, all the boys soon gave up their fags when they saw our stockings, and we all had a bit of fun with a bit of snogging and groping. I reckon one boy, like, come in his pants after Mandy had basically wanked him off, overdoing the rubbing over his privates when we were all, like, groping. I mean, if it was anything like the boy I was having fun with, he had a full hard on under my touch as he pawed at my boobs. I suppose Mandy was just enjoying herself.

Anyway, I'd had, like, a fair few snogs with some of the boys who had a good grope, and I had a hand in my knickers once or twice, and I'd, like, already given a couple of blow jobs to some boys from school.

There was one boy, a right cocky git, thought he was God's gift – can't remember his name for obvious reasons – always acting like he was the school stud, talking to the girls like all he had to do was, like, click his fingers. He tried it on with me out in the playground, and we agreed to meet after school. Then as I walked back to class, he called out across the playground something like, 'And I'll get a blow job later,' for everyone to hear. Like, his usual cocky self, trying to brag.

I stopped in my tracks and, like, went back up to him and said, 'Why wait till tonight?' and I got down on my haunches and began to undo his trousers.

He became a bit defensive then, trying to back away, but by this time we had a small crowd round us and I'd got his cock in my hand, so he couldn't, like, back off now, ruining his own reputation. I like a cock in my hand. Once you've got a boy's cock in your hand, you are, like, totally in control. He was instantly hard, good boy, I'll give him that. And as I began to give him his blow job, it wasn't long before I sensed him coming. Just as he did, I, like, stopped sucking and held him out, so he splashed all over the floor.

I stood up and went, 'That didn't take long; hardly worth getting my knees dirty for. I haven't got time to waste like that, even if it was only two minutes.'

He soon developed a new reputation after that: the two-minute wonder.

And that's why I wanted to do it proper. I mean, like, I didn't want to lose my cherry for the sake of taking one. I wanted a boy that could sustain himself so that I got an orgasm, too. Like, a proper one.

Even though we were still at school, I began going out at the weekends with Haze and Jules to the pubs and nightclubs, and that was when I met this boy called Daniel. I could see that he had the eye for me, as did all the other boys there. I certainly didn't look like a schoolgirl in my figure-hugging dress. I might not've been the slimmest girl in the room, but there was, like, plenty of figure to hug, leaving little for even the most imaginative boys to ponder. My dress was so hugging that I couldn't wear any knickers underneath for fear of, like, you know, them being visible.

I noticed Daniel looking at me out of the corner of my eye, so I, like, played easy to get by moving closer to him and his mates who were all acting like wallflowers. I started dancing near him, clearly flirting, and made my move by bumping into him accidentally on purpose. After a giggle and an apology, it got us chatting, and one of his friends said something like, 'He's only trying to get into your knickers.' So, I let his friend know and made him more jealous that I'd chosen to talk to Daniel by replying, 'What knickers?' Then I moved him away from his pals, leaving them with their mouths open in surprise.

A couple of drinks and a few dances later and we were, like, snogging for England. I knew this was it. I could feel the anticipation down below, getting slightly wet and, like, going weak at the knees and tingling sensations, you know, down there. We stayed till kicking out time, and as we left together he asked if he could walk me home. *You're coming home with me alright,* I thought. *We're not losing bodily contact until we've shared bodily fluids.*

I wasn't nervous or scared; I was excited. I so wanted this. So, we jumped into a cab, and it wasn't long before my figure-hugging dress was hugging the bedroom carpet and we were in my bed, like, kissing and removing each other's clothes. When he took off my dress, he was wide eyed that I really wasn't wearing any knickers. He started to remove my bra, pulling the strap off my shoulder so he could get his hand inside and on my boob. I was, like, oh my God, as he kneaded a sample of my ample and wanted him to keep it going. I shrugged the strap off my other shoulder and grabbed his other hand and put it on my other boob, so he was titting me off with both hands as I managed to unclip round the back.

I lay back and had him straddle me, groping away at me to my heart's content, holding his wrists to keep his hands there. Then I reached round his waist and, getting my fingers in the rim of his pants, I pulled them down. He was fully erect, and his cock stood to attention as he raised himself so I could pull his pants right off. And then I opened my legs to let him in. I was, like, well ready with my juices running riot, his reward all moist and hot, and then his cock came into contact with my fanny and I flinched. Not because of pain or shock or anything, but because of, like, the sizzling tingle coursing through me.

I lifted my hips in response, and he was just prodding his shaft head into my opening, and then he was in, his whole cock sliding deep into me. I, like, squealed with pleasure, and it was glorious. That first time. A cock inside me! Never mind a cock in just my hand or in my mouth; this was proper shagging, and it was amazing, and I soon got my orgasm! I'd orgasmed before when playing with myself and masturbating. I remember the sensations of the first time, coursing through my whole body, making me tremble and convulse with so much intensity, using a toy cock that I also used to practise blow jobs with. And there was one time at school that I had to go to the girls' toilets to take off my knickers because one boy that got his hand in them seemed to know what he was doing and soaked me. That day I had to sit the rest of the school day without any underwear. I think he had a similar problem, too.

But that first orgasm with Daniel was sensational. And when he orgasmed too, it felt like a torrent filling me. I know it was probably only average amounts of semen, but that first time, like, oh my God, the feeling made me orgasm again. We exchanged bodily fluids alright, all mixing together, and I fell in love that night. Not with Daniel. With sex itself.

*

'I bet he weren't twenty-seven years older, though,' Stevie quickly retorts.

'Ten or twelve, I dunno.' I shrug my shoulders again.

'Bloody paedophile, he could've gone to prison.'

'Come on. Lots of people are having sex before sixteen,' I tell him. 'How old were you when you first had it?'

He doesn't answer, just carries on the conversation. 'Doesn't make it right, though, does it? Lots of people drive over thirty miles an hour, but it's still illegal.'

'Whatever. But I'll tell you something, he might not've been no virgin, but it was the best shag he's ever had. If I'd had a dad, he'd probably have a shotgun up his arse. But it was my doing; I told him I was twenty.'

'You told me you were twenty. Oh, my God, you're not really a schoolgirl, are you?'

'You calling me a liar, Stevie?' I narrow my eyes at him.

'Strong words.' He gets serious and raises his eyebrows at me.

'You started it. Do I look like a schoolgirl?' I say, pushing my boobs up and out, even though I've got a full top on – for biking purposes, that is. 'I can dress up for you, though, if that's what you fancy. I can put my hair in, like, pigtails, paint false freckles across my nose, have my shirt fully open but tied at the bottom—'

'No!' Ooh, now it's his turn to get snappy.

Tea finished, Stevie gets up and goes to the counter to pay, and I quickly grab my mobile. Eight unread texts: Amy, Marie, and Haze. *Bloody hell, I don't believe it!* They're all saying the same sort of thing, that if he's hot they all want to find out for themselves. We've bedded boys between us before, but Stevie is not some easy pick-up to be passed around, that's for sure! None of the usual shag 'em and leave 'em, it's your turn now.

I'm about to reply when I see Stevie coming back from the counter, so I hurriedly put my mobile away. We pick up our jackets and helmets and make our way back to the bike, stopping occasionally to look in a shop window or two, but all the while holding hands. It gives me a wonderfully warm feeling to be holding hands.

As we look in the window of an art gallery shop, and Stevie is pointing out the pictures that he likes – although they have no interest to me – I question him about holding hands.

'You like holding my hands as if we *were* lovers, how come?'

'I'm just a very tactile person,' he says.

'Tactile?'

'Touchy, feely. It provides a feeling of security. And I don't want you to get lost,' he jokes, squeezing my hand a little. His squeeze sends sensations up my arm and through my whole body; he really is setting my soul on fire. I can't pinpoint what it is about him, but I love it.

The journey back home is just as thrilling as the one out, and Stevie takes me back to my house to drop me off. As he brings the bike to a stop outside my house, he switches off the engine and we both get off and remove our helmets.

'Don't worry about the coat and helmet, we can sort that some other time.'

'Ok,' I say with a big smile. I've got his leather jacket and crash helmet, and he's got my dress and shoes from earlier today. I'm happy with that, as it means that we will be meeting again besides tonight.

'I will pick you up about seven-thirty and back to mine to take a taxi from there. Ok?'

I'm not sure what Mum will be doing at that time, and she will insist on seeing him. 'It's ok, I'll come to yours. I really don't mind.'

'Are you sure? It's not a problem for me.' He's not so keen for it to be that way.

'It's not a problem for me, either. I'll be fine. I'll see you at yours, seven-thirty,' I say with a smile, taking command. I hug him once more and we share a big kiss. *Wow! That's more like it.* 'See you later,' I say and run up the drive to the front door before he can say anything more.

I get to the door and look back. Stevie's already got his helmet back on. I then hear his soft voice in my ears. 'See you later.' I'd forgotten I'd left the ear phones in. I blow him a kiss, and he pulls away. I wave at him till he's out of sight. I don't know if he can see me, but I wave anyway.

I go into the house and straight up to my room. I don't want to be leaving the jacket and helmet on show, so I put them in the wardrobe. I flop onto my bed and pull out my mobile. Four more texts to read. Again, I can't believe what I'm reading. *What are they all thinking this is?* I've met a guy, they see that he's older than me and make their comments, but they're, like, all over him. I'll show them.

I send them all text messages that we had a hot passionate night of love and that he's all mine again tonight. That should shut them up, but no. Within seconds my mobile is going crazy, so I just put it down. Can't be arsed right now.

Chapter Five

A little while later, I pick up my mobile and look at all the messages, from the same three. I am shocked to read that all three of them basically want to know full explicit details or want to indulge in them themselves – with my Stevie. Then I notice there's a message from Stevie. My heart skips a beat.

Been great day out on the bike, can't wait to see you tonight – Steven x x x

Three kisses! Don't get that many from anyone. I text him back.

Hi Stevie, I love being with you, tonight could be our lucky night – your sexy babe Debbie x x x

I make sure there are three kisses in return. I pick up my tablet and go to Facebook and scroll through the news feed. I also have some private messages in my inbox. It's, like, even here there are loads of comments about last night and me and Stevie. I post a general message for all to see.

'Spent last night and today with Stevie Taylor, and he treats me like a queen. Going out again tonight on a dinner date.'

I sit and think of something else to write, but I can't really add anything, so I just hit post. I may have said a little white lie about his bedroom performance, but I'm sure he is hot. He's very handsome and fit, especially for his age – now it's me getting all 'age gap concerned' – but I shall find out soon, and tonight is where it begins. I start to think of what to wear later.

I take off my jeans and top and look at various clothes from the wardrobe, holding things up against me and posing in the mirror. There's a glint in my eye and a cheeky smile on my face as I look at myself and let the thoughts run through my mind. I rummage through my underwear drawer and pick out some of my best sexy bras and knickers; real seduction stuff.

I'm like, *Oh, Stevie, are you in for a great night tonight?*

*

I'm feeling well proud of myself as I walk along Morley Street, having just gotten off the bus. It's a warm evening, and I've had many a look from, like, men of all ages on the bus and as I walk to Stevie's house. And no wonder. I've got on a really sheer polyester off-white top, really silky and very transparent. Very. Underneath is my black bra – a darker colour to make it all the more visible, just like I did at school. But the best thing is that my top is sliding back and forth across my breasts at my every move, really emphasising them and the pattern and subtle colours in the bra.

I'm also wearing a leather mini skirt, so short that it barely hides my knickers, especially when I sit down. Not that there's much to hide, as it's, like, a matching black thong. And of course, the customary high-heeled shoes. Stevie says he likes heels. With blue eye-liner, dark mascara, and shiny red wet-look lippy. *God, I'm sexy!*

I get to Stevie's house, ring the bell, and watch through the frosted glass as he approaches the door. He's gonna see a super sexy woman standing on his doorstep and get an instant erection and throw himself upon me. *I wish.*

'Hi, Debbie, come on in.' *What? No wow; no darling; no nothing.* It is like I've just turned up out of the blue in a drab overcoat. And certainly no kiss. I actually feel let down by him; I've made an extra special effort to impress him, but I might as well be wearing a diving suit.

'Hey. Come here,' I demand, and as he moves closer I grab him in a full embrace and plant a massive lipsticked kiss upon his lips, holding the back of his head to me. There's no escape as my fingers entwine with his hair. I hold him in the embrace for as long as I can, pleased to feel his arms come around my waist, then I finally let him go.

'Wow. What have I done to deserve that?' he says, catching his breath.

'Nothing... yet. I'm here, like, dressed to kill and you've not even noticed,' I say, and hopefully he hears the annoyance in my voice.

'Sorry. Yes, I did notice, er, very nice. It's just I'm kind of trained to be able to look a girl in the eye without making the obvious obvious. Talk to the face, not the, er...' He's a bit embarrassed by his action.

'Well, I want the obvious to be obvious. Especially from you.' I am annoyed. 'Any normal man wouldn't be able to take his eyes off me, be all over me. Yet you just look past me like I ain't here. I don't want any old man all over me. I want you.'

'You said it. Old. You're forgetting that I'm still old enough to be your, er, mum.'

'But I don't care,' I exclaim, full of frustration. *Oh, what a great start to the night.*

'And like I don't either? Look, can we start again?' He holds my hands in his and looks me up and down, then smiles and says, 'Wow, look at you! What can I say apart from thank you? You look real sexy. If you've made that effort just for me...'

'Yeah, yeah, ok. You're forgiven. But I want more attention, please.'

I'm not really sure what the problem is. He says he's trained to overlook certain things, but surely any man can't fail to notice how I'm dressed and made up. Especially the man I've done it for. I then chastise myself for not actually taking much notice of him. He's in a white long-sleeved cotton shirt, cuffs loose but no tie this time, and some light-coloured linen trousers. They hang from his hips in an almost seductive manner; he's, like, so trendy for his age. I'm doing it again, all age gap and everything, but it must be his physique because he has a nice, cute bum. *God, he's sexy.*

We go to the living room where he has some music playing. I have no idea what it is, but he's got it turned up loud. A load of schoolkids who don't need no education, all going 'Hey teacher, leave them kids alone!' He turns it down as I sit on the sofa, crossing my legs for good effect. Plenty of thigh on show. My dress and shoes from earlier are not where I left them, but I don't bother to ask.

'I've ordered a taxi but it's not due for a few minutes yet.' He joins me on the sofa and sits quite close and takes my hand.

'I spoke to Mum this afternoon about you.' It's me that takes up the conversation.

'Oh yeah?'

'I was telling her about our motorbike ride out for, like, lunch and that, and told her about the thrill of it all,' I tell him, remembering with happy thoughts. 'I said that you had a Harley Davidson and, like, she seemed impressed.' Stevie smiles. 'Then came the difficult bit; she was impressed to think that someone my age had such a top-quality bike.' I go a little silent.

'So, what did you tell her?'

'I told her that you had a high-profile job and earned lots of money.'

'Ah.' He is a bit cornered by that. 'I see. You didn't tell her then that I am old enough to be, er…'

'No. That's why I came to you tonight. If you'd come round and I'm expecting you, she would have been keen to meet you. I'm not quite ready for that. After all, we've only known each other a day.'

'Yes. It's lovely that we've met and here we are planning to go out together, but let's take it as it comes, shall we? Like you said, we've not even got to hour twenty-four yet since you rugby tackled me into submission.' He grins at his own analogy then gives my hand a reassuring pat as he stands up to turn off the music. 'Taxi'll be here any minute. Let's enjoy ourselves tonight and end this talk all the time about are we or aren't we. We met yesterday. We weren't gonna get married today. I come from a time when you spent the first week or so just courting, not jumping into bed immediately.'

He's probably right, I suppose. He is of another generation, and perhaps it's also a culture difference that's, like, getting in the way. I'm used to meeting guys, having sex, and then moving on. I've not had a boyfriend; I've not met a guy and seen him again, especially if I haven't shagged him. If they can't perform in the bedroom, or wherever, then it's over. And normally, even if they have performed. Love them and leave them, that's how it goes these days for both sexes. But Stevie's worth it. He's worth seeing again and again, because I know that eventually we will end up in bed, and I'm gonna give him the ride of his life.

*

The taxi takes us to an Italian restaurant in town, Il Colosseo. 'It's how the Italians say Colosseum. Not the most original name for a restaurant but not many of them are. Il Prezzo, Prego, La Dolce Vita, things like that. But Italian food is my favourite,' says Stevie, as he once again opens the car door for me, and I look up at the restaurant name.

'Wow, can you speak Italian?'

'Yes, but it's hardly rocket science with things like restaurant names.'

'Pizza Hut. That's an Italian restaurant to me. So, come on then, let's put you to the test,' I challenge him to his claim of linguistics.

'I'll say something to the waitress, and we'll probably get "you what?" back,' he suggests.

'I don't care, I wanna hear a bit of Italian. It might be sexy to hear you talk like that.' I beam at him. We enter the restaurant and a young waitress greets us.

'*Buona sera, ho una prenotazione di un tavolo per due, Signore* Taylor.' Oh, wow, he really can speak Italian.

'*Si, Signore, se volete seguirmi.*' I have no idea what's been said, but the waitress leads us to a table, and Stevie helps me into my seat like a true gentleman.

I'm really liking this; it's something I could get used to. Then he takes his seat opposite me. Good, he'll not be able to avoid looking at me and my breasts in my patterned bra under my silky top.

'*Grazie*,' Stevie continues his Italian.

'*Prego. Il menu senorita, signore,*' says the waitress, handing us each a menu. '*Che cosa desidera de bere?*'

'She's asking what we would like to drink. Do you want to join me in a bottle of wine?' asks Stevie.

'Yes, please.'

'*Una bottiglia di Pinot Grigio, per favore.*' He's so sexy.

'*Si, grazie*,' says the waitress, and walks off.

'It's ok, the menu has English details of the food so it shouldn't confuse you, but feel free to let me help you if you have difficulty.'

I ponder the menu. *Antipasti, primo, secondo, carne, pesce*. It's all Greek to me. 'Er…' I begin.

Stevie comes to the rescue. 'Antipasti is like a pre-starter, things like garlic bread, bruschetta, that sort of stuff…'

'You've lost me on bruschetta already.' I look at him for help.

'It's like bread with olive oil, and *al pomodoro* is with tomatoes. Then *primo* is your starter; melon in Parma ham is a strange mix but very nice.'

'Ok, I'll have that,' I decide.

'Yeah, but there's lots more.' Stevie points at the menu. '*Caldo* is hot starters, *freddo* is cold, like the melon and ham, see…' He reaches over the table and points at the items on the menu. I look at some of the items, reading the English; the Italian is just a jumble of letters to me, but I'm like getting the hang of it now.

'Mm. Think I still want the melon and ham, sounds nice.'

'Good, good. Then *secondo* is your main course. Pasta speaks for itself, *carne* is meat, *pollo* is chicken, *vittelo* is veal, *agnello* lamb, *bistecca* steak, and *pesce* is fish.' He's very helpful, and I read through to decide.

Wow is one of my favourite words with everything new that Stevie is introducing me to. But everything seems to be just wow! 'Some of these sound absolutely delicious.'

'They are. That's why I love Italian restaurants. If an Italian can't cook me a decent meal, nobody can. I'm gonna plump for mushrooms with three cheese sauce for starter, and I reckon *pollo vino bianco*, chicken in white wine sauce.' He licks his lips.

'I like the look of this one.' I point at an item on the menu just as the waitress brings us the wine.

'Your wine, sir.'

'Thank you. Don't bother with the tasting, just pour it, please.' *Aw, they've stopped talking Italian.*

'Are you ready to order?' asks the waitress, after pouring us a glass of wine.

'Yes, I think so.' He then asks me, 'What was you showing me?'

I show him the menu again. 'This one.'

'*Ravioli cremonese.*' *Ooh, speaking Italian again.* I'm, like, melting; it sounds so sexy. 'Well, I'm sure you know what ravioli is, and this is basically served in a creamy sauce. Sounds good. Do you want to go with that?'

'Yes, please.' I close the menu as Stevie places our order, and I listen with pleasure at his Italian once again. It is so sexy, even though he's only ordering food.

The waitress takes our order and leaves, and we sip at the wine. We clink our glasses. 'Cheers,' he says.

'Cheers,' I repeat.

It is lovely, like nectar, beautifully chilled, nice and crisp and refreshing. Crikey, I'm turning into a wine expert; I might spit it out if I'm not careful. But I swallow, not spit. Spitters are quitters. 'So, say something to me in Italian; something sexy.'

'Debbie, *si e molto bello e si guarda stasera molto seksi.*'

I let the words wash over me like a warm breeze, I have no idea what he said but it ended in the word sexy, and it sends a hot tingle right through me and into my sexual areas, and my heart jumps a beat. He said sexy. Like, end of.

'So, what did it mean?'

He smiles at me; a sly grin. He taps the side of his nose but says nothing.

'Come on, that's not being fair,' I complain. 'There was sexy in there, even if I didn't understand anything else.'

'I was just saying how lovely you look this evening, that's all.' He shrugs his shoulders.

'And sexy.'

'Yes. You said say something sexy, so I did. It's pronounced the same, probably spelled differently…'

'So how come you can speak Italian, even if you can't spell it?' I ask, perhaps a little too patronisingly.

'I can read and write Italian, but not necessarily every word; I don't know every word in English, either, do you? I mean, how do you spell necessarily?'

'N, E, S, er, double S.' He's smirking at me and gently shaking his head. *Whatever.* 'So, how come then?' I ask again.

'My mum is Italian. And with her side of the family all Italian, I was brought up with two languages,' he explains. He's really intriguing.

'Have you ever been to Italy?'

'Oh, of course, many a time. Most of Mum's family live there. She came here to work and learn English, and she became an Italian language teacher but also used to teach English as a foreign language to Italians here in England. She's retired now, of course.'

The first course arrives. *Anti pasta* or something, he said. 'It's bruschetta,' he reminds me. I love the way he rolls his r, brrrruschetta. 'Just bread with olive oil *al pomodoro*, with tomatoes and garlic and everything. Just a small one to share. Don't want to overdo it before we get to the main course.' *Main course, mmm. Oops, I'm distracted.* 'In some Italian restaurants, and especially in Italy, you would have more courses than we're having. You'd have at least a pasta course as well as a main course.'

The bruschetta is delicious, and with a little more wine, this whole Italian experience is going fine. As we await the next course and the waitress takes our plates away, Stevie tops up my glass. It is a lovely drink; I'm really enjoying it. Never really had wine before, but I could get used to it in the right company. This company.

'Going back to you going to Italy, where have you been, exactly?'

'Well, I've been to a lot of places. Obviously to visit my mum's family, and on holiday a few times. It helps to speak the lingo when you go abroad, and I love Italy. I've been to Rome, Florence, Venice, and all over.' It seems to me that he is deliberately avoiding mentioning his wife and their holidays, then suddenly... 'Me and Debs, er, my wife, loved going on holiday.' This guy likes dropping bombs.

I take a sip of wine to pause and re-assert myself.

'I'd love to go to Rome. It's supposed to be the most romantic city in the world, isn't it?' I'm holding my glass in both hands and smiling up at him. I think the wine is going to my head already, but it's lovely.

'It's a beautiful city, so much to see and enjoy. I'm sure you'd love it. But places like Paris and Vienna and Prague are, too.' He just seems matter of fact; he's not getting the hint.

'Have you been there, too?'

'Yes.'

Bugger the hints. 'You'll have to take me sometime,' I tell him, and he just smiles and takes another sip of wine.

'You'll get there one day if it's your dream. It's so easy to get to these places nowadays, and you don't always need to fly anymore, especially Paris – it's a couple of hours on a train. Breakfast in London, lunch in Paris, they say, sitting by the banks of the Seine sipping French wine in the shadow of the Eiffel Tower. What can be better?'

Stevie is such a romantic; he describes it so beautifully. I'm so glad I met him. I really am falling for him, and I go silent, dreaming of him taking me to Paris to sip wine by the Seine. I'm, like, weak at the knees.

'Where have you been to on your travels?' asks Stevie.

I shrug my shoulders at him. 'Nowhere.'

'What? Not even with your friends to somewhere like Ayia Napa, the shag capital of Europe?' *That was a bit below the belt.*

'I don't have a passport.'

'What about England, or Britain? There's loads of lovely places to visit without the need to go abroad. Or what about hen parties and stuff, to Blackpool or London or Liverpool or somewhere?'

'No.'

'Not even with your mum when you was a kid?'

'No.'

'Crikey, you have led a sheltered life.' Stevie sounds exasperated.

'You know how things were when I was a kid. Mum was left to bring me up alone. When I got into my teens I was, like, seeing my friends and that regularly, and ultimately discovered boys.'

'But you've never even been out on a "girls on tour" trip?' Stevie uses his fingers to air quote. I just shake my head. 'I can't believe it. But it's girls on tour in town every weekend, going out terrorising the male population of the town. You've never wanted to go elsewhere to enjoy your anarchy? 'Specially the holiday destinations. You might meet the man of your dreams.' He grins.

'I don't need to. I've already met him.' I smile back, my sweetest smile.

'Yes, but I carry a lot of baggage.'

'Yep. And you carry it very well,' I say with a glint in my eye as I look him up and down. I emphasise it by rubbing my foot up and down his leg under the table. To my surprise, and delight, he doesn't move away.

'Not that kind of baggage,' he gets serious again, but we're saved by the bell as the next course arrives.

We begin eating in silence until I exclaim about the wonderfulness of my melon wrapped in ham. 'Oh, that's amazing. The sweet of the fruit and the savoury of the ham, you could never believe it could taste so good.'

'Let's have a taste?' he asks, and with a smile I cut a piece of my food and offer it up to him on the fork. He gladly takes the food in his mouth and enjoys the taste. It is such a sexy action; I'm quite stunned. These are, like, the things I've never experienced before, and Stevie is opening up a whole new world.

'Let's try some of yours?' It is the obvious response, and the action is repeated in return as I linger just a half second longer with his fork in my mouth. It is just so sensuous. But Stevie seems to take it all in his stride. He's obviously done it before.

Chapter Six

Our meal progresses as we talk about the food, his motorbiking, even the weather. We repeat sharing each other's main course and order a second bottle of wine. The food, the wine and, of course, Stevie's company is a heady mix, and I savour every moment of it. There's also some soft live music playing.

'One of the good things about this restaurant is that once everyone has finished eating, the music continues, and we can all have a dance. There's no need to vacate the table; it's ours for the night.'

And so, after a limoncello cheesecake – one to share, just like the bruschetta earlier – we enjoy a dance.

Depending upon the music, we sometimes dance apart, and others – the best ones – we dance close and, like, closer still. We sit back at our table and with the wine finished, we enjoy a cocktail.

'You told me that you only do a simple job but, like, you enjoy an exciting lifestyle,' I point out to him.

'I like this kind of lifestyle. I haven't been out like this for ages. A lot of thanks goes to you for that.' He holds out his hand as he speaks, and I take it in mine.

'Then why don't you stay with me tonight and enjoy it totally?' I sound like a man begging a woman.

'We'll see.' He is being coy and uncommitted.

'What is it you do in your simple job?'

'I'm a school teacher,' he tells me.

'That's not a simple job.' I'm actually amazed at his humbleness.

'I've done my job all my working life; it's all I know. But at this stage of life, I can't see myself progressing any further. Headmaster, er, sorry, head teacher is about the only step forward for me, and that ain't happening. Mainly because I don't want that. But you've got a career ahead of you; there will forever be another rung of the ladder to get your feet on.'

'But a school teacher... I would bring you an apple every day.'

'And you've just hit the nail on the head. I was just twenty when I first faced a classroom of kids; secondary kids. Girls of fifteen, most having lost their virginity long before I did. All sexually active. And it's still the same now. I'm forty-seven, and the girls of this generation are more sexy and provocative than ever, even in school uniform,' he says, quite reluctantly.

That explains his meaning of being trained to overlook a sexily dressed girl like me. *Oh my God, and I offered to dress up as a schoolgirl for his pleasure. Oops.* No wonder he snapped at me. And I think of that song playing round his house earlier. All them school kids going, 'Hey, teacher!' It must be his mantra. And it probably explains a lot about his persona, too; his calmness, and the fact that I haven't really heard him swear. 'And do some of the girls, like, still have a crush on you?'

'Not so much now. Not like in my early days. You get to recognise the signs and have to deal with it. You have to be able to walk away from temptation.'

'I can resist everything except temptation,' I say.

He just grins and continues, 'There are strict guidelines. Procedures. Rules. But it's not like it's difficult, I've just got used to looking at a girl and seeing no more than a girl, however attractive, in whatever way. But some do push their luck at times. Don't get me wrong, I love my job and I'd like to think I'm a friendly teacher, so it's never been a problem. Anything like a crush is soon, er, crushed. You have to. But meeting you has put a new angle on it.'

'So, why was it different when you met me? You called me, like, a dark beauty.'

'Did I? Oh.' His eyes widen as he says that, and then went 'But only earlier you growled at me for not noticing how you're dressed tonight.'

Point taken. 'So, what do you teach?'

'Sport, in the main. I actually moved onto it from teaching maths. That's how I started out, but I'm a keen sportsman, a black belt in karate, and when the chance came to become a sports master, well, I couldn't refuse.'

That explains the photo back at his home with the sports trophy. And probably explains his physique. 'You're an expert at all sports?'

'It's not about being an expert at sport; it's all about encouragement and enthusiasm. Some kids' idea of sport is probably Candy Crush on their smartphone, but most are keen. But if there's an up-and-coming Jude Bellingham out there, or an Emma Raducanu, or maybe an Anthony Joshua…'

'I'm sure they're famous sports people, but I've never heard of half of them,' I say. 'This Emma…' *what did he call her?* 'Raddo-something, is she a karate champion or someone?'

'Emma Raducanu,' he reiterates. 'She's a top British tennis player. Won the American Open aged eighteen. I could have said someone like, I dunno, David Beckham or Jonny Wilkinson or Chris Hoy. *Sir* Chris Hoy. You definitely wouldn't have heard of any of them.'

'I've heard of David Beckham. Ain't he married to Victoria Beckham?'

'There you go, you see. If there's a budding David Beckham out there, whatever their favourite sport, I'm right behind them.'

'I've only heard of him 'cause I like Victoria's Secrets underwear. What's he do?'

'Footballer. Ex-footballer. Former England captain.' I must have had a blank expression 'cause he adds, 'You're too young.'

Bang! Right between the eyes.

'I'm not big on sports. Got better ways to spend a Saturday afternoon.'

Stevie raises an eyebrow.

'Do you teach karate?' I – perhaps a little patronisingly – do a 'chop' with my free hand.

'Not really that much call for it in schools. I do a little private teaching at a karate club. I'm known as a sensei. It means teacher.'

'First Italian, now Japanese. Is there no end to your talents?'

'One job is enough, though, and like I said, I do enjoy it. I still do a bit of maths, too. I have to keep my hand in, same as the karate club. I'm too old for serious competition, but I still enjoy a bout at the club and, as I say, I do a bit of teaching, particularly with youngsters. I'm not fully trained as an instructor, but it's great to encourage the enthusiasm. I could teach you if you like.'

I ignore that offer but wonder if it means seeing more of him and getting hands on. Wishful thinking, perhaps. 'What about teaching Italian, like your mum?'

'Again, not much call for it in schools, and where there is, it's extra-curricular and not where I work. I don't intend to move and give up my sports. And again, I'm not fully trained to teach it.' He smiles that charming smile of his, the one that makes my heart flutter and makes me grin.

'But hang on a minute. You say you're all touchy feely, what, with all them schoolgirls falling over themselves to get to you?' I say.

'Tactile only in the right environment. At school, er, work, I'm very professional. I mean, it's probably my karate that goes some way to that,' he tries to explain and just shrugs his shoulders. 'It's all hands on.'

All hands on? I thought that.

'You'll have to excuse me, I need to visit the loo.' Even saying he needs a piss, he's so polite. While he's gone, I take the rare opportunity to look at my mobile phone and am surprised that I've had no messages all night. I had let everyone know I was going out with Stevie so they wouldn't need to pester me, but I'm still surprised no one has. I take a look on Facebook, but there's nothing on there either. Stevie comes back from the toilet, and I lift up my mobile and snap his picture.

Stevie takes a sip of his cocktail – well, I think he's drinking his vodka or gin drink again, whilst I'm having 'sex on the beach'; *I had to, didn't I?* He doesn't sit down but takes my hand and leads me back to the dance floor. We dance close again, cheek-to-cheek, nearly, as he's a bit taller than me. I was still holding my mobile as he whisked me to the dance floor and didn't get to put it down. So, I take a selfie with our faces so close, and he smiles for the camera, so he obviously doesn't mind. Then I lean up and our lips meet in a luxurious kiss. Still holding up my mobile, I take another photo of us in our embrace. Unfortunately, it doesn't come out well, almost missing us. But the chance has gone to try another.

We dance for a little while, but I'm getting tired and ask to sit down again. Back at the table, I call up the two photos I've just taken and post them on Facebook with the comment '00 heaven!'.

'Doesn't your mum do Facebook?' he asks, pointing out that she'll probably see it.

'Oh my God!' Delete. Delete. *Phew*.

We finish our drinks and Stevie asks if I'm ready to go. I think of the things that may be about to happen when we go back home – I'm hoping to go to his house, but I don't mind if it's to mine. I yawn; the wine and cocktails and everything are beginning to take effect. It's not really like me, but it's probably more to do with having the type of drink that I'm not normally used to.

We get into a taxi and Stevie gives my address, putting his arm around my shoulders as we head off. I yawn again, close my eyes, and rest my head on his shoulder.

* * *

I wake up in my bed. It, like, takes a couple of seconds to get my senses together and I realise I'm at home, in bed alone, and completely naked. Even when I've had sex, I still get into my pyjamas to sleep. And my head is banging. *Oh dear.* Last night all comes flooding back to me.

Stevie! He must have brought me home, undressed me, and put me to bed. And Mum might have helped him. *Oh my God.* I look at the clock; it's gone nine. Nothing unusual for a Sunday morning, but I need to know what happened after getting in the taxi. I reach for my mobile and immediately text Stevie.

Hi Stevie. Call me when you can. What happened last night? x x x

Three kisses, I make sure I give three kisses, and I await a response. And I wait, and I wait. I get up, shower, dress, and have some breakfast. Mum is up and about but she says nothing about last night, which doesn't solve that conundrum. She may have been up like she was the night before. So, I bring up the subject.

'Did you hear me come in last night, Mum?' I ask all innocently.

'No, sweetheart, I was dead to the world last night.' *Phew.* 'I went to bed early; I think the lack of sleep the night before caught up with me. It must be my age.' She's starting to sound like Stevie.

'Oh, Mum. You're not old, what's the matter with you? Age don't make no difference anyway.'

'I never said I was old,' she chides me. 'But I ain't got the energy like you youngsters have, partying all night and everything.'

Yeah, everything. I still need to know what happened, there's still no response from Stevie, and it's getting on for an hour now since I texted. Then suddenly my mobile starts ringing, making me jump. My heart skips a beat and I don't even look to see who it is before I answer. It's Stevie.

'Hello,' I say. *Damn. That sounds a bit formal.*

'Hi, Debbie, it's Steven.' He would naturally say something like that to my plain answer.

'Hi, Stevie, how are you this morning? I texted you ages ago to see how you were.'

'I know, sorry, babe.' *He just called me 'babe'!* 'I'm at the gym and my mobile was in the locker. I only just looked at it and saw your message. What's up, babe?'

He called me 'babe' again. 'Nothing, sweetheart.' I'm copying my mum, but it's a reply in kind. 'Hang on. At the gym? At this hour; after last night. I know you're a sportsman but…'

'Just working off the excesses of last night.'

'Oh.' He really is a superman. 'I wanted to know what happened last night after we got in the taxi. Did I fall asleep?'

'You did.'

'And then I woke this morning, totally starkers in bed, alone.' The last word is emphasised to express disappointment. 'And you put me to bed?'

'Yes. Is that ok?'

I'm nodding on the phone, but I can picture the scene of last night.

*

The taxi pulls up outside my house. Stevie pays the driver, then asks, 'Can you call to arrange a cab to pick me up again in,' he looks at his watch, 'twenty minutes?'

'Sure,' says the driver.

Stevie gets out of the car, opens the door on my side, and helps me out. I'm very unsteady on my feet, more than half asleep, and Stevie gently helps me up to the house. 'Come on, Debbie, take your time, take it steady.'

At my door, Stevie takes my handbag and rummages for the house keys and opens the door. The light in the hallway is left on; good old Mum. 'Are you ok to take the stairs?'

I nod dumbly, and Stevie leads me upstairs and into my bedroom. Once in the room, he sits me on the bed. I kick off my shoes. 'Do you want me to help you get undressed?'

'Yes. Mmm.' I lie back on the bed, making it difficult for him to remove my clothes, so he pulls me back into a seating position and attempts to remove my top. As he does this, without me making it easy, I begin to try and undo his trousers.

'Stop it, Debbie. I'm trying to get your clothes off.'

'Yeah, and I'm trying to get yours off. Come on, get your cock out.'

'Don't be silly,' he says, pushing my hands away and then succeeding at removing my top. 'You can lie back now; I'll take your skirt off.'

He pushes me gently and I arch my back so it's easier for him to take off my skirt. It is a natural reaction in that position. 'And my knickers,' I tell him, as I start to pull at the elastic. 'You can't shag me while I've got me knickers on.'

My knickers are off, but he's taking little notice. Instead, he's moved round to pull back the bed sheet to help me in. 'Come on, Debbie, round here.' He walks me round to the bedside.

As he sits me down on the bed, I look up at him with a drunken smile. 'Come on then, get in with me,' I say, reaching back to undo my bra. I drop it on the floor, and he gets his chance to see my beautiful boobs. But, taking no notice, he gets me into a lying position and brings my legs up onto the bed then covers me with the quilt. He leans down and kisses me on the forehead, but I wrap my arms around him and pull him into a full snog.

Stevie pulls away and backs off. 'Goodnight, Debbie.' He's just about to turn off the light when I jump up and go after him.

'Come to bed with me, Stevie,' I say, dragging him back.

He leads me back to the bed, or am I leading him? I get back in. 'Goodnight, Debbie,' he says again, but I hold onto his wrist.

'Stay with me,' I plead in my drunken state, 'please.'

He looks at his watch, then climbs onto the bed and holds his arms around me and we kiss, briefly and gently.

He strokes my hair and kisses me lightly around my face and on my shoulder. Oh, it's so sensual.

I drift off into a deep sleep.

*

'Even my clothes were folded neatly on the chair, knickers and all,' I say to him on the mobile.

'I couldn't leave your room looking like a bomb site,' he says matter of factly, 'so I quickly tidied up before going out to meet the taxi.' Even in a situation like that he was a gentleman.

'You didn't take advantage?'

'What? Like I'm gonna do that. And besides, if I was looking for that kinda thing, do I need to wait till you're disadvantaged?'

Oh no, I've upset him. 'Sorry, Steven.' I even use his proper name. 'I'm sorry, I don't mean to upset you or accuse you of anything. You've been good to me ever since that first minute we met. And last night just, like, proves how special you are.' There's a pause. 'Can I see you again?'

'I think we should leave it for now. I'm busy today with karate club, and then it's back to work tomorrow.' *Please don't say it's over.* 'Let's wait till next week and we'll see from there. A lot can happen in a week.'

I think I'm beginning to cry. There's certainly a tear on my cheek that I have to brush away. It's not that we haven't slept together, and I know he's a lot older than me, but he is a wonderful man and it's the first time I've ever had feelings this way.

'Ok.' I have to go along with him. If I force his hand he might pull further away. 'You're not cross about last night, trying to put me to bed, are you?'

'No, not at all, Debbie,' he says very sincerely. 'I just wanted to make sure you were safe. Last night was, er, fantastic, as you'd put it. It was my sort of idea of going out. The wine went to your head; it happens sometimes. We had quite a lot. And Friday night was your scene, we had a great time then. But it shows that it's not just an age gap that's in our way, it's a cultural difference, too.'

I have to admit he has a point, but that doesn't placate me right now. 'I'll call you in the week and see how you are, if that's alright?' I'm clutching at straws, I know, but I'm not giving in too easily.

'Yeah, sure. I look forward to your call.'

Bastard! *Now he's teasing me.* I keep my calm. 'Ok, Stevie, speak to you later.'

'Yes, bye, Debbie.'

'Bye.' And we hang up. I give a heavy sigh then burst into tears. Mum sees me in distress.

'What's the matter, sweetheart?' she asks, putting an arm around me.

I sniff and wipe my eyes with the back of my hand. 'Nothing.'

'Come on, sweetheart, I'm your mum. Tell me what's wrong.'

'No. It's nothing, honest. I shan't be seeing Stevie all week, that's all.' It's all I can think of to say.

'What about next weekend?' asks Mum, still holding me.

'Yes, hopefully.'

'Well, if he's worth it, it'll be worth the wait. Because you're worth it, too.' She's so lovely, my mum. I love her to bits.

Chapter Seven

Later that day I'm back out with Haze and Jules, just in the local pub for a couple of Sunday night drinks.

'Where's lover boy tonight?' asks Haze, drinking with a straw in her alcopop bottle. She pulls the straw out and says, 'Did you give him plenty…?' And she puts the bottle in her mouth and sucks it like it's a cock.

Both Jules and I grin at her action; it's very evocative and leaves no room for explanation. I do the same with my bottle but shake it just before I 'suck' it, so that some of the drink goes into my mouth, over my lips, and makes me dribble a little. Two lads standing at the bar have been watching us with amazed looks.

'You wish, boys,' says Jules, and we all laugh and rock in our seats and, like, lean against each other.

'When we got back to his place the other night,' I begin to tell them how I hoped it should have gone, my fantasy coming to the fore, 'I couldn't, like, get his trousers off quick enough. But he wanted to play some sensual music and light candles. My fanny was, like, dripping with excitement, my knickers were damp, and I was aching to get them off… for him to take them off.'

Haze and Jules were listening intently, Haze still holding her bottle and rubbing it as though it was still a cock. So, I carry on. 'Boy, does he know where a woman's clitoris is and, like, how to work on it.' I can't help myself; I know I'm lying but I keep on talking. I'm actually getting aroused by what I'm saying.

'He snogged my gob off for ages, teasing me with his tongue whilst his hands were all over me – on my thighs, up the top and over my wet knickers, and over my boobs, before finding his way to undo my dress and my bra. He sucked my tits, hard. My nipples were stiff and ready, his tongue all over them, licking and sucking and driving me wild.'

'Didn't you get his kit off and suck his nipples as well?' Haze's bottle was getting a real working, and I almost expected the drink to suddenly shoot out of the top like a champagne bottle. Or a cock coming.

'I tried to pull off his shirt, as it was undone most of the way, but he was in complete control and I was, like, surrendering to his magic.'

'I would've had his cock in my mouth, like, letting him know who was in command,' says Jules. She's always the dominant type.

'Oh, that came later.' I was really getting a feel for this; I was loving it, picturing Stevie all the time…

They want passionate details, so here goes.

*

He worked his lips and mouth down my body, driving me insane with every tingling touch till he reached my knickers. But instead of pulling them off, or pushing them aside, he put his head right between my legs, pushing his face right into my wet knickers. That made me make them even wetter!

I could feel the features of his face all over my pussy, pushing the silky, but wet, material of my knickers into me. The feeling was surprisingly exquisite. I was longing for him to take them off, but he worked magic on me, just moving his tongue and lips on the edges of the material, teasing me and prolonging the ecstasy, torturing me with pleasure and passion.

Then his fingers slipped under the material of my knickers, and he eased them down to expose my glistening wet pussy. He breathed in the aroma of my sex and the juices as he took my knickers down all the way, over my heeled shoes – I still had them on; I think he liked it that way – and dropped my knickers on the floor. Then he was back down there, his tongue searching round my shag hole, licking, teasing, sending shudders right through my body. I was murmuring sounds of pleasure, running my fingers through his hair, lifting my knees so that my feet were on his hips and so lifting my fanny for him to devour.

Then he reached my clitoris. I don't think he had trouble finding it, as it must have been standing proud, inviting and glistening. But he delayed the act deliberately to tease me further, making me go wild, because when his tongue hit the spot, it made me gasp with, like, ecstasy and I instantly had a red-hot raging orgasm. I screamed out at him, 'Stevie, oh, yes, Stevie!' as he continued to lick me, and I squirmed under him, releasing my juice into his mouth and over his face. He was murmuring sounds of ecstasy, too, loving that I made him wet.

When I couldn't stand it no more, I pulled his head up and drew him into a kiss, tasting myself on his wet lips. He then stood up and took off his clothes. When it came to his pants, I reached forward and rubbed his crotch, my hand over the material, then fingered the edges and pulled his pants down. His rock hard cock jumped out at my face like a cobra striking. I took hold of him, my manicured fingers bejewelling his shaft, pulling back his foreskin, his head wet with pre-cum. I tantalisingly reached out my tongue to taste the honey and licked my tongue over the head of his cock, swirling it round and round, repaying him the torture of delayed pleasure before slipping my lips around the tip and slowly further and further over his throbbing penis. Deeper and deeper I took him in, and slowly drew him out again, then in once more, and out, and in, over and over. His balls were tight and full in my hand. I urged the escape of his honey, drawing his foreskin up and down, running my lips tightly over the shaft of his manhood.

He took his cock from my mouth and gently pushed me back onto the bed, then he moved over me, my legs open and waiting, wanting him inside me. He snogged me once again – this time allowing him to get his own tastes – as his cock neared my opening and he eased himself in. Oh, it was, like, out of this world. The thickness of such a length pushing deep inside me, thrusting gently, raising my breathing patterns. I had my arms under his, with my nails gently scratching his back in a tantalising way, my legs wrapped around him to try and squeeze him deeper inside.

As he thrust, I thrust back, building a gentle rhythm back and forth, getting quicker and faster, our breathing in rhythm to our movement. We went faster and faster until he stiffened and stilled his body, pumping all his honey deep into my soaking pussy. A thunderous orgasm ripped through my body as I clenched my pelvic muscles to drain every last drop from his balls, whilst he panted hotly on my neck. He kissed me gently there before lifting himself up and withdrawing, rolling over to lie beside me. I sat up and went down on him, his cock still hard, smothered in our juices, and I sucked hungrily on it, kissing it and thanking it for such a wonderful, mind-blowing performance…

*

SUGAR DADDY?

When I finish speaking, I am almost sweating and weary, as if the act had really taken place there and then. Haze and Jules are dumbstruck, which is a first, their mouths open aghast. We've talked about boys before, but nothing like that, nothing so descriptive. I was just in the zone; and all of it fantasy! *Oh, how I wish it was true.*

'Wow!' It is Jules who speaks first.

'We've shared before, but not this time. He's all mine. After our motorbike ride yesterday, it was a repeat performance, orgasm after orgasm. His cock is like a piston engine,' I say with a grin.

'I'll get him. I could take him right now. No man can resist me. Watch,' continues Jules, emphasising her words by running her hands over her boobs as the two lads at the bar look on. She runs her tongue over her teeth and licks her lips at them.

She stands up and moves over to them. Haze and I watch as she stands between them, putting her arms around them both. She talks quietly to them and moves away, heading toward the ladies. The lads look at each other in some sort of dismay, then put down their drinks and follow Jules to the ladies.

I can picture the scene.

*

In the ladies' loo, Jules is waiting as the two lads walk in, not quite believing what was promised to them.

'Don't worry, I can handle both of you at once,' she says, leading them to a cubicle. Jules sits down on the toilet and gestures them in closer, and one of them locks the door. She then begins to undo the trousers of the other one, pulls them down, and his pants, to unveil his cock. She takes hold of it, and soon he is hard and ready. Then she turns to his friend and undresses him, too. He already has a hard on, probably from the actions on his mate.

Holding each of their cocks at once, Jules then begins to give one of them a blow job while she wanks the other lad seductively, running her thumb over his bell end. She sucks harder still on the first one and he calls out.

'I can't hold it, I'm coming, I'm coming.' Jules then takes him out of her mouth and proceeds to give the other one a blow job. 'Oh, no!' says the first, 'Don't stop now.' But she takes no notice and continues to wank him off as he shoots his cream, most of it landing on the trousers of his friend. Number two is so worked up he hardly notices.

Jules sucks harder and harder, using both her hands, having let go of number one. Grasping his balls, she entices the sweet cream from out of his balls, sucking and swallowing every drop. Then she takes him out of her mouth, kisses his penis head, and stands up.

'Thanks, guys. That's just what I needed.' She kisses the first lad fully on the lips with a tongue-searching snog. He must have gotten a full taste of his friend, and as she walks away, she grins to herself, satisfied in a job well done; a blow job well done.

*

As I lie in bed that night, alone, how I wish Stevie was lying next to me. Never mind that explicitly described fantasy to Haze and Jules; just to have him next to me. To feel him close, to hold, to cuddle up to.

I take out my mobile phone and write out a text.

Goodnight, Stevie, it's been a wonderful weekend. Hope to see you again very soon. Sleep tight, love Debbie x x x

Three kisses. Has to be three kisses.

I put my head down and snuggle into the covers; I don't hear a reply from Stevie come through before I drift off into a deep sleep.

Chapter Eight

Monday morning, and back to the reality of work. I get to my desk and drop down into the chair. I probably give the image of complete tiredness, but it's more a reluctance of being back in the work environment and not the excitement of the weekend just passed.

'Morning.' The usual pleasantries are bandied around with my colleagues. Louise is more my age and a good friend.

'Did you have a good weekend?' she asks me. I reply with just a big grin, which obviously tells the whole story. 'Oh, you must tell me more. Did you meet Prince Charming?'

'I did. Prince Charming, James Bond, and a knight in shining armour all rolled into one.' Yes, he was a knight in shining armour in the end.

'Wow. I want all the dirty details,' she whispers at me, 'and the clean ones. If there are any.'

'I met this drop-dead gorgeous guy in town on Friday night, and he took me clubbing. We had a real laugh; it was fantastic. At the end of the night, I asked to see him again,' a little fib, 'and we met up the next day and he took me out on his Harley Davidson. Brrmm!'

Louise laughs. 'Oh, brilliant! Anything else?' She gives me a knowing look.

'Oh, yes,' I tell her, just recalling the things I said to Haze and Jules last night. I still dream that it was for real, but sadly it's only a fantasy.

What have I got to do to get Stevie into bed? I'm falling head over heels for his charm and kindness, but I just want to consummate the friendship. 'We went out for an Italian on Saturday, and he *speaks* Italian. He was so sexy with the way he spoke, it made me all unnecessary.' I give a little shudder to describe the feeling of lust that surged through me when he did speak Italian. That bit wasn't fantasy, and the feelings are still there as I remember the evening.

'It's about time you met a fella. When are you gonna let Louise meet him?' She always says her own name and not, like, the word 'me'.

'I've got him all to myself for now. I want to keep a tight rein on him and keep away the scavengers.'

'Have you got any photos?' I show Louise the couple of pictures I took in the Italian restaurant. 'Oh my God! No wonder you want to keep a tight rein on him, he's a hottie.'

'He is.'

'Does that include the bedroom, too?' I almost blush at that. It answers the question for Louise. 'Tell me more.'

'My knickers were, like, wet before we even got to the bedroom,' that bit was true, 'in anticipation of what was to come. And he took his time getting them off, teasing me, and filling me with sensations of lust just running through me from my honey pot right to the ends of my fingers and toes.' Oh my God, I'm reliving my fantasy description of last night, and it's making me feel those sensations again, wanting. 'It was sensational.'

Louise is grinning and about to comment when Alan comes over. 'Anyway, back on the horse,' Louise says with a little clearing of her throat. It cuts off our conversation and we start to look busy.

Alan is one of the office managers, and he spoke to me specifically. 'Debbie, can you go to 'brainstorm'? Mr Jackson wants to have a word with you.'

Brainstorm is the word given for the weekly Monday morning managers' meeting, which was not normally for the likes of me. Mr Jackson is the managing director, but we only ever see him at brainstorm.

Louise looks at me. 'Mmm?' is all she says.

I walk over to the brainstorm office. It's a glass-walled one, so you can see everyone in there. I knock and enter. Mr Jackson stands to greet me. 'Come in, Deborah.' He always calls people by their proper name; no abbreviations for Christopher Jackson. Not even my mum calls me Deborah; except when I was a kid and she was, like, telling me off. 'Take a seat. Have you had a coffee yet?'

'I much prefer a tea, please, Mr Jackson.' He nods to his secretary, and she prepares me a cuppa.

'Milk and sugar?' she asks. An older woman, Gladys must be nearing retirement; her name speaks for itself. I understand she's part of the furniture here, been the secretary to every managing director since she was my age. But she is a very pleasant woman, a good one to have in your corner.

'Just milk,' I say sweetly, 'thank you.' Not 'with biscuits' like I said to Stevie.

'Deborah,' continues Mr Jackson, 'we've asked you in this morning to talk about the Glasgow project, of which I'm sure you're aware, yes?'

'I am, Mr Jackson.' Gladys brings me my tea. 'Thank you.'

'Our engineers and surveyors have done all their work, and now it's up to us in finance to seal the deal. It is worth something in the region of eighty million pounds to us over the next three years. Hopefully that can be doubled and even more with the right strategy, with more construction expected in the Glasgow and Clyde area.' Mr Jackson is showing me some protracted charts on, like, a wall-mounted computer screen of how the project could progress.

'We are sending Philip to Glasgow tomorrow,' he indicates Philip (Phil), 'to seal the deal. You know Philip, of course.'

'Yes, I do.' I look at Phil, one of our top accountants. No, our top accountant. He smiles at me, and I flush a little and look down at my hands. I recover quickly by taking a sip of my tea with a little clearing of my throat. Phil is another hottie, but I've never fancied him because, well, because he's like thirty-four years old, too old for me. *Yeah, right.* Married anyway.

'He's the best man to seal this deal, but he needs an assistant with all the numbers and statistics, and we're asking you to go with him.' Before I get the chance to say anything, Mr Jackson continues, 'Obviously if it's inconvenient with such short notice, then I fully understand, but I'd like you to go to help with your progression within our company. Alan has given a glowing report on you and has recommended you for this project.'

I shoot Alan a thank you smile. Mr Jackson concludes, 'Are you prepared to travel up to Glasgow with Philip? It will be a two-night stay, with the main meeting on Wednesday. But everything will be in place, with a top hotel room for you.'

Like I'm going to turn that down? This is a fantastic opportunity; of course I'm going. 'Thank you, Mr Jackson,' I keep my calm but I'm quite excited about it. I feel honoured to be asked. 'I'll be delighted to go. And I will do all I can to assist Phil, er, Philip in securing the project.'

I go back to my desk and sit with Louise. There's obviously a grin on my face, and she's keen to know what took place in brainstorm. 'What did they say?'

Just for a second, I pull a straight face with another clearing of my throat. Then I smile at her again. 'I'm, like, going to

Glasgow with Phil tomorrow on that Glasgow project. We're gonna seal the deal. Yeah!' High fives all round.

'Oh, great! What an opportunity. Just the two of you going?'

'As far as I know, yeah.'

'You'll have to be on your best behaviour up there,' says Louise. 'That Glasgow project is a big one.'

'We'll sort it easy. Me and Phil, we're a team.'

'What about your new boyfriend? Won't he mind?'

I put my hand to my mouth, a look of shocked surprise on my face covering up the fact that I hadn't thought of him. 'Oh, Stevie!' I actually forgot about him whilst I was in brainstorm. We're not supposed to be seeing each other through the week, but I had intended to go to his house, like, unannounced, before this. 'I'll have to text him.'

Hi Stevie, I'm off to Glasgow tomorrow for three days. Business trip. Tell you all about it when I get back x x x

As the day goes on, I don't receive a message back from Stevie, but I accept that's probably down to the nature of his work.

I'm allowed to knock off early so that I can prepare for the trip. I don't know why, really; it's not like I'm packing for a month away, but I suppose it's what the big shots do with business trips, and I must be in the big shot league now. It's, like, so exciting. And I've never even been on an aeroplane before.

When I get home mid-afternoon, I finally get my reply from Stevie. I put my news on Facebook and everyone else has responded, but my message from Stevie is the best.

A business trip? Wow. Now you're in the big league. Can't wait to hear the news x x x

It is a simple text, but I love the fact he says he can't wait, so he's obviously keen for us to meet up again. And of course, I love the three kisses.

Chapter Nine

Tuesday morning, and they've sent a taxi to pick me up to take me into work. I normally go on the bus, but I'm in the big league now, as Stevie said. And from there, Phil and I are given a chauffeur-driven transfer to the airport. *This is amazing*! It's, like, a whole new experience for me, but for Phil it's probably the norm. I let him take the lead.

He checks on some TV screens once we're at the airport, looking for details of our flight. 'Check in desk fourteen,' he says. I'm still looking at the screen to see how he knows before I realise he's walked off, and I run to catch up with him.

We have to queue for a short while before checking in. It's quite a simple process really and as we are travelling light, there's no luggage to check in. 'What now?' I ask. 'Our flight's not due for like, what,' taking a look at my watch, 'another hour or more.'

'We have to go through to departures and security now, so that could take time. It's not just the people on our plane that have to go through; it's everyone, wherever they're going.'

'Oh.'

'But once we're in, there's plenty to occupy us, you know, cafes and bars, shops—'

I cut him off. 'Shops? Come on, what we waiting for?' and I start to walk off.

Phil just stands where he is, and I look back at him after a couple of steps. He inclines his head in the other direction. 'This way, Debbie.'

We get to the security, and as we queue, we have to dump everything on a conveyor belt and put all small items in a little tray. *What a palaver.* Then a security man comes up to me and asks if I don't mind going through a full body scanner. I ain't got a clue what he's on about so, like, I just nod, and he leads me through a different channel to where everyone else goes.

The security man tells me to stand on a specific spot, hold my arms out and wait. Then he leaves me feeling a like right idiot, standing there playing scarecrows, before he comes back a moment or two later. 'Thank you, miss. That's fine. You can put your arms down now.'

I drop my arms, straighten my clothes, and walk on. 'Thank you,' I say, but I don't know what for. I meet Phil again on the other side.

'That's a full body scan you've just been in. They can see everything,' he says.

Realisation suddenly hits me. 'You mean...'

Phil smiles at me and shrugs. 'I dunno,' he says.

'Bloomin' perv! He's old enough to be my dad.' Then a second realisation hits me. *Oh.*

We go into the departure lounge and I've died and, like, gone to heaven! There are shops everywhere. I can see one with shelves packed with drink, floor to ceiling. Then I see a perfumery. Fantastic. There's designer sunglasses, mobile phones, and stuff, but I can't see no shoe shop. But then I spot the Holy Grail: the lingerie shop. *Yes!* Lingerie. At the airport. Just the word sounds sexy. Lingerie. It just invokes silk, satin, and lace. Vibrant colours and see-through material.

'I'm gonna get a coffee,' says Phil. 'Coming?'

'Are you kidding? Who said paradise was green?' I say with wide eyes, gesturing at all the shops. 'You go and have a coffee. I'll see you on the plane.'

'Well, ok, but don't buy too much. You gotta carry it, remember. Give me your mobile number, just in case,' he says, and we exchange numbers.

Phil moves off towards one of the cafes, and I head in the other direction: shops. He points out where we gotta go when our flight is called, and tells me to keep an eye on the time and listen out for the announcement. But I'm in heaven, looking at all the booze in the shop, alcopops and Jagermeister, and that. And then I'm into the perfumery and all the sales girls are thrusting samples at me, so I fill my bag. Then into the lingerie shop; all that sexy underwear. Bliss. I'm taking items off the rails and holding them over me, posing in the mirror. Bras, knickers, babydolls, everything.

I lose myself in thought, seeing myself in these things and how I could seduce anyone. Stevie wouldn't be able to keep his hands off me. *Oh, Stevie, if only you were here.*

I'm brought out of my reverie by my mobile ringing. It's Phil.

'Hello.'

'Debbie, where are you? They called the flight ages ago. They've almost finished boarding. They'll be closing the gate in a minute.'

Oh, shit. 'Ok, Phil. I'm coming.' I reluctantly put back the undies I have in my hand. 'Sorry. Some other time,' I say to it, and head off as quick as I can without running, and there's Phil waiting for me. *Bless him.*

'Ok. Here she comes,' I hear him say to the boarding crew, and I'm rushed through to board the plane.

We find our seats easily, as everyone else is already seated. 'Sorry, everyone,' I say to all in general. Then as we shuffle past the woman in the aisle seat to get to our seats – mine by the window – I add, 'So many shops, so little time.' She gives a knowing smile.

Once we're seated and belted up, it's not long before the plane is on the move. It's so exciting. Then the plane stops for a while, and as I look out of the window the engines roar louder and the plane moves forward at an alarming rate. I'm like, wow! I watch as the plane leaves the ground, and all the buildings drop away until they look like little models. And then I see the main road, and the cars are like little toys in a shop, and I can see for miles. I never realised that everywhere was so green and the cities and towns so small. This is fantastic, I love it. *Look out Glasgow, here I come.*

*

It's only a quick flight up to Glasgow, and we're met by a man holding up a card with 'Coleman Construction' on it, and again we're chauffeur-driven to our hotel. It's a grand affair, not just any old low-cost place; it's five star and everything. My room is massive, with a big king size bed, shower and bath, lounge area, TV, fridge full of drink, and everything. And I'm told this is only a standard room. *Cool.*

Phil and I meet for dinner in the restaurant and enjoy a fabulous meal and a bottle of wine. I'm reminded of last Saturday out with Stevie and how the wine went to my head, so I restrict myself to just two small glasses.

Phil goes through the strategy of the next day's plan of action. 'I will be giving them a full presentation. The engineering side is all but complete; it's just up to us now. What I need you to do is study the statistics details on the laptop I've given you so that when you're prompted you can reel off the facts and figures. Obviously bring the laptop to the meeting with you. Ok?'

'Yeah, no problem.' I smile at Phil, giving him my most professional stance.

'We'll have an early night so we're refreshed and ready in the morning to be at our best. We'll go in all guns blazing.'

What? No clubbing? We're in Glasgow, for heaven's sake. But he's right; this is not a jolly, or not tonight at least. Tomorrow maybe, when the deal is done.

*

I'm up early, keen to get ready and look my best. I put on a very figure-hugging short dress with plenty of plunge. In red. The colour of seduction. Dressed like this, I can seduce them into agreeing to our deal. With absolutely invisible underwear, so as not to spoil my curves, but to enhance them. I may be a sixteen, but I'm all curves and vivaciousness. Matching high heels – goes without saying – and bright matching lipstick. I'm in for the kill.

Phil is impressed at breakfast. 'Wow! You look gorgeous.' He then coughs and looks away. 'Sorry. I don't wish to, er…'

'That's ok, Phil,' I reassure him. 'That's the impression I'm aiming for. Thank you for the compliment. If this don't get us the deal, nothing will.'

At the meeting in one of the hotel's conference rooms, I'm introduced to the bigwig of the committee we're out to impress, Sir Francis Holmes-Fitzwilliam. *What a mouthful.*

'A pleasure to meet you, Sir Francis,' I say, shaking his hand with one of those feeble, ladylike handshakes. I very nearly curtsy.

'And a pleasure to meet you, Miss Wilson.' *Yep, the dress is working. One-nil.* I much prefer to wear a dress, and I very rarely wear tights; it's, like, either bare legs or hold-ups. The dress is not too short but, like, above the knee. So, when I cross my legs, the silky sheen of my stockings glows and catches the eye.

I've chosen lace-topped, hold-up stockings, as I don't want too many lines, and although the lace isn't on display, they might, like, come in handy. Suspenders are too visible but, like, might've been a good thing on this occasion, I 'spose. My boobs were heaving for Sir Francis's eyes, the cleavage catching his attention, and I'm looking at him looking at my body. He must be in his late fifties, but my cleavage is a sight to behold for any man.

I notice that I'm the only woman in the room with six men, and I can sense them all rise but, like, none of them dare stand up.

As Phil begins his presentation, I sit down and cross my legs. I make sure they're not obscured by the desk, and there are a number of pairs of eyes that are averted away from the presentation momentarily. *Two-nil.*

The presentation goes very well, Phil putting all his expertise into it, and I follow suit, giving all the information in a very bold, unnerved, and professional manner. Sir Francis seems very impressed before calling an adjournment for coffee; tea for me.

As we sit in the more comfortable surroundings of the lounge, Sir Francis comes over to me. 'I must say, Miss Wilson, that I'm very impressed with your professional and confident attitude in all the negotiations.' I'm sitting in a low, comfortable chair, and as Sir Francis towers over me, I can tell where his eyes are targeting.

'Thank you, Sir Francis,' I say, standing up but making sure my cleavage doesn't close, practically pushing my bust at him.

'Please, call me Frank. School teachers are called sir.' I'm, like, all shivers down my spine. That hit home; I know a school teacher. He sits down in the chair next to me and gestures for me to sit back down.

'Of course, er, Frank.' But I don't respond by telling him to call me Debbie; Miss Wilson is fine for now. I know what's impressing him most.

'I'm always in favour of career-minded people like you, with your professional style and confident character. I think there is a good future for you, and if you're looking for a change of scenery, there will always be a position in my company for you,' he says with a smile that underlines the words that are between the lines.

'I don't think I'm ready for a move to Scotland quite just yet, Frank.'

'Oh, I've got business locations all over the UK, and in Europe, too. I can picture you in a position somewhere closer to home. It is a multi-million-pound operation that I own.'

I think he's picturing a certain position that doesn't involve work, and he's probably got the *Karma Sutra* in his back pocket. 'Thank you, it's nice to know my assets are appreciated.' I flash my sweet smile, only too happy to please.

When the meeting reconvenes, almost every time I speak, Sir Francis – Frank – comments with something like 'Thank you, Miss Wilson' and 'very good, Miss Wilson'. He definitely has the eye for me.

And when it comes to lunch, he makes a point of sitting opposite me. At first, I thought he would sit next to me, but then I remember my cleavage and understand why.

'Allow me, Miss Wilson,' he says, holding my chair for me to sit down. He walks round the table to sit opposite, but someone has already taken the seat. 'Come along, Chambers,' he says, 'you know you should let the ladies be seated first.' Then he practically shoves the guy out of the seat and sits in it himself. Of course, when I realise this,

I make sure he gets a good view. Like standing up and leaning over the table to reach for the salt or something, and enlarging the view.

After lunch and coffee, I excuse myself to return to my room. As I'm standing waiting for the lift to arrive, Frank comes along.

'Where are you off to, Miss Wilson?' he asks.

'You can call me Debbie; that's what my friends call me.'

'Thank you, Debbie. So, which floor?' he says, as we step into the lift.

'Third. I'm just popping back to my room to freshen up before we reconvene,' I say.

As the doors open on the third floor, Frank steps out with me. 'Allow me to escort you to your room,' he says as we walk along the corridor.

'It's only just here.' Barely fifteen feet from the lift. 'Which floor are you on?'

'I'm on the top floor, Debbie. I have one of the suites. Would you like to come and have a look?'

I know where this is leading, and I am ready to go along with it. I don't even open my room door. 'Yes, please,' I say, and move back to the lift. I can see his face light up like a beacon. In some cases, this might be seen as sexual harassment. But I see it, like, two ways: I'm gonna get some cock, and I ain't had no cock all weekend; and we get the deal.

We get to his suite and Frank shows me in. 'Wow! This is fantastic!' And it really is. The place is as big as my whole house. There is a lounge area with sofas and scatter cushions, and a large office desk, all mahogany and leather. The bedroom would be big enough to play tennis in, if it wasn't for the giant bed. The king size in my room seems like a doll's bed by comparison. And the bathroom is all polished marble and chrome; it's amazing. It even has two toilets. At least, I think they are both toilets; one has taps on.

'Do you like it?' he asks, gesturing round the room (rooms). 'When you're the owner of a large business empire like me, this becomes the norm.' I think he is trying to impress me, or maybe just boasting.

I look up at him. They say power is a strong aphrodisiac, and I now believe it to be so. He looks down at me with a masterful gaze, and I know this is where we seal the deal, because I am wanting this to happen. Frank's power over me is majestic and I move close to him, putting my hands on his chest, moving gently over his nipples under his shirt and to his tie. I begin to slowly undo it, drawing it from around his neck, and casually toss it onto one of the sofas.

His hands are on my hips, and they search round my waist and up my back. He then brings his hands round the front and over my breasts whilst I'm, like, undoing the buttons of his shirt. I give a little gasp; I just love my boobs being caressed. Our faces come close together and we kiss, just our lips probing and teasing each other, but then passionately. It is a real turn-on for me; for us both. I can feel the juices begin to flow down below in my honey pot, and I can certainly feel Frank's growing hard on. I put my hand down and caress his penis through his trousers. He gives a little moan of pleasure.

I think of Stevie. *Oh my God. This is what I want from him.* Frank is not old enough to be my mum – more like old enough to be my grandmother – and here I am about to shag him. I'm aware that this will get us the deal, but right now I just want sex. I need to be pleasured and have my boobs groped and nipples enticed. I need cock inside me. And I realise that I'm probably a sex addict, and Stevie has starved me since we met.

Stevie has really taken my heart with his kindness and nature, but I need sex. Lots of it. And right now, I'm ready to give this man the shagging of his life.

We part from our embrace, and I begin to undo my dress as Frank picks up his mobile and makes a call. 'Frank here. I think we can make a rapid closure on the deal this afternoon,' he says, as he watches me take off my dress. 'But something has just, er, come off. We'll reconvene this afternoon at…' he looks at his watch, 'three o'clock.'

I suppose that's his power. And I want it. I move over to him, still in my matching red undies, stockings, and heels. I stand before him as he stays seated after his call, and I let him run his hands over my body. He moves his face closer and lightly kisses my tummy, again and again. Oh, it is sensational, and feelings of lust surge through my veins and penetrate my sexual organs. I run my hands through his hair to hold him close to me whilst he reaches up to caress my breasts again through just the material of my bra. His fingers feel for the bare parts of my boobs and run them down the cleavage, and although I love having my boobs caressed and kneaded – especially whilst I'm still in my bra – I, like, allow him to move his hands around my back to encounter the tangible conundrum of undoing a woman's bra and getting it off quickly. There's lots more to explore.

I begin to moan with pleasure at his touch and his mouth on my tummy, and then he pulls me closer still and begins his oral exploration of my breasts, to my joy and satisfaction. His tongue gently sweeps across my erect nipple, his hands covering every part of my body with delicate precision, round my torso, my inner thighs, and over my bum. He then takes hold of my knickers and slowly, almost teasingly, takes them down. He lowers his head as my knickers reach my feet, to slip them off completely over my heels. His face is right in my crotch, and he kisses me there.

'I do believe you're trying to get me into bed, Sir Francis,' I gasp. *And I think you're going to succeed*, I say to myself. Then hopefully I'll suck seed, too.

He sits up straight and regards me totally naked in front of him with a hungry, lustful look in his eye. I am totally at his whim. 'You are beautiful,' he tells me.

'Thank you,' I reply, 'and I'm all yours to do as you wish.'

He stands before me, takes me in his arms, and kisses me passionately once again. My hands drop to his waistline and I undo his trousers. They drop to the floor, but he still has his shoes on, and it becomes a bit comical as he tries to kick off his trousers whilst still trying to maintain the passionate embrace.

I back away from him and smile, holding his hand and slowly letting the grip go as I keep eye contact until the last second and turn and walk into the bedroom.

A moment later, Frank walks in, having removed all his clothes and, like, fully erect. I lie on the bed seductively. Even my heels are off now, but with my stockings still on, I hold on to the headboard as if I am tied there. I'm looking at his cock, so hard and ready; I'm, like, *Come to Debbie*. He might be in his late fifties or even in his sixties, but, like, it's all about the cock.

This is my playground. Taking off a man's pants is like opening a treasure chest, or like a child on Christmas morning. It's all about the cock. It fills me with so much excitement, with a multitude of adventures to explore and playing so many different games with, like, just one toy.

Frank climbs on the bed and lays beside me. I thought he would get on top, but he lies on his back. I get the message, so I turn on to my side and reach down for his cock.

Taking him in my hand, I begin to rub him up and down, up and down. I am now, like, totally in control. I lean in close, still with my hand motion, and kiss him again.

He gives more moans of pleasure with his arms around me, our mouths touching lightly, half kissing, half teasing. Then I feel the gentle push to send me down. I don't need any prompting and I go down on him willingly, wantonly. I want this stiff cock in my mouth, and I'm going to savour every tantalizing taste of it.

But first, whilst still gently wanking him, my tongue runs over his tight balls, just teasing with the tip of my tongue. He gives a loud intake of breath and that prompts me to keep the sensation going. I lick and butterfly kiss his balls and run my fingers over his penis head; it's so wet and ready. My tongue slides up his shaft, slowly, deliberately, until I reach the top. I run my tongue over it just once and follow with my lips, just touching the tip, then slowly sliding them over his cock and taking him deep into my mouth. I draw it back out again, then in, out, and in. Frank is, like, going wild with pleasure. I continue to suck, harder and harder, my fingers caressing and teasing his balls.

'Go steady. I'm gonna come in your mouth if you keep that up,' he calls out.

Oh, yes! That's, like, all the encouragement I need. But I stop, smacking my lips; I don't want to waste it. At his age, he might not be able to go two rounds, and I want this monster inside me. I'm aching for it. So, I climb on top of Frank and straddle him, slipping down onto his stiff cock with ease as we're both so wet. I lean down and kiss him, my tongue probing into his mouth, giving him a full taste of his own cock. I thrust my pelvis, and I can feel an orgasm building, but to my horror, he rolls us over so that he is on top of me... and then withdraws.

I'm, like, *what?!!*

But then he moves his body down and kisses my torso on his way to between my legs and straight in, his tongue plunging into my wet, wet fanny, circling and probing every part of me and exquisitely over my clitoris. The building orgasm is coming back, and I am tensing and arching my back as I thunder to my climax and release my honey over his face and into his mouth. Oh my God, I haven't had an orgasm like that for ages. Has meeting Stevie and hoping to shag him been a mistake? Age means nothing. Frank wanted me, and he's got me. I admit now that sex is, like, the most important thing, and having missed out over the weekend just passed, this is more than making up for it.

'Yes, yes, oh, yes!' I scream out, as I orgasm with Frank's head down between my legs. I pull his head up to kiss him, but he stops short at my breasts, putting his lips around my nipple and his hand over my other breast, kneading me, sucking me. Oh, the sensation! He sucks and licks and nibbles at me, changing over to do the same with both breasts. I can feel it all building up again down below as he keeps up the torment of pleasure.

Finally, he comes away and moves to enter me with his cock. He feels around for my opening, then finds my wet hole and sinks his length into me, easing his way home no problem, with both our bodily fluids mingling together. His penetration takes my breath away and he thrusts in and out, in and out of me; mmm!

He thrusts inside me and rises up on his hands, his arms stretched either side of me, and he encourages me to bring my legs up and over his shoulders. He shifts his body into a kind of sitting position and puts his full length into me. Deeper and deeper, it feels so tight, so thick and big inside me. I'm riding on a wave of erotic pleasure; I'm calling out to him. 'Oh, yes, Frank. Oh, it's so tight.'

For a man that was on the verge of coming earlier, he seems to have found a lot more stamina. And with the intensity of our thrust and counter-thrust, my legs over his shoulders, his cock beating a path right through to my soul, the excitement sends wave upon wave of exotic sensation through my whole body. I feel another orgasm pound its way through my arms, up my legs and down my body, over my boobs and into my fanny, all soft and wet with an enlarged clitoris, as Frank withdraws just enough to keep the head of his penis right on the hot spot of my clit.

Oh my God! The orgasm thunders its way out of my body as I shout out. 'Ohh!' Frank then pushes his way back into me to empty his load deep into my fanny. 'Ohh!' I call out again. 'This is fantastic.' My pleasure is totally fulfilled, my body spent.

Frank rolls over and lies beside me, both of us catching our breath from the passionate intensity of it all, the sensations having driven us both wild to exhaustion.

I'm, like, that's what you call a shag.

But why am I thinking of Stevie?

Chapter Ten

Back at the conference room, Sir Francis asks Phil and me to wait outside whilst he talks with Chambers and them, but we don't have to wait long.

'I tried to call you to say about the three o'clock start,' Phil says, 'but I got no answer.'

'Yes, sorry,' thinking on my feet, 'I heard about the time and went off to have a look around the shops to utilise the time. I'm afraid I left my mobile in my room.' Actually, the mobile in the room bit is true. I had obviously left it there because I didn't want it going off in the meeting, and of course, I never went back to *my* room. I freshened up in Frank's suite.

We are then called back into the meeting and take our seats. Both Sir Francis and I act as normal, and I hope I still have that confident look about me, back in my short red dress and crossing my legs again.

'Thank you, Mr Green, Miss Wilson. I'm sorry that we had to delay our return, but something came up during our lunch break.' *He's kept that sarcasm then.* 'I had to make some important moves before we could reconvene.' It's innuendo in reverse, and I fight to keep a straight face.

'That's fine, Sir Francis. We both understand,' says Phil. 'These things happen.'

'Yes, of course.' Now it's Frank's turn to try to keep a straight face. But then back comes the sarcasm and innuendo. 'I had to get one thing straight first, but the good news is that it has helped in all our negotiations, and I've put forward my ideals to the rest of my committee here, and,' he stands and holds out his hand to Phil, 'congratulations, Mr Green.' They shake hands, the contract is placed on the table, and they both sign it. 'And of course, thank you, Miss Wilson.'

'It was a pleasure,' I tell him. *Well, it was.*

'And as a way of a thank you,' continues Sir Francis, 'I would like to ask you both to give me the honour of taking you out to dinner tonight. Lady Holmes-Fitzwilliam is in town.' *Is she? Oh. Staying here in this hotel? In that room upstairs? Oh.* 'And I'm sure she will join us.'

'Thank you, Sir Francis. That'd be lovely. I'd love to meet your good lady wife,' I say, responding for Phil, too. It's an offer we can't turn down for the sake of the deal, and Phil nods agreement. If our lunchtime shag is what won the deal, then I'm pleased for our company. It's not like I'm a whore or anything; I'm just cock hungry, and after a little starvation, it's no more than I deserve. To meet his wife will be the icing on the cake. A man's semen always tastes sweeter when his wife is in the next room.

I thought he might want to get me alone again, perhaps to straighten things out once again, and I would have been up for it. But to introduce me to his wife, well, that is a bit of a turn-up.

*

Phil and I go back to our rooms, and I begin to get ready to have a shower. I've just taken off my dress when there is a knock on my door. *Sir Francis*, I think, so I don't bother that I am only in my undies. I open the door and Phil is there with a bottle of bubbly and two glasses.

'Can I come in?' He begins to step through the door before he realises I am undressed. He steps back, surprised.

'Oh, sorry,' he exclaims and moves back into the corridor. 'So sorry,' he says again.

I am a bit surprised to see him at my door, but I did open it in, like, my underwear after all. 'Don't worry. You've seen it now. Come in. A little celebration is in order by the look of you.'

'Put something on, though, please. I'm a happily married man.'

'Which bit is happy, and which bit is married?' I joke. *I think he can see the funny side of it.*

I beckon him in and then go to the bathroom to put on the complimentary bath robe the hotel provides before rejoining Phil. He's more relaxed now, and I apologise to him for the mishap. He opens the bottle of champagne, pours us a glass each, and hands me mine. We chink glasses and then high five each other.

'Here's to a job well done,' he says. 'I called back to the office with the good news and spoke to Mr Jackson. He told me rewards are in order, beginning with a bottle of the hotel's best bubbly. So here we are.' He drinks thirstily from his glass.

My mind goes back to the wine at the Italian restaurant, and I sip at the champagne very gingerly. To be honest, I don't really like it, and I'm thinking that there is bound to be wine flowing at dinner tonight with Sir Francis and Lady what-ever-her-name-is. I want to go clubbing in this wonderful city later, to make the most of it. Even with my happily married colleague here.

*

After Phil has gone back to his room, I have my shower and relax on the bed before dressing. Only half the bubbly has been drunk, and the bottle sits on the table with two empty glasses by its side. I think I must have drifted off whilst lying on the bed, because I check the time and realise it's getting near to seven o'clock, when we're due to be picked up.

I pick up my mobile. I've hardly used it all day, due to the way things have gone, and actually feel disappointed that it's only got a couple of missed calls from Phil. I scroll through my directory and click on Stevie. I look at the name for a few moments, pondering to myself whether to call or not.

I think back to my lunch break in Sir Francis's room, remembering how exciting and fulfilling it was just to have sex again after the disappointment of not having it with Stevie. *But I love him.* There, I've said it. The man has cast a magical spell over me, but what I need now is to get him into bed. Just to settle everything and make it proper. It's not even an age issue anymore, having bedded a man at least another ten years older still. Sir Francis's experience shone through, too; his whole attitude was to pleasure me, not just himself, and not just lie back and let me do all the work like most boys I've been with. I believe that will be that same with Stevie, when it happens. And it will. I call him.

'Hello, darling. Still in Glasgow?' he answers, obviously knowing that it is me.

'Hi, Stevie, yes still here. Coming back tomorrow.'

'Good. How's everything been? Are you having fun yet?'

'It's been going great. We're in, like, the poshest hotel in Scotland, I reckon, five stars and everything. The conference went like a dream, and we sealed the contract, and Sir Francis double-barrel is taking us out to dinner tonight, undoubtedly to some Michelin-star gourmet place.'

'With lots of wine, I bet. You take it easy.' *Thanks for the reminder, Stevie.*

'I will. I don't want to make a scene and mess up all the hard work now, do I?'

'I'm sure you won't. It will have been your charm and good looks that would've won the deal, I bet,' says Stevie, and I can only think of how right he is. *No, that's unfair on Phil, but whatever.*

'I did try to make an impression, but me and Phil worked as a team, and we got the result through determination and hard work. Not to mention confidence and professionalism.' *Crikey, I am starting to sound like a professional.* 'Anyway. Have you missed me? I've missed you. That's why I gave you a call.'

'Yes, Debbie, I have missed you, to be honest. I've been thinking about you and how you're getting on, hoping that all's going well. But I didn't call 'cause I know you might not be able to answer. So, I've been waiting on you. I'm glad you called.'

I'm comforted by his words. *Ahh, he's missed me.* 'Can we meet up again this weekend?' I ask, hoping for a yes. 'Not sure what's happening tomorrow when we get back, and then it's Thursday night college. But can we meet up and go into town, a bit of clubbing again?'

'Yes, of course. Your scene this time, after biking and Italian the last two dates out. I look forward to it. We'll arrange something when you get back.' He sounds very keen; perhaps he *is* missing me. Absence makes the heart grow fonder and all that.

'How have you been? At school, I mean, with all them young girls. Did it make you think of me?' I'm teasing him there, but he obviously has no sexual desire when it comes to that sort of thing.

'I gotta be honest, I did think of you,' he surprises me. 'But I think it still makes me wary of our age gap. I dunno, Debbie, let's just see what happens Friday, eh?'

I'm like, *oh*. He sounds keen for us to be together but still has that niggling doubt in the back of his mind. He's hundreds of miles away and I want to give him a hug; I want a hug from him. There's even a little tear in my eye. Oh my God. *How come I'm feeling like this?*

'Ok, Stevie.' He doesn't seem to mind me calling him that now. 'I'll catch up with you before Friday. Must be going, we're getting picked up at seven and I'm not even dressed yet. You've spoken to me completely naked.'

'Well, there you go. Our first all-naked chat. I'm sitting here with no clothes on either.' It sounds like he has a grin on his face; I have one on mine. But I bet he ain't telling the truth. Or is he?

'Oh, Stevie. I'm blushing.'

He gives a little laugh down the line. 'You? Blushing? No, I don't believe that.'

'You know me too well already.' A pause. 'Right, must get going, I'll see you Friday, my love.'

'Ok, bye.'

'Bye.'

'Bye.'

'Bye. Bye.'

'Bye,' Stevie finishes the call.

'Love you.' But I don't think he heard it. And he did say our first naked chat, like there will be more. Hopefully when we're in the same room next time.

I knock on Phil's door, and as he opens it, an older couple walk by toward the lift. 'Oh, hello. You're the girl from next door. Sorry, I didn't recognise you with your clothes on.'

I grin at him, holding back a laugh as the couple disappear behind the lift doors. Then I let out a giggle. 'Oh, Phil, you're a laugh.'

He comes out of the room, and we call the lift. 'I hope they've gotten out,' he says, meaning the couple.

'We'll very likely bump into them in the lobby,' I say as we get in the lift.

'Lobby?' he says. 'You sound like an American.'

Thankfully the couple are nowhere to be seen as we wait to be picked up. A moment later, we're called, and we make our way out.

'Mr Green, Miss Wilson?' the chauffeur asks. Phil nods. Wow! It's not any old taxi; it's a Bentley. A full-on Bentley; a limousine fit for a king. We look at each other with a look of complete amazement on our faces as we climb into the car. It's, like, unbelievable. We were chauffeur-driven to and from the airport, but it was just a posh taxi company, really. This is just out of this world. We sit in the back with more legroom than in my living room. There is a small drinks cabinet, and the chauffeur tells us to help ourselves, but whether it is shock or something, neither of us takes a drink.

The drive to the restaurant is so smooth we hardly feel that we are moving. But it is all too short, and we soon stop outside the grandest restaurant in Glasgow. A doorman opens the car door and we both get out.

'Good evening, Mr Green, Miss Wilson.' *Crikey. Not sir and madam. We're expected.* It makes me think of my first date with Stevie at the Talk of the Town; only this is, like, a hundred times more regal.

Phil and I are taken into the restaurant but not shown to a table. There's an armchair area; I realise that they are pre-dinner seats to look at the menu and order before being shown to your table. Sir Francis and his wife are already there waiting for us, and they both stand to greet us.

'Good evening, Phil, Debbie.' All informal. 'Did you enjoy your drive here?'

'Yes, thank you, Sir Francis,' I say.

'No. It's Frank tonight.' He sounds like Stevie/Steven. 'And this is my good lady wife, Pauline.'

Wow! She is immaculate. She must be about the same age as Sir, er, Frank, but she exudes wealth and style. Her clothes are so well tailored and uncreased, even when sitting down. Her dress, just above her knee, compliments her figure, her legs below so smooth down to her shoes and well pedicured feet. Her hands are manicured and elegant as we shake, and to my surprise, she kisses me on both cheeks, and she does the same with Phil. Her hair is perfect, make-up subtle and precise, lovely jewellery, matching and setting off her dress perfectly, and she's absolutely gorgeous. I don't think I've ever met a woman so perfectly beautiful in my life. I suppose she has the wealth to make the look, but then beauty, real skin-deep beauty, cannot be bought. And she's got it by the bucketload.

'Hello, Debbie, so pleased to meet you,' says Pauline. 'Frank told me all about you.' I flush a little at that. *How much has he said?* 'He told me how he was impressed at your professional manner for one so young. He does have a keen eye for talent.'

Yeah, I know he does. I look over at Frank and say, 'Thank you.'

'It's my pleasure. So wonderful to meet such a beautiful young woman with such a professional air about her. I think you have a very bright future ahead of you. I'm not thinking of just the immediate future, but of your long term. I really believe that by the time you get into your forties, you will be going places, a confident businesswoman.'

I'm actually taken aback by that. I know he offered me a position within his company, but I honestly thought that ideal had already been achieved this afternoon. But he continues, complimenting Phil, too.

'I have spoken to Christopher Jackson already this afternoon, commending you both, and I told him I sincerely hope that these praises are well recognised,' continues Frank. Phil and I can only give each other that astonished look again. 'You look as though you cannot believe your ears, but let's be serious. That deal was far from done. It was never a case of just dotting the i's and crossing the t's; there was some hard work to be done. I think Mr Jackson chose his team well.'

So, was it our hard work in the conference room, or was it the performance in the bedroom? Who cares? I got a double result.

'How did you get to be working with Coleman Construction, Debbie? To be where you are now.' It was Pauline, keen to get to know us.

'When I left school I, like, had no idea what I wanted to do, no immediate job to go to. The day I left school, my world was turned completely upside down; that's when Mum and Dad finally broke up. He was no real father to me, so any plans for after school were never on the agenda.' I begin to open my heart to Pauline. I don't know why, maybe it is her motherly attitude.

'But you got a job, surely?'

'Oh, yes. I was quite a bright kid at school, so at least I had some attributes. I just applied to an ad in the local paper for an office junior, and that was at Coleman's. I was sixteen when I started.'

'Well, you've done very well for yourself in only four or five years. How old are you now?' Pauline was warming to me.

'I'm twenty.'

'As I said, my husband does have an eye for talent. The potential shines through,' she says, as pre-dinner drinks are brought to our table and we are offered a menu. The choices are quite elaborate, nothing like the type of thing I expect to see on a menu. Lobster, venison, duck; all described with strange words like comfit and coulis, langoustine and *foie gras*. I'm like, *what*? I got on with it in Italian better than this. *Like, WTF is foo-ey grass?* Must be some kind of salad or something. I plump for something I recognise. Fillet steak.

When we order, the waiter doesn't ask how I want it, so I tell him, 'Can I have it well done?' There is almost a look of horror on his face but Frank comes to the rescue.

'Good on you, Debbie. That's how I like it, too. I'll have the steak, please,' he tells the waiter. I don't know if he is just trying to save my face or whether he does like his steak well done, but I think it is the former. 'I'll have some wine at the table. Red ok for you, Debbie?'

I nod. 'Thank you.' *What was it Stevie said, a nice juicy steak washed down with a glass of Merlot?* 'Merlot would be nice.'

'Excellent choice, we'll share a bottle of Merlot, Debbie and I,' Frank tells the waiter. I smile and give myself a mental thumbs up. 'And white for you two, with what you're having?' Frank gestures to Phil and Pauline.

'Yes, please,' they say in unison, and Pauline winks at Phil. I'm getting to like her. She's a real down-to-earth woman, no ladylike snobbery about her. Frank orders a bottle of Finca Perdriel Merlot and a South African Chenin.

At the dinner table, we enjoy a really wonderful meal. The red wine is really superb, and the conversation is very informal. We talk about anything and everything from the weather (what else?), sport – Frank's keen to chat with Phil about cricket and that – television, food, and so on. Whilst

Phil and Frank talk cricket, I chat with Pauline, all very girly, particularly about fashion.

'Your dress is beautiful,' I tell her. 'Where did you buy it? And the shoes? I just love your shoes.'

'I'm privileged to be able to afford the best designers,' she says matter of factly. 'The whole outfit is Gucci. The dress, shoes, bling.' I like her use of the word bling to describe such expensive jewellery. 'Even my undies.' She whispers the last bit. 'I always dress in a full outfit of the same design, never mix and match. Prada, Ralph Lauren. Frank's suit is Versace.'

I have a look of admiration for her, certainly not jealousy. 'Oh, fantastic. It must be wonderful to be able to wear such exciting clothes.'

'As long as they look good on some guy's bedroom floor.' Did she just, like, say that? 'You'll have to come shopping with me. Try on some nice shoes.'

Wow! Is she serious? 'You go shopping? I'd have thought the shops'd come to you.'

'Oh no. A girl likes to browse through the shops. I'm lucky enough to go to the designer shops. You'd love it, Debbie.'

We actually swap mobile numbers! I can hardly believe I'm exchanging mobile numbers with this beautiful and wealthy woman. Just as if we were best mates. And she wants me to go shopping with her. *Wow!*

At the end of the meal, we return to the comfortable chairs where we'd had pre-dinner drinks and enjoy coffee before we all make to leave. Frank shakes our hands once again, but I catch him unawares and kiss him on the cheek.

'That offer of a position in my company remains open. If you feel that you'd like to consider it, don't hesitate to contact me.'

'I will, thank you. And thank you for a wonderful dinner. How lovely to meet your wife, too.' Did I say that with a hint of sarcasm? I hope not. Pauline also kisses me.

'Lovely to meet you, too,' she says.

'I've arranged for you both to be chauffeured back to your hotel, or is there anywhere else you'd like dropped off?'

I look at Phil. 'I wouldn't mind doing a bit of clubbing. The night is still young.'

Before Phil gets to say anything, Pauline speaks first. 'Oh, I know just the place. Some great music, a cocktail or two, what can be better? I'll come with you.'

I can't believe what I just heard. Her Ladyship wanting to come clubbing with a little cock-grabbing girl like me, and at her age. I'm surprised she's got the energy.

Well, how wrong can you be? She takes Phil and I to a club in the Bentley, while Frank heads off on his own – back to the hotel, I presume. Or after this afternoon's delights, he might have had something else in mind.

The club is not the standard I'm accustomed to; it seems the type of place that celebrities would frequent. In fact, ain't that guy over there, with the gorgeous girl half his age, him off the telly? Oh, yeah. Stevie and his idea of a charm-on-the-arm of an egotistic celeb. Mind you, she is beautiful and only half dressed. Her clothes barely cover half of her body than, like, they should.

The club isn't too packed – it being a Wednesday after all – but the place is rocking. The dance floor has lights in the floor, and the seating is also quite retro. The music is from the seventies and eighties disco era, just like Bar 8T back home, and the atmosphere is one of utter sensuality with an urge for casual sex, a libido that is drink-fuelled and enjoyed by all. It is almost tangible. *Or is that just me?*

After ordering cocktails to be served by a waiter at our table, not scrummaging at the bar, we all three take to the floor together and begin throwing some shapes to the music, mingling with all the other dancers, getting up close and personal to some of the guys. To my surprise, so does Pauline: Lady Pauline Holmes-Fitzwilliam! I'm, like, amazed! We are all dancing with our arms in the air and bumping into one another with our backsides, quite uninhibited. I dance up near to Pauline and speak close to her ear.

'You old devil,' I say, as she struts her stuff to a young dancer joining in with her. 'You're old enough to be his mother.'

'I can have a toy boy if I want.' She grins back at me with just a small glint in her eye. 'And not so much of the old. *Horny* devil, more like. I'm so hot in bed. There's no such thing as a slut. People like to fuck. Get over it.'

Pauline! I can't believe what I just heard. This is a woman that doesn't beat about the bush, and I love her. She continues, 'I'm a sex addict. Can't get enough. I've actually been diagnosed by a doctor.'

'No. Seriously?'

'Oh yes. Nymphomania. And the younger the better... like him,' she says, giving me a wink and gesturing at the young man she's dancing with. Phil's getting into the spirit, too, dancing with a young bit of fanny in high heels, holding her close with one arm around her waist as she grinds into his groin. This must be the bit of him that's happy.

One guy comes up to Pauline and me and calls out over the noise of the music, 'You two babes are beautiful.' He takes each of us by the hand and we dance together. Me and Pauline make up the circle by holding hands as we look at each other. She winks at me again, and I can't help but beam back at her. I'm, like, loving this place.

We take a break from dancing and flirting to sit down for a breather and, like, another cocktail. I am having Sex on the Beach again; I quite like them after going out with Stevie the other night at the Italian. I make my excuses and go to the ladies, half expecting Pauline to come with me, but she just stays where she is.

A quick pee and making sure my dress isn't tucked into my knickers, then I make my way back into the disco to find Phil and Pauline snogging on the sofa at our table. I do a double take. I can't believe it. I think Phil even has his hand on her breast!

I don't know what to do: just go over to them and politely cough, go back in the loo, the dance floor, what? They break their clinch. Relief. So I move over to the table and sit down. Pauline leans over and whispers in my ear, 'We're in tonight.' And she gives me one of those over-theatrical winks.

'We?'

She replies, 'Oh yes, darling. All three of us.'

*

The Bentley takes us back to the hotel about twelve-thirty. We are all in high spirits as we sit in a line in the back of the limo. Phil is in the middle, one hand on Pauline's thigh, pushing the hem of her dress a little further up. I don't know if he is afraid, or possibly unaware of Paulines's threesome plan, but he doesn't put a hand on my thigh. So, I put my hand on his knee and slowly slide my hand up his thigh, right up to his groin. He actually opens his legs a little wider to allow me full access, so I take the hint and rub over the bulge in his trousers, just to tease him with my little finger. He seems to enjoy it, and so do I.

As the Bentley pulls up, the chauffeur opens the door on Pauline's side and we all file out and into the hotel. We make our way up to the floor where mine and Phil's rooms are, and as we step out of the lift, Pauline takes charge.

'It's been a fantastic night,' she says. 'Let's finish it off in style. Whose room shall we go in?'

'Debbie's still got the champagne in her room,' says Phil, 'if it's not gone flat.'

'Champagne. I like your way of talking.' Pauline lets go of my hand, turns to Phil, puts her now free hand on his cheek, and kisses him. His arms are straight round her waist.

I open the door to my room. 'Come on in, before you swallow each other.'

Once inside, though, we are all three straight over to the bed and kissing each other like we've never kissed before. Yes, even me and Pauline were teasing each other's lips and touching tongues. *Oh my God! It's fantastic.*

Our clothes start to come off, and Pauline is not caring about her Gucci dress one bit. I have to stop for a second and admire her underwear and her amazing body. It just oozes sex. Phil is the first to be totally starkers, and we lie him back on the bed, one of us on either side of him, as we begin to suck on his nipples, one each. It drives him wild with ecstasy. As I move my hand down to feel for his cock, I find Pauline's hand already there, holding his stiff erection up and pulling back the foreskin, inviting me down. As Pauline carries on at his nipples, I go down on his cock, sucking hungrily as Pauline massages him slowly. He growls his pleasure. I thought he said he was a happily married man, not able to look at me in just my undies. But he seems happy now with his full length in my insatiable mouth.

Pauline comes down to join me, and our lips touch as we battle for the territory of the raging hard on at our disposal.

I let her take him in fully as I slip my tongue down his shaft and tantalize his tight sac holding his balls.

Pauline gives him a real long blow job as I stand up and take off the rest of my clothes. My breasts bared, I go straight up to Phil and put them in his face. His hands are on them in a nano second, his tongue seeking out my nipples, his hands kneading and moulding my boobs, his tongue flicking rapidly over my nipple. Oh God, the sensations are electrifying, and I feel myself being worked into an orgasm.

'Oh my God, I'm coming already!' The passion of it all, the excitement, is bringing me to climax so quickly. *What is happening to me?* Coming so easily from just having my nipples sucked; I love it. I think it's the Pauline effect.

Then to my complete surprise, on hearing me call out, Pauline pushes me onto my back, opens my legs and goes down on me. Her tongue probing, her mouth sucking, she licks at my clitoris, and… and… yes! Yes! YES! A thunderous orgasm rips through my body, out through my sex hole and onto her face. Even after she moves her mouth away, my whole body is still shuddering from the most massive eruption of pleasure I have ever had. And it was brought on by another woman; I can't believe it.

'Go on, Phil, fuck her while she's hot,' she tells him, and he climbs on top, his arms at full stretch either side of me. He enters me so easily with all the lubrication that Pauline has created, and I take in a deep breath as he pushes inside me, then I reach up and rub my hands on his smooth chest. I am surprised at Pauline's choice of word for shagging, but I'm still in the throes of my orgasm with another one peaking, my clitoris still sensitive and swollen.

'Oh, fuck me, yeah, fuck…' I pause as another orgasm comes storming out, 'ME!' I scream. I don't know what trick Pauline pulled but it is fantastic. I love every bit of it, the raging torrent of pleasure running through every vein, every muscle in my body. It might be because she is a woman and knows how it feels and can press the right switches in another woman, knowing what she would want. I don't think she is necessarily gay or, like, bisexual or anything, but I get the impression that this isn't her first threesome.

I can't see what Pauline is up to, as Phil and I are too engrossed in each other to notice. 'Oh, Debbie. You're so wet. I can feel you coming all over my cock,' he tells me, and I murmur at the pleasure of feeling his balls bash against my arse.

Then I notice that Pauline has taken off the rest of her underwear and has the champagne bottle in her hand. She lies on the bed beside me and pushes the neck of the bottle up between her legs and into her fanny, allowing a little of the champagne to spill inside her.

Removing the bottle, she tells Phil, 'Drink the wine.' And he moves off me to go down on her. In some respects, this gives me a chance to get my breath back, but my respite doesn't last long as Pauline pours champagne over her tits and tells me, 'Drink the wine, Debbie.'

I do as I'm told, and this woman has the most luxurious breasts, her nipples so prominent and stiff you could hang your Christmas decorations on them. I didn't really like the champagne earlier, but it tastes delicious now. Phil then gets between her legs and rams his cock home. And as he pumps into her like a piston, they both came to orgasm together. 'Oh, yes!' she cries out.

'Urgh. Urgh,' is all Phil can muster as his balls empty into her. Then we all fall into an entangled heap on the bed, covered in champagne, sweat, and each other's sex fluids, the bed soaked from the champagne.

When we all eventually get up, Pauline looks at the wet bed. 'Oh, don't worry about that,' she says. 'You two go and sleep in Phil's room. I'll get this room sorted.' Phil and I look at each other then shrug our shoulders. *What the hell.*

'Will you go back to your room then?' I ask.

'I'm not staying at this hotel,' she says.

'But I thought you'd be in the room with Frank, er, Sir Francis.'

'Frank's not staying at this hotel either.' *Oh. But, like, er, whatever.*

I put on my bath robe and Phil quickly grabs his clothes, then we leave Pauline with a kiss and hurry to his room.

Chapter Eleven

The next morning, I am out of bed making us a cup of tea, back in my robe. We slept together, but while I was naked, Phil liked his pyjamas and put them on before we got into bed together. I would've worn my pyjamas too, but they were in the other room. Phil stirs from his sleep as I make the tea.

'Good morning,' I say to him with a bright smile. 'Did you sleep ok?'

'Like a baby,' he replies. 'You?'

'Yeah. I think it was all the excitement of last night wearing us out.'

'You can say that again.' There is no embarrassment between us; everything just seems normal.

I bring the tea over and we sit in bed together to drink. 'I suppose it's back to reality today then,' I say, sipping at my tea. 'I don't think we're ever gonna have a business trip like this again. You said you were, like, a happily married man and were embarrassed to see me in my underwear. And yet...' I tail off. 'What did Pauline say to you in the nightclub?'

'Nothing much.' He shrugs his shoulders. 'She just said that she wanted to give me a reward for the hard work with Sir Francis's company, snogged me—'

'I saw that.'

'And the next thing we're all naked in your room drinking champagne without glasses.' He grins at the memory, and I can't help grinning back at him.

'She was one amazing woman. Who'd have thought: Lady Pauline double-barrel, rich, incredibly beautiful, and so fucking sexy! She's what wolf whistles were, like, invented for.'

'She was so hot and sexy, so erotic. I can't believe I ended up in bed with her.' Phil is reflecting on our adventures, and seemingly enjoying the memory.

'You're a guy. I'm a woman, and *I* didn't expect to be having sex with her. But it was fantastic. She told me she was, like, hot in bed, but I didn't even think I'd find out firsthand.' I thought about having, like, a private performance with just the two of us in his room. But then my robe gaped a little, baring my breast, and he looked away. The moment was gone.

'It's almost nine o'clock. I think we'd better get our skates on. Got a plane to catch, remember?' says Phil, jumping out of bed and finishing his tea.

I go back to my room and, as promised, everything is clean and tidy. I go to the wardrobe and in there I find the Gucci dress that Pauline was wearing. I take it off the rail and hold it in front of me then pose in the mirror. *Oh my God, she can't have left it here by mistake, surely? How am I gonna get it back to her without any embarrassment?* I pick up my mobile, which I'd left in the room all night. *Should I ring her?* I've got her number. But then I see there's a text message and it's from Pauline.

Hi Debbie. I left my dress for you. I hope it fits. Yours fits me x

No. She can't have left it for me. It's probably worth a couple of grand. I go back to the wardrobe, and my dress from last night is not there. She must have taken my dress to go back to her hotel in. A twenty quid Primark job.

Hang on a minute. She's not a size sixteen. Twelve. Fourteen on a bad day. No, she wouldn't have bad days, I bet. I look through the dress and, yep, it's a sixteen. But she can't be the same size as me; I've seen her naked. Beautiful skin like porcelain, lovely firm breasts, a perfect hourglass waist, smooth silky thighs, her f... *I'm, like, why on earth am I thinking like this?*

I had a three-in-a-bed with another woman. It was Phil that was, like, the lucky one, having two women all over him. Give me three-in-a-bed with two cocks any day. Like that first time with two boys from school just after we'd left.

Oh my God, I remember that like it was only yesterday. Gary and Edmund. I remember their names easily because it was, like, a special time with two boys in one go. A cock in each hand; total control. And Edmund was one of only two black boys I've ever been with. The other was Lance, another boy from school. I fancied him then, but it wasn't till I bumped into him a few years later in BJ's and, like, I snogged his face off and got him to join me in a couple of shots before going back to his place. There I snogged his pants off then went down and spent, like, forty minutes giving head. Then the next hour or so I fucked the living daylights out of him and sat on his face where his tongue was, like, "excess" all areas... especially when he hit the spot, and I showered him before finishing him off by hand, like, all over my tits. It was a bit rushed (lol) but, like, I was so keen after fancying him a couple of years before. He was one of the few boys that, like, got it twice; mmmm, lucky boy. His full name was Lancelot, and I was his Guinevere alright. And there was an Arthur once as well, I think.

I just love shagging. I probably am a sex addict. Like Pauline said, there's no such thing as a slut; people like to fuck, end of. I just need an endless supply of cock. Sex is like my stress relief, my escape from the real world for a while. When I've had a shag, I'm, like, well contented. But nymphomania? Pauline must've made that up, surely.

I hang the dress back up, get in the shower, and let the warm water luxuriate my body, rubbing my soapy hands over myself, enjoying the feel, enjoying the sensations. I dry quickly and put on some clean underwear. Luckily, I brought enough to cover the short time we are in Glasgow, and then an extra set just in case. Before I finish dressing, I try on Pauline's dress and it fits me a treat. I don't get it. It was perfect on her, on her perfect figure. I'm not putting myself down that I'm not perfect, but how can it fit me just as it fitted her? But I don't care. I pose in front of the mirror, turning one way and then the next. I look a million dollars.

I put the dress back on the hanger and get dressed in my normal skirt and top, quickly pack my bag, put in the Gucci dress all folded up, and then meet Phil for breakfast.

The drive back to the airport is ok, in a Mercedes again. Nice, but it ain't no Bentley. Our flight back is good, and we chat about everyday stuff just like normal, and before long we're back on the road and home. At least there's no need to go into the office today.

*

I call Stevie in the early evening.

'Hi,' he says tunefully, answering my call.

'Hi, Stevie. I'm back. How have you been without me?'

'Oh, you know. Same old. I've got karate club again tonight, otherwise I'd bring you over so you could give me all the details of your trip.'

'That's a shame, and I've got college anyway. I'll be off in a minute, so we'll have to wait till tomorrow But there ain't much to say. Business, business, business. Coffee, coffee, coffee and, like, back to the hotel and you can't sleep. Boring really.'

'And there's me thinking you're with the jet set now. Oh well. Till tomorrow'

He wants to cut it a bit short, don't he?

'Do you want me to come to yours on tomorrow night? I need a bit of a boost, let me hair down a bit.'

'I'll come and pick you up, if you like,' offers Stevie.

'I like.'

'About seven-thirty suit you?'

'Yes, please. I'll be dressed to kill. Are you willing to die?' *I nearly said 'Mr Bond' on the end.*

'If you're to die for…' I just hope he means it. 'I'll hold you to that.' *Hold me? I don't want him to ever let go.*

*

Next morning, it's back to work. When I get to my desk, Louise is pleased to see me.

'Hello,' she greets me with her usual bright and breezy smile. I love her to bits. 'How did it go?'

'Very good.' All positive, unlike my chat with Stevie about it being boring. 'We agreed the contract…'

'Oh, brilliant!'

'And we went out to dinner with Sir Francis whatsit, the big boss of Carltons, as a way of celebration. Sir Francis and his wife, Lady Pauline. She was a laugh. I was like…' I pull a face that makes me look full of amazement. 'She was so down to earth.'

Before we get to say any more, my desk phone rings. 'Debbie Wilson.' There's a pause as I listen. 'Ok.' I put the phone down. 'Apparently there's a parcel down in reception for me. Keep me covered, I'll be back in a minute.'

I head off to reception, collect my parcel, and make my way back to my desk. I'm met by Phil, whose been chatting with Louise.

'Hi, Debbie. Boss wants to see us.' I put down my parcel, and Phil and I go off to Mr Jackson's office. His secretary, Gladys, sees us in.

'Ah. Philip, Deborah. Come in, sit down. Gladys, could you bring us all some coffee, please?' says Mr Jackson in a bright manner. *Something's pleased him; I bet it's us.*

'Tea for me, please,' I ask Gladys. She nods.

'Did you have a good time in Glasgow? I heard Sir Francis treated you to dinner.' Our professionalism seems to go out the window, and we are both a little gobsmacked as to what to say. But I suppose that our dinner date would not have been a secret.

'It was fantastic,' I say. 'Came out of the blue, really. Neither of us expected that, did we, Phil?'

'No. And to meet Pauline, er, Lady Holmes-Fitzwilliam, was great. She was so down to earth. I was just saying that to Louise,' says Phil, pointing over his shoulder with his thumb.

'So was I. She was such a character. The whole trip was worth it just to meet her.' Phil and I are all enthusiastic, and again it's as a result of Pauline's influence. We don't even think about the sordid details that resulted in us two shagging and sleeping together.

'Good, good.' Gladys walks in with the coffee and my tea. 'Ah. Here we are. Thank you, Gladys,' says Mr Jackson, as she hands out the cups. 'Sorry it's nothing stronger. Should be, though. I am very pleased with the pair of you, not to mention the virtual nods of approval from the board. The fact that you obviously worked hard and agreed the contract is most commendable, and rewards are being finalised to reflect this. But the glowing report I have received from Sir Francis is recommendation worthy of high praise.'

'Thank you.' Phil and I are back in unison. He actually takes my hand and gives it a squeeze, and I smile.

It's noticed by Mr Jackson, and he coughs lightly then takes a sip of his coffee. 'Yes. I see that you've gotten on well together.'

'That's why we achieved our aim. We worked hard as a team and got the result we needed. That was the key, eh, Debbie? Teamwork.'

'We spent the best part of seventy-two hours in each other's company, not just in the conference, but outside it, too,' I go on, 'to discuss the strategy.'

Mr Jackson nods sagely as we speak. 'Did you enjoy the champagne?'

'Oh, yes. Thank you,' I say.

'We only drank a small amount. We were invited out later, so we wanted to be on our best behaviour. We finished it off later when we got back to the hotel,' finishes Phil. 'Debbie's contribution was invaluable. She was exemplary.'

'As I've already said, I received glowing reports about you both from Sir Francis.' Mr Jackson is finishing off. 'And to say thank you, I'd like to ask you both out to lunch later where I can put forward your reward packages.'

'You're too kind, Mr Jackson,' I say.

'It's the least you both deserve. That was a big contract. You were well recommended, Deborah.'

'And I would recommend her, too' responds Phil. 'As Sir Francis pointed out, Debbie has a bright future, and I think it's in the best interest of Coleman's that she sees it out here.'

I blush at Phil's reference. He's too kind. But it makes me feel proud.

I leave Phil and Mr Jackson talking and go back to my desk, remembering my parcel. 'What is it?' asks Louise, all excited. 'I've been waiting for you to come back to find out.'

'I've no idea,' comes my reply. 'Let's have a look, shall we?'

As I open it, it is soon apparent that it's my dress from the other night in Glasgow, the one that Pauline took from me. And there is a handwritten letter, too.

Dear Debbie,

Here is your dress for you. I borrowed it so that I could check your size to order the Gucci like mine. I hope you like it.

That offer of a shopping trip is still on. I will contact you when I get the chance, and we can do some shoe hunting.

Love
Pauline x

'I don't believe it!' I exclaim.

'What is it?' asks Louise. 'What's wrong?'

'Nothing's wrong.' *Oh my God, how do I explain this?* I'm shaking. Pauline actually bought me a dress just the same as hers. A Gucci dress! Brand spanking new! Oh my God! And I folded it all up in my little suitcase, too.

I pick up my mobile and send her a text message.

Hi Pauline. Thank you so much for the dress. You shouldn't have, but I love it. Can't wait to hear from you. Love Debbie x x x

And it's a three kisser.

Phil emerges from Mr Jackson's office and comes over to me. 'Oh, thanks, Phil,' I tell him. 'My hero. Sticking up for me like that.'

'I was only being honest. Couldn't have done it without you.'

Considering what really took place – some of it unknown to Phil, but a lot that involved him – it was definitely back to normal now.

'Well, he wants to treat us to lunch and says we can take a colleague along, too.'

'Fantastic! Who shall I ask?' With my forefinger on my lips, I scan the room as if looking for someone to ask. Louise clears her throat loudly. 'Louise. Can I take Louise?'

Chapter Twelve

Friday night couldn't come quick enough. I have missed Stevie in a way that surprises me, despite all that happened in Glasgow. I only saw him for two days last weekend, and a whole week has passed, but I'm pleased that I'm finally going to see him again. It's more important to me than the fact it's Friday night – a time when I really like to let my hair down. I just want to be with Stevie.

I am waiting outside my house when he pulls up, as he texted me to say he was on his way. I get into the car quickly. Mum is at home, and I don't want her, like, watching from the window. She probably isn't; she's not that kind of mum, but I can't take the risk. Yet.

Stevie and I kiss, but it is no more than a peck on each other's lips.

'Hi, Debbie,' he says.

'I've been looking forward to tonight all week,' I say to him, and I pat his knee.

'Glasgow must have been boring.'

'It was ok,' I say resignedly, 'just working away from home, that's all. But I got to, like, meet Lady Pauline. She was a diamond.'

'Who's Lady Pauline when she's at home?'

'She is Sir Francis's wife; he is the MD of Carlton's, the company we were negotiating with. Oh, I loved her. She was beautiful, got the wealth to go with it, and she even offered to take me shopping. Can you believe that?' I'm getting excited just talking about it. 'She was wearing a Gucci dress…' I pause to let him take it in as he drives along, and wait for him to stop so he can look at me. 'Just like this one.'

Stevie looks at my dress. 'That's a Gucci dress?'

I nod, running my hands over it at my thighs. Then I take his hand for a second and put it on my thigh. He holds his hand there for a moment before moving it to drive on when the traffic lights change.

'She bought me it. Like, she actually bought me a Gucci dress! I ain't got a clue how much it cost, but I bet it's, like, four figures.'

'Wow. You're kidding. How come she did that?' He is amazed.

I make up a little lie to cover up how she left it in my room, making me think that it was the one she took off when in there. 'We were just talking over dinner and talking shoes and clothes and that…'

'Like women do.'

'And she offered to take me shopping. I couldn't believe it. But just to put the seal on it, there was a parcel for me at work yesterday,' I say, gesturing at the dress. 'And this is it. Exactly the same one as she was wearing on our dinner evening. What do you think?'

'You said you were gonna dress to kill, and you weren't wrong. I like it.'

'Pauline said as long as it looks good on some guy's bedroom floor, that's what matters.' We pull up at Stevie's place and get out of the car. But I don't let the break in conversation stop me. 'I'll need to try that out for myself.' I say it very suggestively, taking his arm and holding it tight.

'A Gucci dress just thrown on the floor? This Lady Pauline must have more money than sense,' he says.

'She knows what she wants. I said she was a diamond. I can't wait to see her again and go shopping. I bet she could teach me a thing or two.'

'How old is she? Like you need teaching.' *Is that sarcasm I hear?*

'She is mid-fifties, I suppose. Dunno. But she is so down to earth.'

'Sounds to me like there was more to it at your dinner party,' says Stevie opening the door, and we walk in and sit down together on the sofa.

I almost blush, remembering what really happened, although I don't think our sexual shenanigans were that much of an influence. I can't let him know what happened, though.

I take Stevie in my arms and bring him into a full-on kiss which lingers just as I want. His arms are round me, holding me tight. *This is more like it. Proper snogging.* I am ready to throw the dress on his floor and make mad passionate love to him right now! We break off the kiss but hold the embrace.

'We just chatted, women's talk. We shared the same interests, even if we are poles apart in reality,' I continue the theme. 'She was so... motherly. I don't know if they've got kids. Probably why they're so rich, but it seemed like I was the daughter she always wished for.' I shrug at that.

'Yes. I know the feeling,' he says. *Whoops. Done it again.*

'Anyway, I was telling Louise at work about my dress, and she said she'd meet us tonight. She's gonna bring Matthew, her boyfriend. I said we'd be in BJ's later.'

*

We get to BJ's about ten, after a couple of drinks in one or two other bars. The place is rocking, just how I like it, with the dance floor packed and the disco in full swing. We go straight to the bar, and Stevie buys me my usual alcopop with a straw. I'm really enjoying this evening, with plenty of glances from both guys and girls at my dress. I feel so sexy.

Despite it being so packed, we manage to find a table and sit down. I put my hand on Stevie's knee, and he places his hand over mine. For a brief second, I think he is going to move my hand, but he keeps it there. It is so comforting, I feel that he is more a proper boyfriend than an acquaintance now, but I need that extra step; and that is to get him into bed. I have some ideas up my sleeve if I really have to coax him into it, but then my hopes hit a slippery slope.

'Did your friend say anything about a time she'd be here?' asks Stevie, as he looks around the room.

It reminds me of the bar in Glasgow, all the drink-fuelled libido hanging in the air. I think about the times I have come in here without a boyfriend, and how I was all part of that. A normal Friday/Saturday night would be to front-load at home with whoever I was going out with, and then basically go on a drink-induced boy hunt. And BJ's was the place above most of the others.

I have a different view of it tonight, though; firstly being with male company, and also not having front-loaded. On a 'normal' Friday night at this time I would already be, like, three sheets to the wind and ready to shag anyone.

There is a clear distinction as to who is single and who isn't, and the sober perspective of it is quite an eye-opener to me. There are all these people getting well and truly rat-arsed and sexually eyeing each other up, and I'm thinking, *that's usually me*.

'No. I just said we'd be in here at some point. Not a problem, is it?' Then right on cue Louise appears and comes bounding over, arm up in the air ready to hug me. I stand and we embrace, air kissing.

'Wow! Look at you,' she says, holding my hands in hers and stepping back to admire my dress. I pose and twirl for her. 'It's amazing.'

Matthew casually walks up behind her, hands in his pockets, like a spare part.

'Come on, Matthew, sit down. You're making the place look untidy,' I tell him. I've only met him once, but it's enough to be able to introduce him. 'This is Stevie,' I say, putting my hand on his shoulder and reaching around the back of his neck to pull him close. 'Stevie, Louise,' pointing at her, 'and Matthew.'

'Pleased to meet you,' says Stevie, but makes no effort to stand or shake hands or anything, which surprises me. Then I realise why.

'Oh, you're, er, Mr Taylor, my old maths teacher,' says Matthew. 'Matthew Ratcliffe. Remember me?'

I think it is a bit odd that he should ask that. But Stevie's response is good. 'I see a lot of kids, why should you be unique? Let's think: Ratcliffe? Ratcliffe? Oh, yeah,' Stevie's eyes widen, 'no mathematical ability, unruly, disruptive, er…'

Matthew's face visibly drops. It is as if Stevie has him to a tee. 'No. I don't recall you.' Stevie smiles, and we all laugh. 'Come on, Matthew, what're you drinking?' Stevie stands and they go to the bar, leaving me with Louise with a kiss on the top of my head.

Once we're alone, Louise is inquisitive. 'He's a school teacher? You never said. And one of Matthew's at that. He's twenty-four now, must have left school, like, seven, eight years ago. You never said he was *that* old.'

'He's not *that* old. I showed you his picture. Surely you saw there that he's older than me?'

'Yeah, but... Matthew's teacher. It's weird.'

I shoot her a look. 'I don't mean like that,' she says to me. 'It's just, well, funny, a small world. But they seem to be getting along ok.' Louise gestures with her eyes at the two of them at the bar.

I follow her eyes and see them chatting as they order drinks. I can picture the scene.

*

'That wasn't really you I described, was it?' asks Steven.

'A bit. I perhaps wasn't the sharpest tool in the box when it came to maths, but I tried.'

'Was that why you thought I'd remember you? Like I said, I see a million kids, one or two might stand out for whatever reason, but...' Steven breaks off as the barmaid offers the drinks and he pays.

As she walks away to till up the money, Steven watches Matthew's eyes following the barmaid. She is wearing a short skirt – in fact, very short – and has her midriff showing under a loose top that barely covers her boobs. Neither leave much to the imagination – certainly not much to Matthew.

Steven has taken very little notice of her, yet he realises with a sly smile that Matthew can't take his eyes off her. It isn't until she comes back with the change then heads off to serve another customer that Matthew finally gets back to the conversation.

'It's just I remember you from school, and it is so weird to meet the boyfriend of one of Louise's friends and it's an old teacher.' He takes a sip of his drink. 'It's even weirder having him buy me a drink.'

'What do you do now then?'

'I'm a sparky; an electrician. I actually went on to college to train,' says Matthew, 'so I wasn't that bad.'

'Fully trained?'

'Yes.'

'And are you working?'

'Yeah, I work at Coleman's, same as Louise and Debbie. That's how we met,' explains Matthew.

'Good for you. A sparky, eh. Worth knowing.'

'Any time, Mr Taylor.'

'It's Steven. Please don't call me Mr Taylor. And certainly don't call me sir,' Steven is eager to point that out. 'Does it bother you that I'm an old schoolteacher and I'm out with a friend even younger than you?'

'I think you're, like, confusing me with someone that *does* give a shit,' Matthew says, to the amusement of Steven.

'But then if you were one of the girls that had a crush on me, it might be different.'

'That's why I remember you,' says Matthew, snapping his fingers. 'My sister had a crush on you. She did extra maths because of you.'

'Yeah. The name Ratcliffe did ring a bell. Karen, wasn't it?'

'Still is. But not Ratcliffe anymore.'

'I'm pleased to hear it. I do remember her; she was bright at maths but kept calling me over to explain or whatever, just to get me to get close. And I'm old enough to be her father.' Steven breaks off whilst he thinks about her.

'I don't know what it is,' he continues, 'but I get a lot of crushes. Maybe not so much now 'cause I'm getting older. I mean, I know I'm fit, that's why I also do sport at school, but girls like me. That's one reason I work in a school out of town, so I don't get recognised. Didn't work tonight, though, did it? But I think that's what it is with Debbie; she's got a schoolgirl crush on me.'

'But you're still going out with her?' Steven nods. 'There's nothing wrong in that. She's not a girl anymore…'

'I know, but it's still not easy. I'm actually giving in to all that I've learned not to.' Steven starts to walk back to the table. 'Come on, I bet Louise is spitting feathers.'

*

Stevie and Matthew come back to the table and sit down. 'What have you been talking about?' Stevie asks.

'You,' I say. 'And dresses and shopping and stuff,' I quickly add. 'What about you two?'

'What about us?'

'What you been talking about?'

'Matthew has been telling me that he's an electrician, so that's good. His schooling must have been up to some good.'

A favourite record of mine comes on the disco, and I jump up and brush out the creases in the infamous dress. 'Come on, Lou. You dancing?' I ask Stevie.

'You asking?'

'I'm asking.'

'I'm dancing,' says Stevie, as he turns back to Matthew. 'Are you getting up?'

'No. I don't dance,' he says all embarrassed.

'What d'you mean you don't dance?' By this time, Louise and I are on the floor whilst the boys continue to barter. 'I'm an old boy pushing fifty. You just get up a move about like no one's watching. You shouldn't have inhibitions, not when you've got a nice girl to dance with. She'll love it.'

Before the conversation goes any further, I see that Haze and Jules have come in. Seeing Stevie without me, they make a beeline for him.

'Hello, lover boy,' says Jules, putting an arm around his shoulders as she tries to kiss him. Stevie pulls away from the attempted kiss, but I see that she puts her other hand on his crotch and gropes him. 'Is it my turn tonight for the sexual olympics? I've heard you've got a gold medal.'

Stevie backs away from her, but she takes a second to remove her hand, so he has to push her away. By this time, I'm off the dance floor and over at the table.

'What the fuck are you playing at?' I snarl at Jules.

'Hello, Debbie. I didn't realise you were here. I'm just sizing up lover boy here.' *She is so fucking cocky*! No, that's the wrong phrase. Whatever. 'He seems to be rising to the occasion, too.'

'You bloody leave him alone!' I bark.

Stevie takes my arm and leads me away. 'Leave it, Debbie. Let's not get into a fight.'

'But she was groping you.' I'm affronted, angry, ready for a fight. 'She was saying you're getting a hard on.'

'Don't be silly now. She was just being obnoxious. Just walk away and calm down a bit.' Stevie takes me back to the dance floor, but I'm in no mood for dancing, so we lean against the perimeter rail.

'What did she say to you?' I ask, still buzzing but cooling off a little. After all, I can't be mad at Stevie, it was all Jules' doing.

'She wanted to know if it was her turn tonight. Bloody hell, Debbie, what have you been telling people?'

'Her turn for what?'

'Sex. She actually said sexual olympics. Someone has put that in her head,' he says, his eyes looking at me accusingly.

'I only told them you were good in bed just to make them jealous.' I try to sound casual, but I don't think it works.

'We've not been to bed. But now I've got loads more twenty-year-olds trying to…' He breaks off when he realises what he is about to say, implying that that's what I'm trying to do. 'You see? I knew I'd made a mistake when I came to your rescue the other night.'

'What does that mean?' *Oh no. We're having our first argument.*

'I end up meeting old pupils.' He tuts, shakes his head, and carries on. 'Good job it wasn't a girl, like his sister. Good job it's not someone from the education authorities. Or my headmaster. Seeing me with all these young girls, groping me and everything. They'd have my balls in *their* hands alright.'

'You can't blame that on me,' I plead.

'Heard so many things about me, she said. Crikey, I bet it's all over Facebook and everywhere.'

'It's not on Facebook.' I try to think back. *What did I put on Facebook?* 'Just a picture from the Italian restaurant, that's all.'

'Oh, so you admit to telling tales, then?' He's gone all schoolteacher on me. By now, Haze and Jules have gone, so we return to the table. Stevie takes a large gulp of his beer and I follow suit, with a big suck on my straw. Louise and Matthew are sitting quietly.

'Can't you see, Debbie? This is why we can't have a relationship, why I can't go to bed with you.'

Louise and Matthew are in earshot, but they just put their drinks to their mouths and look away.

I'm almost in tears at that. No relationship. No bed. I think about everything that's happened in the short space of time since we met, thinking more of how much I missed him when I was in Scotland. And how he, like, admitted to missing me and that. I can't let that all come crumbling down around our feet. I need to throw an ace on the table, and quick.

I take another gulp of my drink and empty the bottle. 'I'm ready for another,' I say. 'Let's try some shots, eh? Get the party started again.' I get up, ready to head for the bar, and I encourage Louise to come with me.

'Forget that little scene,' I say to her. 'Ever since I met Stevie, they've been trying to get into his pants. Can't believe Jules did that. Stevie calls them the fat slags.'

Louise gives a little snorting laugh. 'I can see why. She was so brazen. But what was that Stevie said about relationships and everything. I thought you two were, like…' She makes a gesture with her first two fingers of one hand.

'We are… or at least we will be if I can keep him caged.' There's wishful thinking. 'Keep the predators away. I mean, we all like a shag, but I see it all differently now. I shoulda kept my mouth shut when I was telling them all about him. And what I said was a bit made up.'

'Made up?'

'I just made up some story about us shagging just to, I dunno,' I pause to think what I'm meaning but I'm not sure myself, 'make them jealous?' I say it as a question, more to myself than to Lou.

I order some drinks from the barmaid. Gracious me, that girl's skirt is short. Never mind above the knee, that's like damn near above her hip! It's a pleated affair, one of the kind a cheerleader would wear. No wonder the boys keep asking for drinks off the bottom shelf. As she pours our drinks in front of us, I give her a big Debbie smile and that certain, like, eye contact usually reserved for the boys to let them know I'm interested. She beams back at me.

Wow! That, like, sent a real charge through me, like an electric shock. My spine is tingling, my heart jumping.

I don't even get that kind of feeling when a boy is drooling over me. I've had sex with another woman, sort of, and I get an urge that I felt last week with Pauline. The urge that swept over me when I had no hesitation in, not just, like, having a threesome but all the woman-to-woman sex. God, I loved it. And now, suddenly, here's a sexy blonde woman my age-ish, and she's making me quiver all over.

'Nice dress,' she says, looking me up and down. It's got the cleavage that Pauline's had for her, and I'm wearing a necklace that draws the eyes down to it.

'Gucci,' I tell her, all casual like.

'Really? Wow! Dead sexy.'

'My name's Debbie,' I say as she takes payment for the drinks. *Oh my God, I'm chatting her up!*

'Yasmin.' She says it so sweetly. 'Give me your mobile number; I'll call you some time. We could meet up when we're on the same side of the bar,' she says, pointing at the floor on my side of the bar.

Oh. My. God. Is this really happening? 'Yes. I would like that.'

Yasmin retrieves her mobile from behind the bar. Let's face it; she has nowhere to keep it on her person. I tell her my number, and she loads it into her mobile. I get a text straight away. 'That's from me. You'll have my number now.'

I check my mobile and load the number into my contacts list. 'Thanks,' I say, and give her another of my big Debbie smiles.

'I'll call you. We'll have some fun together, I'm sure,' she adds. 'See you,' then she's off to serve another customer.

I pick up the drinks, and as I turn to go back to the table, Yasmin smiles and waves at me. *Did that all really happen? Or did I dream that?* Suddenly I remember that Louise has been with me all that time and has seen and heard all the conversation. She looks at me with a glint in her eye.

'Now who needs to keep the predators away?'

'I know. I couldn't help it. I have no idea what came over me, but she is beautiful.' Isn't that what I said about Pauline? 'But at least I know she won't be drooling over Stevie.'

'You hope, but if you've not bedded him yet, that will capture him. Two of you in bed.'

Again, I think about my night of lust with Pauline and Phil. Mmm?

I put the drinks down on the table and pass round the shots. 'Come on, boys, all four of us together in one. Last one is a cissy.'

We take our drinks and knock them back. I then take a swig of my regular alcopop whilst everyone else follows suit. Louise sits down with Matthew and puts her arm around his shoulders, while he responds by putting his hand on her thigh. As he slides his hand up and down, shifting her skirt a little, it reveals a little more of her leg and I can't help but look. *Oh my God, what's getting into me?* I hold out my hand to Stevie and ask him to dance.

'Are you guys coming?' I ask.

We hit the dance floor en masse and dance close. That drink-fuelled libido feeling from Glasgow is back again. But is it because of my close proximity to Stevie, Yasmin at the bar, or Louise's smooth, silken thigh? Never mind all the libido in the air, I'm gagging for a shagging. My hormones are going wild, and I need Stevie tonight more than ever. I need cock more than ever, and it's gotta be Stevie's.

He holds me real close as we dance. It's not a slow dance, but we're in a tight embrace and I can feel him through his trousers. He's not got a hard on, but I can feel him all the same, and I can feel the sensations swirling around my pleasure pot, wanting him to fill it, my juices flowing. It's a fantastic sensation; I could have an orgasm here on the dance floor. I can't believe this is happening to me.

Chapter Thirteen

We dance for a while longer, and I hold Stevie so tight, not wanting him to move away. It's not quite skin to skin, but I dream that it is. A couple of more drinks and dances later, we say our goodbyes to Louise and Matthew. Louise and I embrace and kiss, fully on the lips this time, no air kissing, and she whispers in my ear, 'Good luck.'

It's only just past midnight and we're heading home. Midnight? Like, an early night for a Friday. The taxi takes us to my house, and when the car pulls up, Stevie leans over and kisses me on the cheek.

'Give me a call some time,' he says, and sits back in his seat.

'You're not coming in then? I thought that was why we came home early.'

'No. I think we need to have some of our own space. I didn't intend to get involved like this, and tonight has just proved why.'

Well, I ain't gonna cry, if that's what he thinks. 'Ok. I'll call, like you say.' I pat him on his knee and get out of the car.

I walk up to the door, look back, and wave as the car drives away. I go into my handbag, not for my keys, but my mobile. I get Stevie's number up, count to ten, and hit call.

'Hello,' he answers. 'I said give me a call, but I didn't expect it that quick.'

'Stevie. I'm locked out. Mum's not in.' It's all a lie, but I'm not letting him get away so easily.

'Have you given her a call?'

'She went out to some do with her work. She's not answering.'

'And you've got no keys?'

'No. I must have forgotten them when I came out. I was outside waiting for you, remember?' All sweet and innocent.

'Ok. Wait there, I'll get the driver to turn back.'

'Thank you,' I say, and we hang up. In no time at all the taxi is back, and I run up to the car. Stevie opens the door and I gladly get in.

'You'll have to come back with me,' he says, and the driver is off again. 'Flipping taxi'll cost a fortune.'

'I'll make it up to you,' I say and move closer to him, holding his arm, my face close to his. I see the taxi driver's eyes looking at us in the mirror, and I wink at him. He looks away again.

When we get to Stevie's house and go inside, we don't even go to his lounge, but he makes his way upstairs.

'I'm not sleeping on the sofa. You can, by all means. I'm happy to share my bed, but only to sleep.' It's a firm statement but said calmly; that's the teacher in him. We get to the top of the stairs and go to the bedroom. 'Do you want a hanger for your dress? You don't really want to leave it lying on the floor, do you?'

'No,' I say. 'Thanks.' And he hands me the hanger.

'I'm just gonna brush my teeth and have a wee.' He heads off to the bathroom, and while he has gone, I take off my dress and hang it up, then take off my bra, leaving me in just my knickers.

Stevie comes back into the bedroom but takes very little notice of my nakedness, actually looking away almost exaggeratedly.

'Can I borrow your toothbrush?' I ask.

'Yeah. Sure.'

I go off to the bathroom and brush my teeth and have a wee, and when I go back to the bedroom Stevie is already in bed, although he's not covered from the waist up. He has a hairy chest – not bushy, but hairy – and it looks good enough to eat. He's seen me naked, although he didn't look, but I haven't seen him. It is a wonderful sight, and I wanna get my teeth and tongue on those nipples, get my hands all over him.

He points to a t-shirt on the bed next to him. 'That's an old t-shirt of mine; should fit you. Can you wear it, please?'

'Of course.' I hold the t-shirt up to look at it; it has logos on it, something to do with karate. I put it on and turn to look in the mirror. It's a bit small but emphasises my assets beautifully. *God, I'm sexy*. Even in Stevie's old t-shirt with my bum peeking out.

I climb into bed. It's a weird feeling, just climbing into bed to lie alongside someone. The only time I get into bed like that is when I'm sleeping alone. With a boy, it's usually in a state of lust with clothes half on, half off, all limbs entwined and, like, snogging.

I snuggle up to him, not daring to find out if he is wearing anything from the waist down. But he accepts the closeness and puts his arm around me.

'To be honest, Debbie, I've got a bit of a headache. Probably all the excitement of tonight, and that's why I wanted to come home early. I've had my paracetamol and I just wanna go to sleep. It's not an excuse to not go any further than this. I like you, Debbie, I really do. But I can't help but feel as though I'm at a brick wall. Meeting ex-pupils and stuff. Then the fat slags turning up like that…'

He's not totally naked, I can tell, and I've got the t-shirt on, but this is, like, the closest we've ever been. And if it's all that's going to happen tonight, then I'm going to enjoy it.

I snuggle up to him just that little bit more and say, 'I understand.' I kiss him on the cheek and we continue to lie holding each other in silence before drifting off to sleep.

*

I wake in the morning to a little light coming in around the curtains, and it takes me a second or two to orientate. *Stevie's bed... I'm alone, though.* I look at the clock: eight thirty-three. I must have slept like a log, which is a surprise as it was quite early for a Friday night for me, and I'd only had about half my usual drink – probably less, with no front-loading. I remember being in Stevie's arms and must have just drifted off into a deep, deep sleep.

I sit up in the bed just as Stevie walks back in, wearing pyjama trousers and a t-shirt, and carrying two cups of tea.

'Oh, good morning, sleeping beauty. I thought I was gonna to have to wake you with a kiss.'

'You still can. I'll pretend to be asleep,' I suggest, and as he puts my tea down on the bedside table, he leans in and kisses me. Three kisses, just like his texts.

'I won't ask if you slept alright. You were off before I even switched off the light, snoring away. Took me ages to get off,' he says, getting back into bed and starting to drink his tea.

'Did I really snore?' He nods with his cup to his mouth. 'No one's ever told me before.'

'You've probably never been asleep with anyone before.' *Ooh, that was a cutting remark.*

'What about you? You say you took ages to get off, and yet you're up before me as well.'

'I slept for a good six hours; that's enough for me.'

'I slept well, and I was happy and comfortable and secure in your arms. I would have liked a bit of action, but I was still just as happy lying in your arms.' There's a silent pause; it's almost deafening. 'Stevie? Why won't you have sex, er, make love to me? We go out together, we dance close, we hold hands, we kiss, we have a laugh. Now we've even slept together. But you won't shag me. Why not?'

'Just before you fell asleep, you told me you understood.'

'But tell me more. Please.'

'When we first met, I just felt sorry for you after what the fat slags did to you. I could see what had happened, saw them running and laughing and hiding, and when I bumped into you, I saw the situation immediately and I wanted revenge for your sake. It went totally against my instincts – my instincts as a teacher: you were a girl that could be, or could've been, one of my own pupils. Just imagine if you were. How would that look if my superiors saw it? I'd be hung, drawn, and quartered. Or is it just the fact that you are so much younger than me? I get girls – not so much now, but more when I was younger – all having crushes on me.'

'I can see why. You're a really dishy guy. Don't put yourself down,' I say, complimenting him.

'But we went out, had a laugh, and got your revenge,' he continues, 'and now look. Going out like we did last night is not really my scene. The bins go out more often than I do. But I come out with you because I like you, and I do wanna have you as a friend. But like last night, we get a situation where I meet an ex-pupil. Luckily it was a boy, and he wasn't bothered by it, but he could've been. Or he could've been a girl that had a crush on me. Like his sister.

Or someone like a colleague or a parent, or someone from the authorities. Heaven only knows what might happen.'

He shakes his head whilst thinking of the consequences. 'Then I get the fat slags groping me and wanting to have this wild sex they've heard about. It just goes against all my instincts. We're a generation apart: you, Louise, and her boyfriend...' he pauses.

'Matthew,' I fill in his blank.

'Matthew, yeah. And then them,' he says, referring to Haze and Jules. 'I mean, I could get to know them and probably like them. I like everyone, it's in my nature, but they are just over the top wanting to have sex with me, and not beating about the bush about it either.'

Oops. 'Yeah, sorry about that. That is my fault, I admit it. But they were so over the top about it, like you say, so I told them a story to make them even more jealous rather than be, like, you know, sceptical.' Stevie nods his understanding as I continue. 'We're all chasing a falling star, but why do people try to stop you when you catch one?'

'Debbie, you're so poetic,' he says, putting his hand on my knee, even if it is with the bed quilt over my legs. I smile at his touch.

'I'm meeting Haze and Jules this morning for our usual Saturday shopping sojourn in town.'

Stevie tuts. 'Haze and Jules? They even sound like a pair of fat slags. What's wrong with Hazel and Julie?'

'I dunno.' I shrug my shoulders. 'That's how I've always known them.'

'Well,' says Stevie, getting out of bed again, 'you haven't got any clean clothes to put on, but you're welcome to a shower if you want. I'll get some breakfast for you. What would you like? Cooked breakfast, cereal, what?' He begins to get dressed, taking off his pyjama trousers. I am a little disappointed that he is wearing underpants.

'I'll have a cooked, please. And I'll have a shower; these clothes are clean enough till I get home.'

'Ok,' he says, heading off to the kitchen. 'You'll find the towels on the rail.'

After he leaves, I lie on the bed a little longer, just contemplating everything that has happened between us and all that he's said about not sleeping together... well, not having sex. I can see his point of view, but I'm not ready to just leave it at that yet. I have strong feelings for him, not just a desire to shag him. He's kind, caring, and above all fun to be with. It's just all so different and alien to me. My head is in a spin, my heart in a whirl, and all over a man older than my mum. *Oh, Stevie, what are you doing to me?*

*

I have my shower, get dressed, and go downstairs to the smell of eggs and bacon cooking in the kitchen. I'm back in my Gucci dress, which feels weird, but I've dispensed with my knickers. If only he knew. *Should I tell him?* I decide not.

I sit at the table. More tea is already made, and the cutlery and condiments are neatly laid out. He really is a little house husband... and I'm the lager lout. He brings over two platefuls of cooked breakfast: egg, bacon, sausage, beans, mushrooms, the lot. A full Monty. It looks so daunting but delicious, and I tuck in.

'Where are you going shopping with, er...?' asks Stevie.

'Just in town,' I say, between mouthfuls of food. This breakfast is lovely; I don't normally eat like this any time, but this morning it is fantastic.

'Do you want me to drop you off?'

'I need to go home first and change. Put some clean knickers on.' I don't quite tell him I don't have any on, but it must put an image in his head.

'I'll take you home and come in while you change, if you like?'

'No,' I snap; a little too snappy. 'Er, no. It's ok,' I reassert myself. I don't want him coming in with Mum at home. 'Just, er, drop me at home. I'll be fine, thanks.'

'I bet you've got your keys in there, haven't you?' he says, pointing at my bag with a sideways look. I look away shyly and nod. 'And your mum was in last night, too?'

'I just wanted to be with you.' I'm trying to find the words to explain how I feel, what I want. 'I just love being with you.' I get all assertive. 'It's not about shagging. It's about being with you, having a good time together. Lying in bed with you all snuggled up; that's why I slept so well. I dunno.'

Stevie continues eating his breakfast, while I've stopped eating. But the food is so lovely, I get back to it.

I can see Stevie is contemplating what I've just said; in fact, I'm contemplating it myself. *Am I really looking for the L word?* We've only known each other a week, only been out three times, but I can't stop thinking about him, even when I was in Glasgow and all that went on there.

'I love being with you, too,' says Stevie, finishing his breakfast and washing it down with his tea. 'This is the problem I'm faced with. I couldn't stop thinking about you all last week when you were away, and it was great to see you again last night. I was looking forward to it all week, I can tell you. But this whole thing has to stop. You need to go and pick on someone your own size,' he says with a slight grin. 'You're young, you're beautiful. You're sexy, if you want me to say it.' *Yes, I want you to say it.* 'One day you'll find Mr Right, and don't forget to invite me to the wedding.'

I clear my breakfast plate. That was absolutely delicious. If that is anything to go by, it's him I want to marry. 'Can't we just be friends?'

'Yes, of course. You go off and do your shopping. Have a nice day, but keep the stories to yourself. We've got each other's number, eh?'

Chapter Fourteen

Stevie drops me off at home, and after a quick change and putting on some knickers, I make my own way into town to meet up with Haze and Jules. We go down the high street and look in most of the stores, especially the shoe shops. In one, we spend ages looking and trying on shoes and taking up all the assistant's time, but still come away without buying anything.

We call in one or two other shops, looking at skirts and dresses, then we try on tops, and Jules buys one. Our next stop is the lingerie shop. This is my favourite shop; this is how I've become so sexy. *Thank you for making me the sex goddess that I am and giving me, like, loads of fun.* As a result of coming into this shop, I can tease, tantalise, and twist any boy around my finger. Well, most boys; I think of Stevie. And I get some of the most wonderful sensations and pleasure to boot.

We look at some of the underwear, so daring and so sexy. Haze holds up a pair of very brief knickers. 'These are what I need to capture that man of yours, Debbie,' she says, and holds them against me at knicker level. Then she holds them against herself, actually lifting up her skirt, and looking in the mirror. 'He wouldn't be able to resist.'

We all three laugh as Jules says, 'It makes a change to see you in knickers.'

We move through the shop and look at the sex toys. There are dildos and vibrators on display, and the usual quips are there. 'Bit small,' I jokingly say about one.

'Much prefer the real thing,' says Haze.

'Yeah, but some of the real ones malfunction too quickly,' I say, and we all laugh.

But some of the goods look quite inviting. I ponder over them a second, thinking of Stevie. Even in here he's on my mind; looking at artificial cocks, I'm still thinking of him. *Should I buy one just to satisfy my curiosity?* About him, that is.

Jules picks up a pair of red fluffy handcuffs. 'These are what we need,' she says, holding them up. 'No escape. Satisfaction guaranteed.'

'No. This is what you need.' Haze is holding up a red lurex dress. It is short, figure-hugging like a body stocking, long-sleeved, and completely see-through. 'There'll be nowhere for him to hide, every inch of my body will be on show.'

'You wouldn't dare,' says Jules. 'There'll be nowhere for *you* to hide.'

'I don't need daring and I don't need to hide. If I wore this tonight, I'd easily get my money back; I definitely wouldn't need to take a handbag with all the fellas drooling over me. I'd just go up to any of them and ask them to buy me a drink. They wouldn't refuse. It's not for the bedroom; it'd be off by then.'

She goes to the changing room and tries it on. She shows it to me and Jules. *Oh my God, she looks so sexy I could fancy her myself. Oh.* My mind flashes back to last night in BJ's. Yasmin. Er…

'You look fantastic,' I tell her.

'Would lover boy be able to resist?' she asks me. That's a good question. She goes back into the changing room to dress then goes off to pay for it.

'You're really gonna wear it? Out?' Jules is incredulous.

'You just wait. Keep a close eye on him, Debbie,' says Haze, and I think about what I said to Stevie and catching a falling star.

I decide to buy the fluffy handcuffs and also see a basque, a tight-fitting baby doll with suspenders. In red. Yes, that's how I'll keep Haze's hands off him. The way to a man's heart is through his penis, and this is where it starts.

We stop off for a quick drink and actually call in at BJ's. It's a totally different place in the day – quiet, serving food. I rarely go in during the day, and it's quite surreal. It makes me think of Yasmin again. I take out my phone and just look through my old texts.

Yasmin x

That's all it says. I'm about to put the mobile away then I, like, change my mind and press call. I let it ring a number of times, but with no answer, I lose my bottle and hang up before the voicemail comes in.

I think no more of it and carry on chatting with the girls before we pick up our bags and head home. I make my way to the bus stop alone. It's a glorious day, and I think about Stevie; we could have gone motorbiking again. A motorcycle goes past and I have to look twice, my heart skipping a beat thinking it might be him. I'm almost disappointed when it isn't.

Daydreaming, I'm quite oblivious to the fact that my mobile is ringing. I quickly rummage through my bag to retrieve it before whoever it is hangs up. I don't even look at the name in my hurry to answer it. 'Hello,' I say.

'Hi, Debbie. It's Yasmin. Did you try and call me?' My heart skips another beat.

'Hi, Yasmin.' I copy her cheery voice, despite the nervousness shaking through my whole body. 'I thought I'd give you a call after last night. See if you were doing anything.'

'I'm at home right now. Not been up long, working till the early hours and that.'

'Yeah, I'm sure. I didn't wake you, did I?' I say apologetically.

'No. I was in the bathroom and only just saw that I got a missed call.' She is so cheery, it gives me a warm feeling inside. 'What you up to?'

'I was, er, I bought some new clothes and wondered what you might think.' I deliberately omit to say that it's underwear I bought.

'Oh, Debbie.' She is so cheery, so full of beans. 'I'm honoured that you even thought about me like that.'

'I thought I might get your address and come over,' I say, letting the words just roll off my tongue. 'Whereabouts do you live?'

'Fitzwilliam Street.'

Fitzwilliam? How ironic. That name takes me back to Glasgow and a woman I met. 'I know it. That's the number 17, isn't it?'

'Yeah. Are you in town?'

'I am.'

'Look, give me half an hour and I'll come down and meet you,' she says, and I can sense her starting to get ready. *Half an hour? What am I gonna do for half an hour?* Apart from fret.

'Where do you wanna meet?'

'We can meet at AJ's if you want?'

'AJ's?' I query. 'Oh, yeah. AJ's.'

'Yeah, I know everyone calls it BJ's, but staff are not allowed to. Do you wanna meet there? I might be able to wangle us a free drink,' she says, and I can literally hear her smile down the line.

'Ok. See you in half an hour. Bye.'
'Bye.'
'Bye. Bye.'
'Bye.'

To kill my half an hour I just look in a couple of more shops, and in one underwear shop I buy some stockings to match my suspender basque, as I hadn't bought any earlier. I choose some nice sheer, barely black stockings with a pretty red lacy top to match the red basque. I thought that if I put on the basque to show Yasmin, I would really need the stockings to go with it. The thought of wearing these undies for another woman to see is actually a turn on. If she likes it, I'm damned sure Stevie will like it.

I walk back into B, er, AJ's and I can't see Yasmin. 'Hi, Debbie,' that cheery voice calls me from behind. She's just coming in the front door behind me. I hadn't seen her out in the street.

'Hello, darling,' I say, looking back. *Oh, wow!* She's wearing pink hot pants that barely cover her cheeks, with matching heels to accentuate her legs and bum. She has a sleeveless cotton top with buttons all down the front, but only the middle two buttons are fastened, leaving her navel on show and her breasts wobbling like two pink blancmanges. She has beautiful smooth skin and long blonde hair that frames her pretty face, with just the right amount of make-up. She is, like, absolutely gorgeous. I am quite stunned at her beauty.

We kiss each other's cheek. 'Oops. Sorry, I've put lippy on your face,' she says, wiping it off with her hand. 'There. Better.' Her soft touch on my face is quite delightful. I put my fingers to where she has just kissed and touched me.

'Thank you.' I'm not sure if I mean for the kiss, the touch, or the removal of the lipstick. *All three, I think.*

'Shall we just have a coffee, or are you ready for something else?'

'Coffee is fine. Well, a cup of tea, actually. I like my alcopop, but I'll save them for tonight,' I say with a grin. She gives me a wink.

'See you in here tonight, then.' Yasmin goes off while I take a seat, and she brings back a tray with our drinks. She has a cappuccino.

'Will you be working again tonight, then?' I ask her.

'Yes. I work here on the busy nights, Friday, Saturday, sometimes Thursday, depends.'

'Not your full-time job?'

'No. But it's my main job at the moment,' she says, drinking her coffee.

'So, what do you normally do? You're so beautiful you should be a model,' I tell her.

'Thank you. I *am* a model…' she begins.

'Seriously?'

'It's not all glamour like these supermodels you see in the papers all the time,' she says with a little reluctance in her tone. 'My height doesn't help much to find work, but I get some assignments and I get paid well for them, but they don't come in regularly.'

'So that's why you work here then?'

'I enjoy it here. It's like having a night out and getting paid for it. It's great fun, meeting lots of people, having a laugh, everything. I love it. Gives me a chance to dress to kill and tease all the boys; they just drool. But if a girl doesn't like being looked at, she shouldn't make herself so attractive. I like being looked at.' She winks at me. 'It's when they stop looking you wanna worry.'

Her cheery persona really reflects the enthusiasm for the job she does, and I'm sure she loves flirting with the boys and dressing provocatively for it. She certainly did last night, and it even caught my eye. And the way she's dressed now, in the afternoon, is certainly making me feel good again.

'You enjoy flirting with the boys?' I begin to ask.

'No. Teasing them. I don't really try to attract them for, like, trying to get a date. I've never been with a boy that can give me an orgasm,' she says a little dejectedly. 'I dunno, it's like that song that goes, like, you never make me scream.'

'But orgasms are not all about, like, penetration. Yeah, there's nothing better than, like, a good hard cock inside you, but it's not designed to stimulate the clitoris, it's just, like, a reproduction organ.' *Oh my God, I've gone all agony aunt.* 'If you want your clitoris stimulating, get him to use his finger. Or better still, his tongue. I mean, at the end of the day, how does a woman, like, get you going?'

'The thing is, boys get to the bedroom, it's all me, me, me. At least, that's all the boys *I've* been with. All they want is a blow job and then can't get my knickers off quick enough to shag me, while I'm, like, wanting lots more pre-intercourse action. Like you said, with their tongue and that. And lots of kissing,' she says almost sadly. 'What's the point of dressing sexy and having exciting underwear when they don't take the time to even look and admire it and caress it and stuff? And then when I'm just getting warmed up, they're, like, crossing the finish line. They just have their fun – don't get me wrong, I give them a good time – but afterwards I'm, like...' she shrugs, 'left wanting. Now, with a girl, it's so much better.' Her enthusiasm lifts. 'I know what I want and can give it; equally, I *get* what I want because a girl can do what she knows she wants. Don't you agree?'

'Yeah.' *I think so.* I think about Pauline last week and that thunderous orgasm she gave me. She certainly knew what to do, and it's probably all to do with knowing what *she* wants. I get it. 'But not all boys are, like, wham bam, thank you, ma'am. Some have a bit of skill, 'specially if they're a bit more experienced.' My mind drifts a little, thinking of Stevie.

'Yeah, no. I'm more inclined these days to be behind the camera,' says Yasmin, going back to the original subject, bringing my thoughts back to earth. 'I'm studying art and photography at Uni; I mainly do a lot of stuff for the girls aiming to be models. And some boys, too. It's a two-way thing. That's how I sometimes get modelling assignments myself.'

'Sounds like a glamorous world to me.' Actually, I'm a bit jealous. There she is going round showing off her wonderful body to boys that can't have it, and flashing it at the camera or eyeing other beautiful women from behind it. 'You've had no one come in here and recognise your talents?'

'You.'

It is a straight answer, and one that makes me blush. 'I didn't mean like that...'

'Why don't I take some photos of you?' She quickly comes to my rescue. 'You're a beautiful woman and you'd look good in photos, a bit of glam, a bit sexy.'

'Well, that was what I wanted to show you. The clothes I bought this morning are underwear.' I hold up my lingerie bag.

'Oh, lovely. You could put them on, and I could take some photos, yeah?' Her enthusiasm knows no bounds. *How can I refuse?*

'Yes, please.'

'Come on, drink your tea. My car is right out front.' I realise that's how I missed her in the street before I came in.

'I've got the key to the studio, so we can go there, and you can, like, dress up and pose for me. Or undress.'

'Great.' Meeting Yasmin is proving to be a stroke of luck in more ways than one. Just as it was meeting Stevie.

We go outside, and there's Yasmin's car right on the doorstep. A Mercedes Benz SLK convertible. We climb in, and she takes the top down on such a gorgeous afternoon. 'How did you get a sexy beast like this?' I ask her.

'I've got a rich daddy. Bought me it a couple of years ago for my eighteenth birthday, after I passed my test just a week earlier. It's coming up to its first MOT soon, so might have to ask him sweetly for a new one.'

That tells me how old she is; same as me. 'Rich father. How lucky are you? My dad hardly existed.'

'You'll have to meet him. He got rich because he's the one that started up the modelling agency. He supplies models all over Europe for all sorts of clients, some very famous ones; catwalk models for top fashion designers, clothes advertising, children, older people, wherever a model is needed. It's not all beautiful women in lingerie.' She says the word lingerie just as it's spelled. Lin-ger-ree. Takes me a second to work out what she means. 'And he also owns a couple of lap dance clubs and provides the girls through his agency. He likes to call them gentlemen's clubs. That's how I got into it, through the agency,' she tells me, as we drive through the streets.

'You do lap dancing?'

'No. The lap dance clubs are not in this town, they're in the bigger cities really. I've done it a few times, but it's too far to go to the nearest one when I'm at Uni. Summer's coming, so I might give it another go. It pays well. And I do like to dress like this. I get excited with the "you can look but you can't touch" side of it. If you've got it…' She shrugs. 'My height lets me down for much modelling, as I'm only four foot ten... and a bit. So, I started the photography bit. Like, behind the camera instead.'

'But you said you still do a bit of modelling...'

'Now and again.'

'But you're stunning. You are so beautiful...'

'All they want most the time is, like, tall size zero girls,' says Yasmin, resignedly.

'That counts me out then.' I point out. 'So how tall do you need to be?'

'Five ten and upwards, I s'pose. And skinny as fuck.'

'That counts me out again. I'm only five six in my bare feet,' I say, 'but hang on. You said it's not like, all glam girls in ling...' I'm saying it like it's spelled now. 'Er, lingerie,' I correct. 'You could model for petite sizes and stuff.'

'Exactly. And that's why there's work out there for girls like you, especially in larger size clothing advertising. You'd be perfect.' *It's ok, I'm not insulted by that.* But she quickly adds an explanation. 'For a bigger woman, you're both beautiful and very curvy. There's no "fat" about you. All smooth lines and sex appeal. That's why I like you; you've a body to be proud of. I can't wait to take some photos. I think you and I are gonna get on like a house on fire.' She touches my thigh, high up, higher than the hem of my skirt – and it ain't that long in the first place. It sends a shiver right through me. It's like... mmm.

It makes me smile. *Am I a lesbian?* Absolutely not, but... *Thanks, Pauline... I think.*

We get to the studio, and she opens up. It's a bit eerie at first because it's dark and there are no windows in the main studio. It's quiet, too. Yasmin puts that right by putting on some relaxing music that fills the room yet has no distinct source.

'Normally, there are a few of us, lighting people, make-up, etcetera, and of course tutors, as I'm a student. But I think we can get by with just the two of us for now.'

'Is this all your stuff?' I ask, looking around the whole room.

'No, unfortunately. But one day. It's the Uni's, but I have a key so that I can come in any time I like. Though this is the first time.' She says it mischievously, and I can only keep smiling at her. She is so bubbly and wonderful.

Yasmin gets a laptop computer booted up and beckons me over to have a look. On the screen there are photos of models in all sorts of poses and states of undress. Some are men – not many, but they catch my eye – and all of them are, like, sexy, glam photos. Women in bikinis, in underwear; men without a top, or with a shirt fully undone. Women topless; sexy poses like those that advertise my favourite shop.

'Are these what you've taken?'

'Yes.'

'They're very good. I like them. And I like the clothes, too. And shoes,' I add with enthusiasm.

Then Yasmin shows me some pictures of herself. Wow! They are fantastic, and so sexy. She, like, dresses in a way that emphasises her body anyway, but seeing her posing is actually a turn on. Apart from the fact that she is not naked in any of the photos, they could easily be seen as soft porn.

I put my hand on her shoulder and move close. 'They are wonderful. You are so beautiful.'

She leans her face onto my hand and turns her head to kiss it. 'Thank you,' she says humbly.

We actually hold the pose for a moment or two, just enjoying each other's touch, however casual. It's almost at the point when we should start to kiss and snog and... then Yasmin gets back to the point.

'Let's have a look at this new underwear you've bought.' I pick up my bag and lift out the basque. 'Oh, wow. Very sexy. There's a proper changing and make-up room over there,' she says, pointing, 'but there's no one here but us chickens, so you can change here if you like.'

'Yeah, I'll do it here.' I stand up and start to remove my top. I can hear Yasmin's camera shutter clicking away, and after I've lifted my top right off, I can see her taking photos of me as I undress. It, like, spurs me on as I reach round to unclip my bra.

'That's right. Keep that natural look and carry on,' she says, snapping away.

I undo my bra and allow it to slip off my shoulders. I hold it in place against my boobs, then I hold it with one outstretched arm, with my other across my chest over my boobs, before dropping my bra to the floor with my arm outstretched in an evocative way.

'Oh, Debbie, that's so sexy.'

I'm not sure if she's saying it for the photos, or her pleasure, or both. But I carry on undressing. Still in my short skirt and heels, I begin to unzip my skirt.

'Turn around and let me see you from behind as you drop your skirt.'

I do as I'm told and slowly reveal my bum in my silky knickers to the camera, to Yasmin. She lets out a little sigh.

She puts down the camera then and helps me into my new basque, assisting me to remove the labels and stuff, and straightening it out. 'You might need to brush your hair after being in my car with the top off,' she suggests. 'I'll go get a brush.'

She heads off to the make-up room while I take the stockings out of my bag, open them up, and put them on. I'm actually sitting on a *chaise longue* to do this – obviously a prop for the photos – and when Yasmin comes back into the studio, she sees me fastening the first stocking.

'Oh, that is so sexy,' she says in her cheery style. 'Let's brush your hair a bit, and then I'll take some photos as you put the other one on.'

Yasmin brushes my hair, and I'm loving her running her hands through my hair, tilting my head back as I luxuriate in the feel of her caress. Then she goes back behind the camera as I continue to 'dress'.

'That's it, Debbie, slowly, sexily. Pout for me,' she says, going all professional. It makes me think of Stevie and how he sometimes goes all schoolteacher on me. *Oh, Stevie, if only you were here right now.* Then she stops taking pictures. 'Let's have a bit more lipstick, make them fuller. Have you got the same lippy on you?'

'Yes,' I say, pointing, 'in my handbag.'

Yasmin goes over to the chairs where we were sitting and where my clothes and bag are. She picks up my bag and is looking for my lipstick when I see her do a double-take at the underwear bag. She rummages and pulls out the fluffy handcuffs, then holds them up and looks at me in that oh, so sexy way. 'We could have some fun with these.'

'That was the idea,' I say to her.

She comes over to me and hands me my lipstick and a mirror, then she opens the handcuffs from their packaging. After I apply a bit more lippy and practise a bit of pouting, she's got the cuffs ready. And without words or persuasion, I hold out my hands and she locks me in. We look into each other's eyes and the lust is there, glinting in her eyes. I'm sure it is in mine, too.

'I've got you where I want you now,' she says, holding the cuffs.

I lift my arms up and back down over her head and around her back, then pull her a little closer. 'And I've got you where I want you,' I say. There's a second's delay and then we kiss. Full on, lips on lips, tongues touching in a real lustful snog. I'm, like, oh my God! *Is this really happening?*

My hands are bound but hers are free to explore my body, running them all over me, over the basque and over my breasts. I break from the kiss enough to keep my lips in contact with hers but enough to gasp as she rubs my breasts, bringing my nipples to attention and sending shockwaves pulsing through my body. It is sensational!

I manage to move my manacled hands down her back and onto her bum. It is a beautiful shape in my touch, smooth and round, and I feel her cheeks clench under her pink shorts. Oh my God. It is so horny, I can feel my heart racing and my sex organs tighten. I've never felt this horny before. I'm in the sexiest of underwear and in the arms of a young, sexy, so sexy woman. Yes. A woman. Snogging. Who knows what's gonna happen next, but whatever it is, I want it.

Then suddenly we freeze. There's a noise. 'Hello.' Someone is coming in; a male's voice by the sound of it. Oh no! Not just because of my state of undress and capture, but the interruption has thrown cold water on the lust coursing through both of our bodies.

I quickly lift my arms and allow Yasmin to 'escape', and she rushes over to the door to stop the intruder coming any further. 'Hello. Yes, we're doing some photo shots, er, naked ones,' I hear her saying, as she goes out of the door.

I move over to where my clothes are, but I'm handcuffed so I can't really do anything. I pick up my clothes and stuff and head for the make-up room to sit and wait. 'Shit.' Total frustration overwhelms me, and I say it again. 'Shit.'

Yasmin comes into the make-up room. 'Ah, there you are,' she says, then her shoulders drop and she lets out a heavy sigh. 'Apparently, they've got the studio booked for a big family shoot. I asked him to give us five minutes so you can get dressed,' she says very reluctantly. I hold up my manacled hands. 'Oh, crikey. Sorry. Where's the key?'

'I don't know, you opened the packaging,' I say. 'Don't tell me…'

'It's ok, they're here,' she says, and unlocks me. I get out of the basque and stockings, with a little help and giggling from Yasmin, and get dressed again.

*

Yasmin gives me a lift home in the SLK with the top off. 'You'll have to come round and have a look at the photos I did manage to take. I'm sure there'll be some good ones of you.'

'Yes,' I say, 'I will. And we have some unfinished business to deal with.'

Yasmin looks across at me and smiles. She stops for a red light, puts a hand on my knee, then leans across and we kiss. It's only a quick kiss, but we must have let it linger a little too long, as the driver in the car behind sounded his horn because the lights had changed. Or was it because he got the horn seeing two sexy babes kissing in the car in front? Yasmin pulls away, and as she picks up a bit of speed, we look across at each other and laugh at the situation.

'I'll have a look at the pictures as soon as I can, and if there is anything I think worthwhile, we'll try and arrange a proper shoot with all the make-up team and dressers and hair people, get you a good portfolio, and I'll pass them on to Daddy.'

'Yes, that sounds great.'

'I'll have a look later, and if I see you in AJ's tonight, I'll speak to you, then we can arrange something,' says Yasmin, as she drives down my street.

'I want to see you again, if that's alright with you.' There's no point beating about the bush. 'For, like, friendship, I mean.'

'Yes, of course. You don't think I'm just gonna leave it at that, do you? No way!' She has that glint in her sparkling eyes; she is one hell of a beautiful woman. 'As you say, unfinished business.'

She pulls up outside my house, and I lean across and we kiss again. It's a quick smack and I open the car door.

'Thanks, Debbie. It's been great. Just a shame it ended like that, but we'll make up for it, I promise.' Yasmin squeezes my hand and pulls me back, and this time the kiss is a full-on snog again. And this time it's my turn to give her breast a quick caress, my hands free. Yasmin puts her hand to my face and through my hair, pushing it behind my ear.

I break off the kiss. 'Enough, or we'll end up finishing the job right here.'

Yasmin just gives me a look to suggest 'why not?' *Oh, she is so beautiful.*

Chapter Fifteen

It's early evening and I'm walking up to Stevie's door again. I've got a dress on over the top of my basque and stockings, my handcuffs are in my handbag. It's a bit warm to be dressed in such underwear, but I'm planning it to be hot, hot, hot in the bedroom tonight.

I ring the doorbell, and as I see Stevie coming to the door my heart skips a beat. It's still there, that fluttering feeling that Stevie creates even just by his apparition through the frosted glass.

'Hello, Debbie,' he says, opening the door wide and welcoming me in. 'I wasn't expecting you tonight. For what do I deserve this pleasure?'

'I wanted to see you. Maybe a night out, maybe a night in,' I say suggestively as we kiss. Three kisses.

'You only just caught me. I was about to go out and get a takeaway. They charge for delivery when you're only paying for one, but you can join me if you like?'

'Yes, that'd be nice. What sort of takeaway were you thinking of?' I make myself comfortable on his sofa, crossing my legs to emphasise my stockings and show a bit of thigh, and he sits beside me. He's only got shorts on, so I put my hand on his thigh and give it a gentle rub, up as high as I dare, and then pull my hand away. After this afternoon's activity with Yasmin and the way I'm dressed making me feel sexy, my hormones are racing around like crazy. I need to keep control, but I could rip his shorts off right now.

'Chinese. Is that okay for you?' I nod approval. 'I've got a bottle chilling in the fridge, yeah?'

'Pinot Grigio?'

'Er, Sauvignon, I think. Do you want me to order and get it delivered, or shall we still go to the shop? It's only a five-minute walk.'

'If it's only round the corner, we'll go for a walk.'

'I like your way of thinking,' he says, as he stands up then offers his hand to help me up. To my surprise he puts his hand around my waist, and I move in closer. I hope he's not teasing, but after this morning's conversation, I know I've got my work cut out tonight.

'I just need to powder my nose.' I make my way to the stairs for the bathroom, but once I'm upstairs, I quickly pop into the bedroom and look at the headboard. It's a full one, not like my wooden rails at home, so it'll make it difficult to handcuff him to the bed. I'll think of something. I go into the bathroom and flush the toilet even though I didn't go, just to make it sound that way.

We leave the house to head to the takeaway; Stevie holds the gate open for me and follows me out. I take his hand, and we walk along together like a proper couple.

'Are you okay walking in those heels? You like your heels, don't you?' he asks, looking down at my shoes.

'Don't you? I wear them all the time.'

'I've noticed. Very nice, too.' *That's a surprise.* 'But they're car-to-bar shoes, not for walking.'

'Carterbar? What's that?'

'Only suitable to walk in from car to bar,' he explains, emphasising each word individually.

'Oh.' *I get it.* 'No, I'm fine. So, you like them?'

'Yes, of course. I like to see them; they emphasise a woman's figure.'

'Now there's a bombshell. I thought you were trained to overlook such things.'

'Yes. But I can still look if I want,' he says assertively.

'It's been a lovely day. Did you go out on your motorbike?' I ask.

'No, not today. Yeah, it was nice enough to go for a ride, but I stayed at home apart from a quick nip to the shops after I dropped you off.'

'I could've come with you, and we could've, I dunno, had a picnic somewhere or something,' I say sweetly, swinging our arms as we walk.

'That would've been great. You should've said.'

'You said you wanted to leave it for a while and give you a call when I was ready. You didn't want me calling you as quick as I did last night, did you?' *Get out of that one!*

'*Touché*. I walked straight into that, didn't I?'

'And now you're taking me for a takeaway to have a night in. Tut, tut, Steven Taylor. I've made up my mind; have you made up yours?'

We walk along a little further in silence. I'm happy just holding his hand but I am still hoping for an answer to my question. We get to the takeaway and look at the menu. 'What do you fancy?' *Like he doesn't know the answer to that!*

'What are you having?' I ask, and he tells me his choice. 'That sounds good, I'll have that, too.'

'Yeah, but if you have something different, then you can have some of mine and I'll have some of yours. The best of both worlds,' he says it with such vigour that I study the menu and choose something else.

'So, it'll be like when we shared at the Italian last week?'

'You're getting the idea, Debbie,' he says and squeezes my hand, then he goes to the counter to order. He sits back down with me but keeps his hands to himself. 'What about your day?' he asks. 'Your shopping with what's their names?'

'Yeah, the usual browse round the shoe shops and that. Nothing special.' I shrug my shoulders. 'We just go in for a laugh, really. Sometimes we buy something but not always.'

'Sounds like it's a bit of a chore, the way you dismiss it as nothing.' *There you go, he's gone all schoolteacher on me again.*

'No. It's fun. We have a laugh.' I try to sound enthusiastic about it, but how can I tell him what we did actually buy? My basque and stockings. My handcuffs. Then there's that dress that Haze bought. Oh my God, I dread to think of the scenes she'll be making going in the bars dressed like that. 'We have a laugh, that's what we do. It's a girly thing, you won't understand.'

A young girl walks into the takeaway; she can't be any more than sixteen or seventeen. She's not quite Yasmin, but she's got skimpy shorts on and a top that reveals her midriff. She goes to the counter and has to raise herself onto her toes to rest her arms on the counter, making the top she's wearing rise even further, giving everyone a full view of her waist and her bum in her shorts, emphasised by the fact she stands on tiptoe. There are one or two other men in the shop, and their eyes go straight to her. Even mine do. She's got a lovely bum. *Oh my God, I am turning gay.* But Stevie takes no notice of her at all. I look at him as if to say 'can't you see her?'

'What?' he says, doing a double-take at me.

'Nothing.' I say it with surprise in my voice.

The girl turns away from the counter and beams a smile at me. I can't help but give her a sweet smile in return. *Oh, stop it, Debbie! What's getting into you?*

We collect our food and head back home, walking hand-in-hand once again. I feel overdressed in my flowing dress and stockings whilst Stevie is in just shorts and t-shirt. But I feel sexy in my dress and knowing what I'm wearing underneath. I swing our arms again, acting like a kid; it makes me feel so carefree.

'I met up with a friend this afternoon. She is at Uni doing art and photography and she took me to the studios, asking me to do some posing.' I continue our theme of my day.

'A model now. Is there nothing you can't do?'

'It was only like, the two of us, but she wanted to have a go. She reckons she could get me some work, said I'm a natural. We didn't get far, though, because someone else came in that had booked the studio.' I omitted exactly what had been interrupted. 'But we'll look at the photos and maybe next time we'll do it properly with make-up artists and everything.'

'Great. You'll have to let me see them,' he says encouragingly.

'They're sexy,' I point out. 'I was only in underwear.'

'Oh.' He raises his eyebrows and seems to have second thoughts about seeing the pictures.

I turn and walk backwards in front of him, still holding his hand. 'Don't you wanna see pictures of me in my undies?' I say, all innocent. 'You've seen it for real.'

'Of course I do. I'm sure they're sexy.'

'Very sexy.' I stop walking and he collides with me. At least it means I get him to put his free arm around me, and I make the most of it by pulling him close and stealing a kiss. 'I've got the same underwear on still,' I tease him.

'Haven't you changed?' He says it like a sledge hammer, bludgeoning away the sensuousness of the moment.

'It's not just any old underwear, it's real seduction stuff.' I take my arms from around his waist and turn, and we carry on walking. 'No karate t-shirts for me tonight.'

We walk along quietly. I've struck him dumb. The schoolmaster has been out-mastered. 'What's the matter, Stevie? Have I frightened you off?'

'Not at all. I'm just processing what you said. It sounds exciting, but you really are determined, aren't you?'

I stop walking again as Stevie takes another couple of steps before turning to face me. If I'm honest, I'm a little angry.

'Yes,' I snap, 'it's very exciting. Look, Stevie, you're a single man living alone, no girlfriend – apart from me – not been in a relationship since, er…' I look down at my feet, 'you know, and you're with the sexiest girl in town who's making it quite clear that its access all areas… You tell me you're not celibate or impotent. Don't you get frustrated at all?'

He takes my hand again and holds it gently. He sighs. 'When I was a boy, about thirteen or fourteen, just coming into puberty, I got into a fight with another boy.'

Here it comes, I think. Here comes the real truth about why he rejects me. Not this schoolgirl nonsense. He starts to walk on again and almost drags me with him.

'He kicked me. Hard. Fucking hard,' he swears, catching me off guard. I don't think I've heard him swear. 'Right between the legs.' He says that bit politely. 'I was in pain for ages, and I ended up going to my doctor. I didn't tell anyone. Not my parents, friends, teachers, no one. To be honest, I was a bit embarrassed at losing the fight to a boy I should have beaten, considering our sizes. It's one reason why I took up karate, so that it didn't happen again.'

We come to his house, and his story is abandoned for the moment as we go into the kitchen and prepare to enjoy our feast. 'I'll carry on later,' he says, referring to the conversation about his childhood fight. 'I don't want to spoil dinner.' He gets the wine from the fridge and pours us each a glass.

We lay the food out over the table in front of us and tuck in. 'I don't know about you, Debbie, but I'm starving.'

'Yeah, me too.' I smile at him, and we begin to chat about other things, and his schoolboy fight is forgotten.

'Ever since I can remember I've tried to have a takeaway at least once a month. Not too often; it's never the treat if you have it too much. I would like to make it dinner out if I could, but on your own it's not so good,' he says, while we share the food between us.

'Well, that's all changed now. Debbie's here, and I'll be your dinner date in future.' I say this with a grin, despite a mouth full of noodles. 'You say you want to be, like, friends and have someone to, like, go out with,' I say, when my mouth is empty and the food washed down with a sip of wine.

'And takeaway night. Staying in; it's the new going out,' Stevie says, lifting his glass. 'Cheers.'

I pick up my glass again to clink with him, but he takes a sip of his drink, and the moment is gone.

'This bit of modelling you did…'

'It wasn't really modelling, I just had some photos taken by a friend,' I try to put it in perspective. 'She's into photography, and she felt that I would be good, especially for, like, larger women's clothes advertising.'

'Yeah, she's probably right,' he agrees. 'You told me that you are a sixteen, but I'd never had said that. A fourteen more like, though I'm not a women's clothing expert. But you're all curves and smooth lines…'

'That's what Yasmin said.'

'There you are then; we can't both be wrong.'

'I usually buy sixteens, as I need them to get over my boobs and hips. But the bit in the middle is probably fourteen.' I stand and run my hands over my waist and middle. 'I can wear fourteen in some stuff but it's tight in places.' I emphasise which places by running my hands over my bust.

'This Yasmin. She can get you modelling work?'

'Not as such.' I think about her main motive in photographing me. 'Her daddy, er, father is in the modelling business, and she wants to do some pictures because she believes I'd be perfect.'

'I can't disagree.' He gives me that smile that melts me.

'I can only give it a go. I mean, if nothing else, it'll be fun, and we should get some nice photos. You could have one as your screen saver on your mobile.' He smiles, and again I melt.

Stevie pours more wine, but I remember last week and how it went to my head. 'Have you got anything else?' I ask, in hope of some alcopops or something.

'Lager. Vodka.'

'Any Red Bull?'

'Er, no. Sorry. If I'd known you were coming, I'd have got something in for you,' he says as I sip at my wine. *I mean, it's nice, but I want to stay alert this time.*

'The wine's fine,' I say. There's still some food on the table but eventually we both give up on it.

'I'm stuffed,' says Stevie, with his hands on his belly. 'I'll have to do an extra five miles in the morning now.'

'I'm just about ok,' I tell him. 'But enough is enough.'

'Let's go sit on the sofa, it's a bit comfier.' He takes the wine bottle, and we move to the lounge and plonk ourselves down with a sigh. I kick my shoes off and lift one leg to lie across his. It makes my dress ride up a little, and I'm sure he catches a glimpse of red stocking top. He doesn't mind the contact, though, and actually puts a hand on my ankle. *Come on, Stevie. Higher.*

'The school holidays are coming up soon,' I say, in a complete change of direction. 'Do you have all that time off?'

'Yeah. One of the best things about being a teacher, but it restricts me if I want time off any other time of year. And holidays are more expensive; it's unfair to people that have kids, but even more unfair when you don't.'

'Are you going on a holiday in the summer?'

'No plans. What about you? Going away with the fat, er, girls?'

'No. I already said that I haven't really ever been on a holiday before,' I say. 'I was hoping you'd take me to Italy.' I've been on an aeroplane now and I can, like, picture myself sitting on one with Stevie next to me, heading for Rome.

'Oh, yeah, I remember, but you haven't got a passport,' he says, picking up his tablet computer. He taps a few icons and brings up a page on destinations in Italy. 'Where would you like to go?'

'Are you serious?' *Is he asking me just offhand or is he genuinely looking at where he could take me?* 'You'd take me to Italy?'

'I didn't exactly say that, but get yourself a passport and we can review it. 'Bout time I went back again.'

'I'll be ordering a passport on Monday morning, make no mistake. You can be my professional referee,' I say, putting my feet back down and snuggling into him. 'Let's have a look.' I hold the tablet so we can both read it.

Italian images flash before my eyes: the Colosseum in Rome; gondolas in Venice; the Leaning Tower of Pisa; they all look lovely and romantic. We chat about Italian cities for a while, then look at scenes from other European cities, such as Paris, Barcelona, and Bruges.

As I dream about visiting these places with Stevie, he takes the tablet and calls up a game. 'Fancy slicing some fruit?'

'Eh?'

'Fruit Ninja,' he says, as if it should be obvious. And he starts to play a game, swiping his finger over the screen and 'slicing fruit'. It looks fun.

'Give us a go then,' I say, trying to pull the tablet off him.

'Hang on.' He keeps a grip on it. 'Aw, look out.' Fruit is falling everywhere, and he keeps losing lives. I pull on the tablet again, and we have a childish tug of war. 'Stop it,' he says, trying to concentrate on his game. 'Argh!' an exclamation of a near miss, he keeps slicing and holding tight to the tablet as I try to steal it from him. Then he hits a bomb. Crash! He's out.

'My turn.' I take the tablet and begin a game. It's trickier than it looks. Crash! I hit a bomb; that didn't last long.

'Let me show you.' He tries to take back the tablet, but I hang on.

'No, I wanna go again.' I start a new game. 'Oh.' 'Ah.' 'Argh!' This is fun, and my finger is jumping all over the screen. I get a high scoring fruit; oh no. Lost a life. 'Argh.' I keep going. 'Whoa!' Lots of fruit come at me, I can't keep up. Crash! A bomb.

Stevie takes the tablet off me. 'Look and learn, baby. One fruit salad coming right up,' he says, and starts up another game. I let him play unhindered this time as I watch him. His concentration is absolute, and he racks up quite a score, but eventually – crash!

I take the tablet off him and try again. It's crazy, fruit all over the place, 'Argh!' 'No! No!' 'Argh!' Crash!

Whilst I'm playing, he leaves the room and comes back carrying a box. I put the tablet down when my game is over and look at what he's got now. 'Buckaroo!' he says, setting it up. 'What's the point of being grown up if you can't be childish now and again?' I can't believe this; I'm playing children's games with a forty-seven-year-old. It's great fun.

We play a few games of Buckaroo!, sitting on the carpet and watching as we keep score over who sets off the bucking bronco first. And we are falling around in fits of laughter, helped by finishing the bottle of wine. We sit back after he makes the bronco buck again, and the toys are all over the floor. Still on the carpet, we lean against the sofa with playful sighs, and I turn to him.

'This is the best fun I've had in ages,' I say to him, holding his hand.

'If you've still got some energy left, I've got a dance machine, if you wanna go.'

'No more games. Not yet.' Feigning exhaustion, I lean in to him, our faces close. This is the moment: we kiss, a quick peck at first, followed by another. Then another and, holding his face, I keep him there. Our lips together, his tongue sneaks out and caresses my top lip, just as he did that first time on the dance floors of the town centre clubs.

The kiss prolongs as we tease each other with our tongues clashing and lightly biting each other's lips. I run my fingers through his hair while he has his hands around my back, pulling me into the kiss. We break for a brief second, and I breathe heavily and sensuously, then the snog resumes with full passion.

I bring my hand down over his shoulder and down the side of his body, across his hip and along his bare thigh. I don't touch him there, not *there,* but I can sense the beginnings of an erection as his shorts tighten. He brings his hand to my cheek, and I put my hand over his, gently rubbing it. All the time our lips are engaged in a blissful, uninterrupted kiss. I take hold of his hand and move it from my face and onto my breast. *Oh my God, that is so beautiful*, and I groan and breathe heavily across his cheek.

'Oh, Stevie,' I murmur, and as I take my hand away from his, I'm thrilled that he doesn't move his. He keeps it on my breast and kneads me, bringing my nipples to full erection. I pull up my dress to reveal more thigh and my stocking tops. I know Stevie can't see, but I know that they're there and it heightens my pleasure. The sensation runs through my body, from my lips against his, from my breast in his hand, up my thighs and to my sexual area.

'Oh,' I breathe again. 'Oh, Stevie.' *Oh, yes! Yes, keep that going Stevie. Yes, caress me more, squeeze my tits. Oh...*

Then the phone starts to ring! Still kissing, my arms around his neck, my fingers running through his hair, my eyes pop wide open. He's got a landline phone. *Who the hell has a landline these days?* For a second, Stevie ignores it. I hope he lets it ring off, but my hopes are dashed as he breaks the magic and gets up to answer it.

'Sorry,' he says. 'I've got to answer it. To ring at ten on a Saturday night it must be important. Hello?'

He listens for a while, and I can just about make out the sound of the caller. I get up off the floor and sit on the sofa, straightening out my dress and covering my stockings. I put the heel of the palm of my hand against my forehead in frustration. It's like being slapped in the face.

Stevie starts talking to his caller. I'm not paying that much attention, but I then realise he's, like, talking Italian. I look up at him and he mouths at me – 'Mother'. He talks a little more, but I have no idea what he's saying, although he has a calm tone.

'*Si, si. Ciao.*' He ends the call and looks at me. His shoulders drop and he lets out a sigh. 'I'm sorry. So sorry, Debbie,' he says with a look of utter devastation. 'I'm gonna have to go.'

Twice in one fucking day. First Yasmin, now Stevie. I don't believe it. 'I'll come with you,' I suggest in a vain attempt to keep the mood going... but it's already gone.

'She's old and she's not well. She always talks Italian these days, but it's not fair to take you with me. I probably won't be back till the early hours.'

He dials a number on the phone and makes another call. He orders two taxis, one each. 'I can't even drive with half a bottle of wine inside me,' he says, rolling his eyes. 'Great.'

Stevie comes to me, lifts me to my feet, and puts his arms around me in a real heartfelt hug. I bury my face into his chest, and he kisses me on the top of my head. 'I'm so sorry,' he says quietly.

I look up into his eyes. 'Don't worry. If it was my mother, I'd jump too. You've gotta do what you've gotta do; it can't be helped.'

He runs off upstairs, and a moment or two later he comes back down with trousers and shoes on. He goes to the kitchen where all the takeaway dishes and everything are lying around. He takes one look and closes the door again, coming back into the lounge where I'm picking up the toys off the floor and putting them back in their box. He looks down at me and says 'sorry' again and helps me to my feet.

'It's ok, Stevie. It happens.' I'm being reasonable with him, but I'm as frustrated as hell. *Twice*, I say to myself again.

We walk out of the house together when the taxis arrive, and we kiss at the gate. 'Call me or text or something next week. Let me know how you get on with the modelling,' he says, and we kiss again.

He gives me some money to pay my taxi bill. I take it from him silently and reluctantly, looking at the money with a confused expression. Then I shrug and look up at him.

'Sure will. Can't wait to see the pictures myself.' We get into our taxis.

Stevie's taxi pulls away, and we wave to each other as his car passes mine. The driver looks over his shoulder at me. 'Where to, love?'

'Town centre. AJ's,' I say.

Chapter Sixteen

I walk into BJ's and straight to the bar; I need a drink. Straight away I see Yasmin serving another customer, but she sees me, waves, and gives me that gorgeous smile of hers. *Thanks, Yasmin, that's cheered me up.* She's in hot pants again, black glitter ones this time and a matching black t-shirt with sequins down the front. I realise that all the guys are looking, too. But when she's finished serving the customer, she comes straight over to me, regardless of who is next, leans forward over the bar on her tiptoes to me, and we kiss, fully on the lips. I sense all the guys' chins, like, hitting their chests.

'Hiya, darling. Alright?' Her cheery little voice, I love it.

'All the better for seeing you,' I say. *She called me darling.* She gets me a bottle of my favourite alcopop, and as I offer the money, she doesn't take it. 'On me. Or him, or him, or him,' she says, pointing around at random. 'They all want to buy me drinks. I take the money and, like, put it in my purse. Do you think it's the shorts?'

'I do.' I look down at her as she turns and pushes her bum out.

'I've had a quick look at some of those photos,' she goes on, taking no notice that anyone else wants serving. 'They're, like, well sexy. I'll text you tomorrow and we'll have a look together.'

'Yeah.' I smile, knowing that there's a few boys listening in. 'Look forward to it, Yasmin.' And for good measure, we lean across the bar and kiss again. She then turns and carries on serving.

I make my way away from the bar, and I spot Haze and Jules on the dance floor. I join them.

'Debbie,' calls out Haze and raises her arm, inviting me into a hug. We air kiss. 'Hello, sweetie. Where's lover boy?' *Lover boy? Why do they call him that?* I mean, it's not like they haven't shagged half a dozen boys since I met him. Even I've shagged two. And a woman.

I hug Jules, too. 'He's had to go see his mother. She's not well. I don't know, it was all in Italian.'

'Well, that's perfect,' says Haze, pointing over to some boys watching us. 'We've been plied with drinks by those three guys. Him on the left – He's snogged my face off already.' She gives me a wicked smile.

Jules joins in. 'That's the point. Like, there's three of them, and now there's three of us. D'you know what I mean?'

I look over at the boys. Mmm. They look good, and I need a bit of cock tonight after the day I've had. 'Ok, which one's mine?'

'Well, that one I've snogged is definitely mine,' says Haze.

'I'm surprised you've, like, had a problem with two of you and three of them,' I say with a suggestion. 'I mean, why not go back to your place or somewhere, all five of you, and have a shag fest?'

Haze and Jules look at each other in disbelief. 'Why didn't we think of that?' says Jules. 'But ain't you interested?'

'Oh my God, yeah. That one with long hair, I like the look of him.' His hair's not that long, a bit tousled like Stevie's – that's probably why I like him – but the other two have cropped hair. 'What's his name?'

Again, they both look at each other, then shrug. 'I dunno,' says Jules.

I take a suck on the straw of my drink. 'Come on then. Let's find out.'

We walk over to the boys, and I immediately go to the one with the hair. 'Hi, I'm Debbie.' *Please don't be a minger.*

'Grant.' He points with his bottle of lager at his friends. 'Mikey and Dave.'

He sounds ok; not a minger so far. *Try this.* I lean up to him, put my free hand behind his head and kiss him, slow and lingering. After I break the kiss, I look him in the eye.

'That's, like, broken the ice nicely. Congratulations, you've pulled. And tonight is your lucky night.'

All three of the guys are looking at me in disbelief. Even Haze and Jules are a bit taken aback at my brashness. If they only knew how horny I was feeling after the day I've had. And I'm not letting this seductive underwear go to waste.

Come to think of it, where's Haze's lurex dress? I knew she wouldn't have the bottle.

'Do you like to dance?' I ask, er, was it Grant? I'm practically pulling him onto the dance floor to get him alone. He looks over his shoulder at the other four. I hope it's with a smile and not a look for help. On the floor I dance up to him, thrusting my hips at him. He has his hands on my waist but seems very distant.

'Come on, babe,' I say, grabbing his hands and pulling them around my back so that he's close and holding me tight. I can feel his cock through his trousers, rising to the occasion like it's been alerted to temptation. 'I don't bite. But I can use my mouth in lots of different ways. Like this.' And I kiss him once again.

We dance like this for a while, and I pull him into a kiss once more. 'All this dancing is making me horny. And thirsty. Are you gonna buy me drink?'

'Yeah, sure.' I think he is glad to get off the dance floor. Perhaps he's one of those guys that's a bit self-conscious when it comes to dancing. Like most of them. They don't wanna dance with you, but they still expect a shag at the end.

He goes off to the bar, and I rejoin Haze and Jules. 'Any good?' asks Jules.

'He's shaping up nicely; very perky,' I say with a glint in my eye. 'And I've come prepared.' I delve into my handbag and pull out the handcuffs. Haze and Jules laugh.

The boy – *what was his name?* – comes back with my drink. I take it from him using both hands, making sure there's a lot of hand touching. He pulls away from the contact and says he needs the loo.

'I think he's nervous about you,' says Haze, watching him go.

'He's gonna have the time of his life.' I emphasise my words by lifting my dress quickly to show off my stockings. 'Told you I've come prepared.' I look around briefly. 'Where are the other two guys?'

Haze and Jules both shrug their shoulders at me. They don't seem too bothered. They've had their drinks supplied, so if someone else takes over the mantle, so be it. But then we see all three guys coming out from the corridor that leads to the toilet area, two of them laughing.

'I wonder what they've been talking about.' asks Jules.

I can picture the scene.

Mikey and Dave are already in the gents as Grant comes in and goes straight to the cubicle. They hear him lock the door and pull the toilet roll.

'What's the matter, Grant?' asks Dave. 'Having trouble keeping the champagne in the bottle?'

There's a grunt from behind the door as Mikey laughs. 'At least you'll be able to break your duck; she's all over you like a rash,' he says.

'Let's hope she doesn't leave you with a rash,' laughs Dave.

The toilet flushes and Grant comes out. He's a bit red-faced; there are others in the toilet, too, and he's still arranging his trousers. 'Why do you keep saying things like that?'

'Everyone knows you've still not lost your cherry. She did say tonight is your lucky night,' points out Mikey.

'Make sure you keep it clean for her, no tissue remains sticking to it,' advises Dave.

'I actually fancied the one in the red top,' says Grant.

'She's mine,' boasts Mikey. 'She's already kissed my face off. I thought she was gonna go down.'

'Go down where?' asks Grant, and the other two just laugh as all three walk out of the toilet and back to the dance room.

*

As the boys approach us, we put our drink bottles between our lips and all suck like it's a cock. It's done deliberately so the boys see us as we take the bottle out of our mouths and wipe the corner of the mouth with the middle finger. Then we smile at the individual boys that we've 'paired up' with. The other two smile back, but mine – *what's his name?* – is still a bit sullen. Obviously, the joke they were laughing at when they came out of the toilets was on him.

I put my arm around his neck and whisper in his ear. 'Later for you, baby,' I say sweetly.

'When do you want to go?' he asks.

'Crikey. You're keen. You need to buy me a drink first.'

'I've bought you a drink,' he says, pointing at my bottle.

'Yeah, but it's nearly empty, and I'm in the mood. Do you just wanna go round the block, or do you wanna go round the world?' I look at him inquisitively, but seductively.

He smiles. 'I wanna go round the world,' he says, and actually kisses me. That's the first move that *he's* made. I make sure it's a good one as I seek out his tongue with mine.

*

As the night comes to an end and the bars start to thin out and close, we make our way to the taxi ranks. Me and whatshisname get in the first taxi before Jules and Haze and their boys, and on the journey home we continue kissing. It's passionate snogging that we've been practising all night, showing my intention of what's to come. *I can't wait to get his pants off.*

The taxi drops us off at my house, and we go to the door. He kisses me again. 'This ain't goodnight just here,' I say, feeling him shaking. 'Are you cold?'

'No. If I'm truthful, I'm a bit nervous.'

'Don't be nervous. Look, try this.' I take both his hands and put them on my boobs. 'How does that feel?'

'It feels good,' he says with a smile.

I keep his hands there. 'Give them a good squeeze. I just love my tits being squeezed.'

After a moment or two, I let go of his hands, and he's quick to remove them from my boobs. 'I didn't say stop.' And he gropes me again.

I let him carry on for a little longer as I breathe heavily at his touch. 'Come on then, let's go round the world.' He lets go as I search for my keys and let us in, and we go straight upstairs to my bedroom. I put my bag on the bedside table as he rushes off to the bathroom.

While he's there, I take off my dress and wait for him in my baby doll and stockings. I'm, like, still in my heels, lying on my front on the bed, my chin resting on my hands, up on my elbows, my legs crossed, and my feet in the air. He comes back in, and I hold out my hand to invite him onto the bed where once again we snog passionately. A good snog is the best way to get a girl going, but my juices are flowing already. After the day I've had, I'm ready for take-off.

He's a bit better this time, pawing me and groping at my breasts and bum. I push him back on the bed and start to remove his shirt. Throwing it on the floor, I begin to kiss his chest and lick his nipples. He just breathes heavily and, like, moans his delight.

I check he has his eyes closed, then reach out for my bag and take out the handcuffs. Taking one of his hands, I move his arm above his head. I'm pleased that he leaves it there as I take his other hand and move it over his head. I then quickly snap the cuffs in place, and he looks up.

'What are you doing?'

'Giving you the time of your life.' I give the cuffs a playful tug, as if testing their security. 'Now you are totally at my mercy.' I grin. 'Don't worry. I won't show you any,' I tease as I finger his nipples. 'Sit back, hold tight and, like, enjoy the ride.'

I then move down, undo his trousers and pull them off, pants and all, and throw them down with his shirt. His cock is erect and, glistening and wet. I take hold of him and run my thumb over the tip, spreading his juice all over, and then go down on him, opening my lips just enough to put them on his round head and moisten my lips with those lovely fluids.

He moans and groans and squirms in my hand as I slowly open my lips more and more and let them slide down over his bell end. I run my tongue around the tip of his cock and work my lips up and down, assisted by my hand around the girth, while my other hand gently teases his balls with, like, featherlight touches.

He continues to moan as I work on him, then I feel him shudder, his legs shaking uncontrollably before he lets out a heavy sigh – almost a growl – and takes me by surprise as he empties himself into my mouth. Hot torrents of salty cream pour over my tongue, and I swallow hard, taking his full load.

As he begins to still and I can't feel anymore cum escaping, I take my lips away, swallow, and move up to him, like I do with all the boys that come in my mouth. And he gets a taste of his own medicine as I kiss him full on, tongue as well, with splashes of semen still on my lips and in my mouth. I don't really know why some boys don't like it much. I think it's lovely.

'Oh, Stevie,' I breathe, holding his head in my hands and lifting myself to put my boobs into his face, still wrapped in my sexy underwear. 'That was unexpected, but I loved it. Do you always come so quick?'

'I'm just excited, sorry,' he says. 'And my name's not Stevie.'

Whatever. I look down at his cock and his hard on is abating. 'Looks like we gotta try something else to make you hard again. I need that cock inside me; there's no getting away.' I emphasise my words by pulling lightly on the handcuffs.

Grabbing the rails of the headboard, I sit up over him and pull down my knickers to reveal tonight's star prize. I then bring my body up, with my legs either side of him till I'm over his face, and slowly drop down so that he can reach with his tongue. I widen my hole with my fingers, wet and inviting for him, and command him, 'Lick me, Stevie. Lick my clit.'

I don't know why I'm calling him Stevie; I might as well say Yasmin. Or Pauline. Or Phil or Frank, even. But I can't remember his name, and it should have been Stevie tonight anyway. I think back to earlier this evening and playing with kids' toys and then kissing and groping before the phone rang and killed the moment. We were *so* close.

He's licking me good but, oh... oh yeah, he probes deep, I'm having to move to make my clitoris find his tongue, as he doesn't seem to know where it is. I suppose I've made it difficult for him by handcuffing him, but now I've got his tongue there – wow!

'There, there. Lick it. Oh, oh! Stevie! Don't move from that spot. Don't stop.' It's fantastic; his tongue has hit the bullseye and, yes, yes, oh yes, he's got it now. 'Yes! Yes!' I'm thrusting forward, rocking on his face, hanging onto the headboard. God, it's sensational.

I'm conscious that he's down there, trapped, but he's driving me crazy, his tongue is... oh... oh! Wild sensations run up through my clitoris and through my body, tingling through me, pulsating through me from the sensuous lapping of his tongue. My fanny is so wet, my sex rippling.

'Oh, yes. Yes!' I scream, and I orgasm all over his face. I come down off him and snog him to return the compliment and get a taste of my own medicine.

'My God,' he says, gasping for breath. 'I've never done that before. It was, like, so sexy with you all over my face.' At least he enjoyed it and didn't feel a prisoner.

'I'm sorry. I was aware you were, like, trapped down there, but you were so good, I couldn't let you stop.'

He smiles at that, pleased with himself that he's given me so much satisfaction.

I look round to see if his penis is hard again yet. It's on its way; a little persuasion should get it stiff. I take him in my hand and gently stroke away, running my thumb over the top again, and he comes back to life, thick and erect. The head of his cock is still glistening with his cum, and I kiss it. I then climb on top and slide down his full length, putting my full weight down on him. And we ride. Oh yes, we ride. I'm up and down his cock, slowly bouncing on my knees, taking his full length as deep as I can, then rising up so the tip of his cock is just touching my fanny lips and teasing my clitoris. Then back down on him all the way to the hilt. Again and again. Oh yes. Oh, oh. The hard penetration of his renewed erection is driving me wild.

He's moaning sounds of pleasure and breathing heavy. I'm calling out. 'Stevie, Stevie.' Suddenly his cock slips out as I rise just too much, but as I go back down, we miss, and I can feel every inch of him sliding along my lips and over my clitoris. The swollen head of his cock inflames the sensitivity of my clit. I slide back down and into his balls, then back up again till his balls are at my bum, his penis tip against my clit. And again, and again. Rubbing me, caressing me and, oh, oh…

I reach down to him, my hands on his chest, his nipples between the thumb and forefinger of each hand, tweaking him, brushing him. He moans his pleasure, arching his back as he thrusts to give me the full length of his cock, still running along my lips.

'Yes, Stevie! That's good. Keep it there. Oh! Yes. I'm coming, coming good,' I growl. 'Yes! Stevie. Stevie,' I cry out as I feel the hot shudder of another orgasm pulsating through me. 'STE! VIE!' I almost scream through clenched teeth as he stills his movement and also shudders to orgasm, the discharge coming along with mine as the two vital outlets engage, and the thought that our juices mixing together heightens the pleasure. I love a cock inside me, but that was incredible. Just constant contact against my clitoris taking me higher and higher into the clouds of ecstasy.

I let the orgasm finish its throes before I climb off him and take the opportunity to suck his cock whilst it's still hard. Tasting all the juices of his cum and mine, I savour the nectar before sharing it with him once again with a snog. He lies back exhausted, still manacled to the bed as I lie alongside him.

After a while I get up and head for the bathroom, leaving whatshisname alone on the bed, still manacled. Whilst I'm in the bathroom, I hear movement on the landing and quickly realise it's Mum. I can hear that she goes to my room. Oh my God, she'll find him lying there totally naked, covered in sex juices, and tied to the bed.

I can picture the scene:

*

'Oh, so you're Stevie, are you?' says Mum, as she goes in without knocking and finding a naked young man attached to the bed. 'I'm Debbie's mum.'

'Argh!' he cries out as he shuffles about making vain attempts to cover up his nakedness, all to no avail because of the handcuffs. 'No, no. My name's Grant.'

'Oh, I thought I heard Debbie calling out.'

He still attempts to hide his body as Mum sits on the bed beside him. 'No, no. I don't know why she kept calling me that.'

'That's a shame. I was hoping to meet this Stevie,' said Mum.

'What is this?' asks Grant in panic, completely exposed to Mum. 'A nymphomaniac's convention? Untie me. Please. I didn't think it'd be like this; I'm a virgin.'

*

I come back into the room, having taken off the seduction wear, to find Mum sitting on the bed whilst the boy is still tied up. 'Untie me. Please,' he says. 'I didn't think it'd be like this. I'm a virgin.'

'You were,' I say, 'and, like, I've got your cherry. You were fantastic.' I take hold of his cock, abating once again. 'And so were you.' I move over to retrieve the keys from my bag and let him free, before putting the handcuffs back in my handbag. He straight away covers himself up, putting his hands over his privates.

'It's a bit late for that now,' says Mum.

He gets up off the bed, still covering himself, and goes in search of his clothes and gathers them up. 'Can I use the bathroom?' he asks shyly, making his way out of the room. He doesn't wait for an answer.

Mum and I sit quietly on the bed, and we listen to him shuffling about in the bathroom before the toilet flushes. He comes back to the bedroom fully clothed. 'I'm off,' he says, and disappears down the stairs.

I call after him over the banister as he runs down the stairs. 'Thank you. You were fantastic. The girls will love you.' The door slams. If he heard me, I'll never know.

I go back to my room and Mum's still sitting there. It's only then I realise that she is totally naked. We've never been inhibited about nakedness, though it's a rare thing to be seen like this. I thought she normally wore pyjamas. No wonder, er, whatshisname was a bit scared. Although my mum's got a beautiful body, even if she is in her mid-forties, so he should've been delighted.

'Pity. He looked like a nice young man. I could have gone three rounds with him myself,' Mum says, as she gets up off the bed.

'You're old enough to be his mum.' *Oh my God, did I just say that... aloud?*

'Ok. So, when I've finished, I'll pick his clothes up off the floor and put them in the wash.'

'I think you scared him off, coming in starkers. He probably thought he was gonna have to do it all again, tied to the bed, and at the mercy of a house full of naked women.' I ponder things. 'A virgin? He was good for a first-timer.' Another cherry in my bowl.

Mum smiles at me in the doorway. 'Goodnight, Debbie.'

'Goodnight, Mum. Love you.' I love my mum; she is so beautiful for her age. She should find herself another man. She deserves one.

As I lie on the bed, I'm thinking about what has happened today. It could easily have been Yasmin here tonight. And I was so close to it being Stevie that I even forgot that boy's name. So close! I think I was fantasising with the love cuffs. I wanted it to be Stevie and just not let him get away.

Chapter Seventeen

Late Sunday morning, still going round in my dressing gown, I receive a text. It's from Yasmin. My heart lifts and I smile. She's asking if we can meet up to have a look at the photos. I decide to ring her.

'Hi, darling.' That cheery voice makes me melt.

'Yasmin, I'd love to meet up. I can't wait to see the photos, can't wait to see you, too.' *Am I being too pushy?*

'The photos are on my computer. They're on my laptop, but it'd be better if you came here to have a look, as I can get them up on my TV. I'll make us some lunch.'

'Oh, yes please.' There's a big grin on my face.

'Come round when you're ready. We'll have a look at your sexy poses, and I'll get lunch for about one.'

'Ok.'

She gives me her address. 'Can't wait to see you. Wear your best underwear. Love you, bye.'

'Bye.'

'Bye.'

'Bye. Bye.' I end the call. *Wow*. She's like the second sexiest woman in the world, and she told me she loves me. *And* she said to wear my best undies. My heart skips a beat.

I rush off to get dressed and select my best knickers – my pink and black shorts – and matching bra that gives me the best cleavage. I take off my dressing gown and pose in the mirror, holding my knickers across me, turning first one way then the other. I'm getting good at this posing lark. *God, I'm sexy.*

I throw my knickers onto the bed and look at myself in the mirror, totally naked, wearing nothing but a grin. I run my hands down my sides, over my hips. I think of Yasmin – not Stevie, but Yasmin. I run my hands through my hair then shake it down, letting it fall naturally. I head off to the bathroom for a shower and let the warm water run over me for a moment before washing. As I stand there under the water flow, I'm now thinking of Stevie and what his reaction might be when he sees the pictures of me posing in my underwear. Underwear he should have been seeing for real last night. *Oh, Stevie. How am I gonna make you love me?*

*

I get a taxi to Yasmin's; buses are not so good on a Sunday. She lives in a more affluent part of town, which is not surprising with her rich daddy. I assume it's his house and she still lives with him.

I ring the bell and Yasmin opens the door. 'Come in, darling.'

She called me darling again, and I love it. I enter her house, and she closes the door before we kiss – only a greeting kiss, but fully on the lips.

'Wow! Look at you,' she exclaims. 'You look beautiful,' she says, as she steps back to look me up and down but keeps hold of my hands. I'm in a top that plunges to show the effect of my 'meet-in-the-middle-cleavage' bra, along with a leather-look mini skirt. And it's all for her.

'What about you? You're so sexy.'

'Thank you,' she says, giving me a twirl and making her skirt fan out. I think I got a glimpse of knickers, but they were so brief I'm not so sure. 'Nothing special.' She's wearing a short skirt, black and white check – one of those skater skirts that are high over the waist. Not really suited to me, but it looks stunning on her. She has on a very chiffon type, tight-fitting black top, and you can clearly see her bra, all lacy and colourful. She's in bare feet, which is a shame because it doesn't accentuate her beautiful legs. But she tiptoes when she twirls.

'I think you'd be sexy with nothing on,' I say matter of factly. Then I realise what I've actually said.

She looks at me with a cheeky grin. 'Well, I'm, like, totally naked under all these clothes,' she says, and takes my hand to lead me into her lounge. 'Welcome to Chez Yasmin.'

'Is this your place?'

'Yes. Do you like it?'

'It's fantastic.' I look around; everything is so neat and clean, the décor bright but not over vibrant. 'Do you live alone?'

'I do. I like my own space, but I also enjoy sharing it, too.' Her cheery voice is so uplifting. Even if you don't need it, just hearing her speak you find there's a little more room for your heart to be raised.

'How come you're so bright and bubbly all the time?' I ask.

She shrugs her shoulders. 'What's the alternative?'

Point taken.

Yasmin picks up her laptop, which is already switched on. 'Come on, let's go in the kitchen, we can look at them better at the table.' Then with a second thought, she adds, 'Look at me, not offering you a drink. Coffee, tea?'

'Tea, please,' I say, as we go to the kitchen, and she puts the kettle on. I think about what she said about getting the photos up on the TV, and then I see she's got a TV in the kitchen.

'Tea it is. One of the best things about being English, I think. Don't you? The great tea drinking nation.'

'Yes. But what about China? And didn't you have a coffee yesterday?'

'Yeah, but this is home-made tea. Much better.' She smiles and makes the tea. Her personality is so infectious. *I love her.*

She sits down with me and positions the laptop between us, then calls up the photos from yesterday. She presses a couple of keys and they're up on the TV, bright and bold. They come up in a batch, and there are hundreds of them. She double clicks on the first picture, and there I am, standing amongst the studio equipment. Then Yasmin clicks through the pictures one by one; it's almost like seeing a film in slow motion, watching myself get undressed. First my top, then my bra.

Yasmin takes hold of my hand. It's not a gay move, I think, especially as we watch me undress, now topless. It's more her affection, and I love it.

'These are fantastic.' I actually can't believe I'm saying that, seeing myself topless, breasts on display.

'You are a sexy girl, so natural.' Yasmin squeezes my hand just a little bit.

'I was just getting undressed, that's all.'

'You were at the start but, like, in an evocative way, like putting on a show, and then you began to pose for me. Look.' Another photo comes up in which I'm holding my bra out at arm's length, and the next couple of pictures show me drop it theatrically on the floor. 'Is this how you undress for the boys?'

I'm taken aback by that question, and I give her a quick look. I thought she was gay, and that she thought I was too. I'm distracted from my reverie by the next run of pictures. I'm taking off my skirt, and with the camera at my back, revealing my bum in sexy silk knickers. All provocative.

I'm amazed at these pictures. Yasmin had shown me some photos of other girls in similar sexy poses, but these pictures are of me!

Then the photos change slightly. I've got the baby doll on and one stocking, putting the other one on. As the pictures flash by, the stocking is getting further up my thigh. It's me. But the photos are so sexy, it's a turn on.

But then there's no more. 'That's as far as we got before we were interrupted.' Yasmin clicks back to the gallery.

'Oh, Yasmin. They are fantastic.'

'You've said that already.'

'I'm just overwhelmed to see such pictures like that of *me*. They're fan... er...' I put my hand on her knee and gently run it up her thigh to the hem of her skirt. I turn to bring our faces together and we kiss.

She puts her arms around me to hug me closer as we prolong the kiss, our tongues searching for the other and gently touching whilst I keep my hand high upon her thigh.

Yasmin moves her legs slightly more apart to allow me more access and my fingers go searching. She *is* wearing knickers – probably the briefest of G-strings – as I feel the small piece of material, all soft and silky, covering her sex. But it doesn't matter; I can feel everything through the thin material, and Yasmin murmurs her approval of my touch.

I shudder with pleasure as Yasmin responds to my gentle touch. I can't believe I'm doing things to another woman that I would like the boys to do to me, but they're always in a rush and can't get my knickers off quickly enough. I continue the probing of Yasmin's pleasure pot through her knickers. It feels good having the material on my fingertips but also feeling what it conceals, knowing there's a pot of gold at the end of this particular rainbow. And Yasmin is purring and, like, squirming to my touch.

I remember what she said about a woman giving pleasure to another woman, because she knows what to do and how it feels. As I'm doing it, I can imagine the sensations myself.

Yasmin breaks the kiss. 'Shall we go somewhere a bit more comfy?'

'Yes.' This is the moment. I have never felt so horny in my life, wanting sex so much as I do now. I know I got a shag last night, but this is just a whole new world, and I'm so excited. I can't explain why. I don't know whether it's just because Yasmin is so lovely and beautiful and sexy, or if I'm love with her, or that I really am gay and I'm just finding out. I just feel so fucking horny.

Yasmin takes my hand and leads me upstairs. How many times have I led a boy upstairs by the hand, and now here I am being led myself? By a woman. Going into the unknown.

We get to the bedroom, and she closes the door, despite no one else being in the house. She leads me to the bed, and we sit down at the bottom. 'From the moment you smiled at me in the bar, Debbie, I've wanted this,' she breathes heavily in my ear, taking the lobe between her lips and then her teeth.

One hand is at the back of my head, her fingers running through my hair. The other is moving up inside my top, running over my torso, sending shudders of pleasure through my body. She reaches my breasts and it, like, takes my breath away.

'Oh my God. Yasmin. I love you,' I manage to whisper hoarsely as I gasp for air. She has moved from my ear and is smothering my neck with kisses, nuzzling me. It is utterly amazing, and I just let her do it, her hand on my breast searching for my nipple through my bra. Ecstasy. I can feel myself getting wet down below.

Yasmin then lifts up my top and, breaking the kiss, takes it right off. She then takes off her own top, and I quickly put both my hands on her boobs over her bra. The material is soft and silky to the touch, her breasts smooth and round, her nipples protruding against my palms. Her head falls back, exposing her neck, and I kiss and nuzzle her as she did me.

'Oh, Debbie.' She too is muttering hoarsely, feeling the sensations flood through her. 'Take off my bra. Suck my nipples.'

I do as she asks, revealing the beautiful, silky-smooth skin of her breasts. They quiver for me as I cup one in my hand and caress it, finding her wonderfully erect nipple with my fingers, whilst I put my lips to the nipple of her other breast and lick it, circling my tongue around it. Round and round and round. Mmm. This is delicious, I love it when boys do it to me, and now I'm doing it to another woman. I'm like, oh my God, this is amazing.

'Oh, yes,' she cries out, and it encourages me to work harder with my hand and tongue. 'Oh, Debbie,' she says, putting her hands either side of my face and bringing me up to hers, snogging me, kissing and tonguing me, biting my lip lightly. It's a passionate kiss like I've never known. It is fantastic!

I still have my hand on her breast, but I move it away and stroke her delicious torso, over her belly to the top of her skirt. I pull her towards me so that she is not lying on the fastener, and I reach round and undo it, pulling the zip slowly down, feeling the anticipation of what lies beneath, conscious of the urge that Yasmin felt as I pulled her skirt away.

Her knickers are no more than a thong, leaving her cheeks bare for me to stroke and caress. Her bum is so smooth, just like her breasts, and sensitive, too. My touch is driving Yasmin wild with lust, and she exaggerates my groping by pushing her bum out and I am given the excitement of feeling the small piece of material of the strap of her silken thong.

'Pull them off,' she almost begs me. 'Pull them off and finger me.' She *is* begging.

I take down her knickers and drag them slowly over her feet and drop them to the floor. Then I put my hand back on her ankle and sensuously, with the lightest of touches of my fingertips, I make my way up her calf, over her knee, and along the inside of her thigh. As I close in on her vital area, she opens her legs to invite me in once again, as she did at the kitchen table. Only this time she is naked and exposed, her fanny warm and moist from my earlier work.

My fingers find her fanny and I have no difficulty entering her. I rub my finger lightly at the roof of her sex hole and, with my thumb pressed down, land a bullseye on her clitoris. She shudders at my touch, squirming under my fingers, jerking her hips as I rub with my thumb and probe with my finger. She is so wet and, like, good enough to eat. So, I move my face near and, trying not to break the spell, I put my tongue there before I remove my hand, only keeping my fingers there to help hold her open wide as I tease her clit with my tongue.

'Oh, yes. Yes. There, lick me, baby, oh, oh,' she squeals, or something like that, arching her back and thrusting her hips as I lick and suck her clitoris. 'Oh, oh,' she keeps crying out as she brings her knees up so my head is framed by her thighs, and I feel her shudder as she climaxes and her juice comes flooding over my lips and face. *Oh, the feeling, the sensation, is just fantastic.* Soaking in another woman's juices. *Heaven.*

She again pulls my head up to meet her face-to-face. 'Let me feel my juices on your face,' she says, and we kiss and snog. She goes down and kisses my bare midriff whilst kneading my breasts gently with her hands. The soft kisses are so sweet on my body, and although I want Yasmin to kiss and caress me in other places, I luxuriate in the pleasure from her kissing alone, breathing deeply with every touch of her lips. Oh, oh.

Then, without breaking the momentum, Yasmin takes my bra straps off my shoulders, pulls back the cups and bares my breasts. I can feel my nipples so erect, calling out for attention, and Yasmin duly obliges. Just as I did to her, she cups one breast in her hand and teases the nipple with her fingernail, whilst she puts her beautiful lips to the other nipple, kissing it, licking it, sucking it.

Oh my God. I've had my nipples sucked many a time, but this is, is, is, oh. I am coming already! All the momentum of the passion, and now the perfect manipulation of my nipples, brings me to a climax and I orgasm, shuddering and convulsing in pleasure. It is totally unexpected, as Yasmin hasn't even touched my honey pot, let alone my clitoris. I still have my undies on, but she has certainly found a delicate spot. I think it is the Pauline effect.

'Oh, Debbie, you are glorious,' Yasmin tells me, and for a second she breaks off from sucking my nipple to change position and suck the other one. This time she runs her hand over my midriff again and slowly moves over my skirt, which has ridden up to expose my knickers. Yasmin's hand strokes over my knickers, and she murmurs her delight at the sexy material in her hands. They must've been wet. 'You really did put on your best underwear.'

I want to reply, but my breathing is too shallow. Then she slips her hand inside my knickers and over my wet fanny, rubbing her finger up and down the lips and then on my clit. Oh my God! With just a couple of strokes, I am coming again.

This time the orgasm is much more thunderous as I cry out. 'Yasmin. Oh, Yasmin, oh yes.' And it doesn't stop. She keeps up the stimulation and I keep up the orgasm. 'Yes! Yes!!'

I almost have to push her hand away to give me some respite. But she stops and brings herself back up to face level, and we kiss once again.

She has only sucked my nipples and gently, but briefly, stroked my clitoris, and I am having multiple orgasms. She hasn't even penetrated me with her finger or used her tongue down there, but in the space of a couple of minutes I'm coming and coming again. And here I am, like a quivering wreck, soaked in sweat and pleasure. Apart from shoes, I was only wearing four items of clothing, and three are still on. And I've just had the best sex ever. No boy has stimulated me that much. Like, ever.

And as I lie there, still half clothed, alongside this naked sexy woman, my juices are still flowing, my body still trembling, my head rushing. 'Oh, Yasmin…' I begin, as she takes hold of my hand.

We lie on the bed, silently for a minute or two, just coming back down to earth. I turn and look at her, naked and flushed after the exhausting activity, and she looks beautiful.

Slowly she sits up on the bed. 'Shall we have a shower?'

I sit up with her, thinking about my orgasms, and take off the rest of my clothes. 'Yes, good idea,' I say, and I follow her to the bathroom. It's a big room with a bath and separate shower cubicle – both big enough for us to get in together.

Yasmin starts the shower running, 'Plenty of room,' she says, and she steps in. 'Come on in. The water's lovely.'

'Cool,' I say, as I step into the shower with her.

It's one of those big, round soaker showers, and we stand underneath it and let the water run over us, soaking our hair and our bodies. I luxuriate in the warmth of the water, tingling my skin and reviving my senses that were so erratic earlier.

We rub each other's bodies as though washing, but not using soap, then we start to giggle, feeling like little girls again. The stroking of bodies becomes more intimate as Yasmin rubs my boobs and caresses them, tweaking my nipples to erection despite the warm water. All the sensations and urges come flooding back into my body, and I hug her close under the water, brushing her hair back and wringing out the water. Her head tilts back and her mouth opens invitingly, and I put my mouth to it sensuously and we kiss once more.

This is something else that's a new venture for me; even in the throes of full-on sex, I don't kiss the boys this much. And once again the passion is reignited and I drop my hand down to her bum and stroke it, feeling the full roundedness of it. It's so beautiful, so sexy. I then bend my knees and slowly drop down in front of her, kissing my way down her body, her breasts with the water cascading over them, kissing down her torso to her sex.

She opens her legs for me, and I kneel down under her until my face is level with her crotch. I tilt my head back, open her honey pot with my fingers, and reach out with my tongue. As she moves forward, covering my face, I find her clitoris immediately. It's not the most comfortable position, but I don't care. My mouth is pressed hard against her, my tongue licking round and round, as the water runs down from her body and over my face.

'Oh, yes. Debbie, yes. You are insatiable. Don't stop,' Yasmin murmurs, as I realise that she's turned the water off. I can feel her legs and body shuddering, and I wonder how she still manages to stand. I open my eyes to see her arms outstretched and she is leaning, almost pushing, against the tiled wall of the shower. I continue to lick, and her legs continue to tremble, and I can taste her juices mingling with the water of the shower. Then *her* shower starts.

'Yes! Oh, oh!' She climaxes over me; it is so beautiful. I feel one of her hands on the top of my head, practically pushing me deeper into her, my face covered by her fanny, my tongue deep inside, my hands groping wildly at her bum. 'Oh, Debbie.'

Then Yasmin bends her legs and crouches down. Still astride me, she takes my face in her hands and again we kiss. More kissing. 'You are sensational,' she tells me as we sit there at the bottom of the shower cubicle, dripping wet, splashing in the water in the tray.

She sits down on her bum and puts her legs out straight either side of me. The shower is that big. I look at her, just admiring her beauty, her nakedness. I think for a moment about the boy I shagged last night, that he was a virgin, and how I took his cherry. And here I am with Yasmin, my first encounter with, like, girl-on-girl sex. Yes, Pauline had a bite of the cherry, but this…

'I love you,' I say, and I have no embarrassment in saying it.

'I love you, too,' she replies.

'I never thought I could, like, look at and think of a girl the way a boy should be looking at you and thinking of you. But, like, you are so perfect and I love you. It's not just because we've just made love; that was like the icing on the cake. Everything about you. Your looks, your personality, everything. I'm so glad I gave you that smile that I normally reserve for boys to let them know I want them.' I'm babbling.

She looks at me for a second, her beautiful eyes wide, taking it in, but with her eyebrows raised, smirking, as if to say 'shut up, Debbie'. Then she laughs and leans back. As her skin touches the glass of the cubicle, she jumps at the coldness of it. 'Argh!' It makes me laugh, and we laugh together.

We get up and out of the cubicle, and Yasmin fetches us some towels from the airing cupboard. We dry ourselves and rub our hair before going back to the bedroom where we dry our hair with the dryer. Unfortunately, I have to dress in the same clothes I've just made love in, but they're ok. My knickers are not really that wet.

I help Yasmin choose some other clothes, some skin-tight, calf-length jeans and obligatory heels, with a string-strap top over a real ego-boosting bra.

'Don't bother with making lunch,' I say to her as I help her dress. 'Take me out in that sexy beast car of yours and I'll treat you to lunch.'

We go out, and as it's another beautiful sunny day, we have the top off. We go for a drive, stop off for a pub lunch, and spend the afternoon just enjoying each other's company, talking shopping, shoes, handbags, underwear. We chat about my work, and I briefly mention Glasgow but don't give her all the dirty details. What happened in that room stays in that room. Yasmin talks about her photography, on both sides of the camera.

'I think that's why I like girls more than boys, 'specially when it comes to making love,' she begins. 'I'm not out-and-out gay, but the female form is, like, much more sexy than men's.'

'How did you first, like, you know, with a woman?'

'I had my fair share of kissing and groping with some boys in my early teens, but when it came to actual sex, that first time… nothing. I put it down to first-time nerves, and I bled for a week, so that put me off a bit. Then when I tried a couple of more times, still nothing. I just felt, like, unfulfilled.

'It was like shaking a bottle of Prosecco or something,' she continues, 'the wine all bubbling and fizzing, but the cork just won't come out. Like a rocket firework. The blue touchpaper is lit, and it shoots to the sky, higher and higher and higher.' She reaches up with her arms high above her head. 'But there's no…' She describes a firework using her hands, with her fingers shaped like she's holding a small ball. 'Boom!' she makes the sound of an explosion and spreads her fingers as if they're the flash of a firework.

'Then I was, like, seduced by an older woman.' It makes me think back to Pauline again. 'It was the most amazing thing, like, ever,' she says, her eyes full of excitement and delight. 'And I just… exploded!' She does the explosion thing with her hands again with a little more exaggeration this time, spreading her arms up and wide. 'And then the next time, boom.' More hand gesturing to emphasise her words. 'And again. And again. I can't say I'm out-and-out gay, but sex is more…'

'Do you have… er, you know, with some of the models?'

'No. It's all serious stuff when I'm doing that.'

'Don't you even think, like… you know?'

'Not really. It's all professional.' She's starting to sound like Stevie.

'So have you finished with boys then?' I'm very inquisitive.

'If a boy catches my eye, or my imagination, then maybe something might happen. Who knows? I quite like older men really.' *That strikes a chord.* She shrugs her shoulders. 'I'm not saying I won't settle down one day; I'd like children. But I'm still young and enjoying life. I mean, straight women don't, like, get so many orgasms, because a woman knows what another woman wants.'

She grins, and I can't help but smile back. Is she right? I'm not sure, but I'm learning. I think, *Oh my God. Is this me?*

'I mean, what do boys know about want?' she continues. 'They're always easily aroused yet all they want is a blow job.'

'But I love giving a blow job,' I say. 'I just adore cock. Of course, yes, I want an orgasm too, as many as I can, and I know it takes more to stimulate a woman.'

She intervenes. 'That's my point. Women are better at it; they understand what's going on. If you're pleasuring me, you know all the sensations I'm going through and what I'm feeling.' She gives a little shudder. 'I mean, you're, like, so good at making me splash.' *I like that analogy: splash.* 'And it's 'cause you know where to touch, where to feel, because you want it doing to you. A boy gets a hard on by just saying "hi", and all they want is for me to go down on it. That's it. Like I said the other day, where's my fun, where's my orgasm?'

Crikey, I get the equivalent of a hard on by her just saying "hi" to me. 'That first time we met, I dunno what it was, like some sort of electrical charge or something, but OMG it was instant,' I tell her. 'But don't you like sucking cock?'

Yasmin continues, 'I want to have my body pleasured, tantalized, worshipped. I mean, look at it,' she gestures down her body with her hands, and I'm looking, 'it just has to be adored.'

'Yes, that's it. I'll worship and adore your body, and we'll both get our pleasure, but it's the same with a cock. I get most of my stimulation from having a good workout on his cock. Most of my satisfaction comes from giving him the ultimate satisfaction. A job well done. A blow job well done.

It's all about the cock. I mean, I'm not gonna, like, go with just any old minger; the more handsome, the more fit, the better. But it's all about the cock. It's like being a kid on Christmas morning when you unwrap your present and play with it for hours because it gives you pleasure. There's so much you can do with a cock. You can lick it, you can suck it, bite it, wank it, stroke it, kiss it, fuck it, squeeze his balls, tickle them, lick them. Empty them,' I say with a glint in my eye. 'Up your fan, on your face, all over your tits. In your mouth. Oh! The fun is endless.'

Yasmin smiles at me then pulls me into a hug. 'Oh, Debbie. I love you.'

Later, Yasmin drops me off at home and we kiss goodbye. It has been the most perfect day. I walk up to my front door and hug my handbag to my chest. I have, like, the widest grin on my lips. I am in love.

Chapter Eighteen

Monday after work I decide to go and see Stevie to let him have a look at the photos Yasmin took. She has emailed them to me, and I've uploaded them to my laptop. So, I set off to see him. 'I'm going to Stevie's,' I tell my mum. 'Don't wait up.'

'Debbie, sweetheart.' She comes out to the hallway to speak to me. 'Do you want me to give you a lift?'

Good grief, no. 'It's ok, Mum, I'll get the bus.' I try to sound calm and offhand.

'Are you sure? It's raining out.'

'Yeah, welcome to England in the summer,' I say, rolling my eyes. 'I'll be fine, got me brolly.'

And so, laptop under my arm and brolly in my hand, I head to the bus stop and take the short journey to Morley Street. I ring the bell and see the distorted image of Stevie approaching through the glass. My heart skips a beat as he opens the door.

'Debbie,' he says with surprise and glee. 'Lovely. Come on in. That's twice you've caught me off guard like this.' He steps aside to let me pass, and once inside he kisses me on the lips before closing the door. 'Laptop.' He points at it.

'Observant,' I reply. 'I've brought it to let you have a look at the photos I had taken that I told you about.'

'Oh great,' he enthuses. We go to the lounge. 'I'll put the kettle on. Make yourself at home. I don't mean sit about in your underwear with your feet up and the remote control in your hand. Just make yourself comfy.'

In my underwear? That would be comfy. He goes off to the kitchen and I boot up the laptop. I call up the photos and can't help but have a quick look at myself 'getting undressed'. I hope Stevie likes them.

He pops back in from the kitchen. 'Have you eaten? Do you want anything?'

'No thanks, Stevie. I'm fine, ta.' Did he get a quick peek? The one on the screen at that point was of me topless. I know he's seen me topless for real, but I think he's in for a surprise. *A pleasant surprise, I hope.*

A moment or two later he comes in with two cups of tea, sets one down on the coffee table for me, and begins to sip at his.

'There's a lot of them,' I say, quickly resetting the file. 'Are you ready?'

'Yeah, I've been looking forward to them, I just didn't think you'd get them so quickly.' Still drinking his tea, his eyes are on the screen.

The first picture comes up, and it's just me standing there in the studio amongst the equipment. I then click through just as Yasmin did, and it's like the slow-motion action again, seeing me get undressed.

Stevie is quiet as he basically sees me taking my top off. Then he asks me to stop to go through some of them again. 'Were you aware these were being taken? It's just like a film of you, rather than posing.' He puts down his cup, not yet finished but keen to take a closer look at the pictures.

'I wasn't aware straight away that she was, like, taking photos. I was just getting undressed to put on the underwear I'd bought, so they get better,' I point out, eager to get to the sexier ones, to gauge his reaction. Ok, he's seen me naked and stuff, but these pictures do get better. I go through them again.

'You see,' he begins his critique. 'Firstly, you're not smiling. I suppose you could say it's the sultry look, but you can see it's just you.' I move the pictures along, my top lifting up and my boobs, in my bra, coming into view.

'This could be a good one. If you do it again, start off without your bra, and when you get your top up this far, the view of the bottom of your breasts will be very titillating – if you excuse the pun – in anticipation of what comes next. And also try not to lift the top too high and block your face.'

Quite the expert.

'Of course, that's posing. This,' he points at the picture, 'is just you caught on camera getting undressed.'

'Yeah. I take on what you say, but I, like, started posing when I realised she was, like, taking pictures. Look.' I move on, and we see me taking off my bra, smiling at the camera. 'See?'

'Mmm.'

Then my boobs are bared, and I drop my bra sexily to the floor. He's quiet. I look at him and his attention is fixed to the screen. He notices I'm looking at him, and he looks back, doing a double-take. 'What?'

'No comment?'

'Very nice. You've got a lovely body, be proud.' He picks up his cup and finishes off his tea. I haven't even touched mine.

The pictures move on, and they show me taking off my skirt with my back to the camera, looking over my shoulder, my black hair down my back, and me pouting at the camera as my knickers come into view and my bum protrudes erotically.

'I like that one.' He points at the picture on the screen where I'm looking over my shoulder as I take down my skirt. The skirt is still high enough to be classed as on, but my knickers – red against the black skirt; yes, I was wearing *red* knickers – are coming into view. And, as Stevie points out, one of my boobs is 'deliciously on show with the nipple invitingly erect'.

He puts his hand on my knee and moves it to my thigh. It gives me a tingle and I put my hand on his. I think about sliding his hand further up my thigh, but just rub his hand instead.

'I think they were erect because it was a turn on for me,' I say, emphasising the words 'turn on'. 'I've got lovely nipples, like, anyway. I began to get a taste of the posing and how the pictures would be a turn on for anyone who sees them. Like you.'

I'm waiting for a reaction.

'They are.' *Well, it's at least positive if not, like, enthusiastic.*

The pictures continue as I finish taking off my skirt, and there are a couple with me just in my knickers, but I'm not really posing.

'You could've posed there by holding your boobs.' He shows me by putting his hands on his 'boobs'. 'That would be enticing. What man wouldn't want them to be his hands?' I raise my eyebrows at that. 'And when you stand, you should have one leg straight, with the other bent slightly at the knee and across the first. Didn't your photographer say that?'

'No. She just took the photos. But she did get into telling me what to do with the next lot.' I move on to the photos where I'm in my baby doll basque and stockings, one on while pulling the other one up my leg and over my thigh. Pouting at times, sultry in others.

'Yes.' He seems a little more enthused at these. 'Very sexy.' He smiles at me. 'I like them.'

'Maybe I could get Yasmin to do another session in my stockings and underwear, with me draped all over your Harley, you know, like in some of those boys' mags and that,' I suggest, and Stevie raises an eyebrow.

Then, unfortunately, the pictures come to an abrupt end. 'That's as far as we got before someone else wanted the studio,' I say.

The disappointment in my voice is probably more to do with exactly what Yasmin and I were doing when we were disturbed. But we've made up for it since.

'That was the real seduction stuff that I was wearing the other night,' I tell him.

'I thought you had stockings on,' he says, like getting a question right at the quiz night.

'You seem to be very, like, ready to give advice,' I begin. 'Like holding my boobs or how I should stand. Quite the expert.'

'Not at all. But you seem very assured with yourself in front of the camera; the fact that you're not so much as naked, but exposed. I can see that with a bit of advisory help, and a bit of preparation and stuff, and some proper posing, you could easily be a proper model.' I actually feel he's being more schoolteacher-like, like how he told me he encourages the kids' potential.

'Do you look at magazines with, like, those sort of photos?'

'Not much. I don't really take much notice of stuff like that. I'm not necessarily turned on by such pictures. An attractive woman is one with a pretty face; a beautiful woman is one with charm and a pleasant nature. She doesn't have to be semi naked for me,' he says.

'Don't you feel you wanna shag them?'

He pulls a long face at my question and shrugs. 'Why do you ask such a thing?'

'Most boys' attitude is, like, "I would".'

'Yeah. But I'm not most boys.'

'It's just you have a strong opinion about how to pose, yet you're not interested…'

'Oh, I see,' he says, with a tone that cuts through me. 'It's back to the "why won't you shag me, Stevie?" bit again. Show me some erotic pictures of yourself and then it's a live performance.'

I'm almost crying; I'm quite hurt by that. But I'm not gonna cry in front of him. 'If it hadn't have been for the phone ringing the other night, we would have been sh— … making love.'

'Yes. Saved by the bell. I should've known better.'

When he stabs you, he always hits the heart.

'I'm not a schoolgirl!' I snap at him through clenched teeth.

'Debbie,' he takes my hand, 'I know you're not. Oh, I don't know. I can't explain…'

I snatch my hand away; fury has gotten the better of me. 'Well, you need to explain. I can't wait for you forever because "you don't know". We've been through all this more than once: you tell me you're from a generation where you court for a week or so. Well, we've done our courting. You go out with me, you treat me, you wanna see all my sexy photos,' I say, waving my hand at the laptop, still showing a picture of me half naked, 'we've even been to bed together. But where's the sex? Just what is it with you?'

I'm guessing there's not going to be any activity tonight, and I'm beginning to tire of my fruitless chasing. I can pick up boys no problem. I did it the other night, even if I can't remember his name. I can't remember them all. But shagging is not the be all when it comes to Stevie. There's something else there; I just can't put my finger on it. But I'm hungry for cock, and now I hunger for Stevie's cock. It's only natural now. We've done our courting; it's time to up the ante.

And then there's Yasmin. Sex *and* love. There's many a boy who would like to be in my shoes when it comes to Yasmin.

'You're young. I'm old. End of. What more can I say?' He seems confused. 'I could've gone with any of those girls that had crushes on me, but I didn't. I learned not to get in too deep.'

'That's different,' I say exasperatedly. 'They *are* schoolgirls. And it's your job.' I'm getting frustrated. I just wanna beat my fists against his chest.

He continues, regardless of my rage. 'When I was younger, I kept my distance with girls, and then I got the teaching job and I learned to overlook such things. And it's the same with you. I feel it's just like those girls: you've got a crush, and my natural feeling is to keep clear.'

Oh. 'So, it *is* the age gap. Most men of your age would kill to be able to have sex with women my age. That guy you knew, you know, on our first date. Couldn't keep his eyes off my tits.'

'Yeah, I know.' We sit without speaking for a moment, then the laptop goes into energy saving mode, breaking the silence.

'When can I see you again?' I ask, knitting my fingers and looking down at my hands.

'I can't see you Friday. It's our end-of-term dinner. Saturday, hopefully the weather will be nice again, so we could go motorbiking if you like.'

I look up at him, shaking my head to force my long hair back. I beam at him. 'Yes. I like.'

Am I clutching at straws? I need to hang on to what I've got, as my feelings for this man are strong. He's, like, turned my world completely upside down.

'Can I still have a copy of the photo I chose? For my mobile wallpaper.' He once again puts his hand on my thigh. *The bastard's such a tease.*

I revive the laptop and scroll through the pictures.

'That one.' Stevie points at it when the one he likes comes back up.

'What's your e-mail address?' I ask. He tells me, and I work on the keyboard for a couple of seconds and hit send. His mobile bleeps and he receives the photo. He then hands me his mobile. 'Save it to wallpaper for me.'

Oh, yeah. The age gap. 'Don't you know how to do it?'

He shrugs and smiles a real 'pleeeeze' smile, and I can't help but smile back. He just makes me melt, despite his defensiveness.

'I'll send them all and you can look at them to your heart's content.' He can have them to wank over. He must masturbate because he doesn't shag. I know he doesn't shag, because he's not shagging me.

*

College after work was cut short, thankfully. It being the last Thursday of the term, some of the guys are going for a drink together, but I decide to go home.

I let myself in and it's quiet. Mum must be out; it is still early. But wait a minute. I can hear a noise upstairs, so she must be up there. I walk up the stairs quietly, listening to the noise. It sounds like… No, it can't be. I get to the top of the stairs, still listening, and it is definitely the sound of shagging. The moaning of the lucky couple, the movement of the bed. *Oh, Mum. You old devil. Good for you.*

Her bedroom door is slightly ajar, and I can see through the crack. There she is, on the bed on her knees, her arse in the air, rocking on her elbows as the guy thrusts into her. I can just make out the torso of the guy, and he looks quite fit for his age, assuming he's Mum's age. Ish. Then I catch his face in the mirror.

I stagger back as if I've just been electrocuted. *Oh my God! Oh my God! Oh, my God! It's Stevie!*

It's Stevie. He's… Oh my God. He's shagging my mum.

I have to put my hand over my mouth to stop myself crying out. Thankfully, they haven't heard me, and as I run back down the stairs, I can still hear them at it.

I run back out into the street, careful not to make any noise. I start to cry. I can't hold the tears back this time, but at least there's no one here to see them. I don't know what to do. I don't know which way to turn. I can't go back in the house, even if they've stopped shagging. *Oh no. Help.*

I run to the bus stop and the bus is coming. I get on and head for town. I need a drink. I'm gonna find Yasmin; I need someone to talk to.

I get to BJ's and it's not very busy, but it's not even nine o'clock yet. Yasmin is behind the bar. She's got skinny calf-length jeans on again, but painted-on leather ones this time. High heels, of course, to compliment the jeans, and a strappy t-shirt cut off just below her boobs. If she raises her arms, her boobs just come into view, in the way Stevie suggested I should pose. And she's not wearing a bra, or it seems that way. She looks absolutely delicious. No wonder the boys are asking for drinks off the top shelf so she has to reach up. I'm looking at the, like, top shelf drinks myself, wondering if I should ask.

She sees me and blows a kiss with her hand, finishes serving her customer, picks up a bottle of my favourite drink, and brings it to me. Doesn't matter who needs serving next.

'That guy back there,' she gestures to the customer she's just served, 'he bought you the drink. He don't know it, because he, like, thinks he's bought *me* one.'

She leans forward on the bar to kiss me, but as our faces get close, she pulls back. 'Debbie. What's wrong? You've been crying.' Without any consideration to the customers, she comes out from behind the bar, takes my arm, and leads me to a seat. She gives me a big hug before we sit down. 'What's the matter, Angel Cake?' She holds my hand. That and her calling me 'Angel Cake' make me smile.

'I just got home from college, early tonight, like, end of term, to find my mum in bed with a guy,' I begin, taking a large gulp of my drink.

'Urgh. Gross.'

'And then I caught a glimpse of the man... and it was my boyfriend.'

'You've got a boyfriend? You never said.'

'Are you cross with me?' I give her my puppy eyes look.

'Of course not. It's not a problem.' I'm not sure if she is a bit resentful or not; her cheery voice disguises any resentment. 'The bloody granny-grabber. He don't upset my Debbie and get away with it. I'll pull his balls off. I mean, there's cheating and then there's this.'

'My mum is not a granny; she's beautiful.' But despite the way I'm feeling, Yasmin does make me smile. She called me *her* Debbie.

'I didn't mean it like that. But she must be twice his age at least.'

'No, they're, like, the same age. I mean, ish.'

'What? Debbie, you've kept that a bit quiet.' She can't quite believe it.

'Well, he's not exactly my boyfriend as such.' I give her a brief history of Stevie and how he's refused my every attempt to get him into bed, apart from the other night when we, like, *slept* together, but then I find him shagging my mum. 'The biggest problem is, I can't work out which one of them is doing the dirty on me.'

'Oh, Debbie. You're so mixed up. Stay here and have another drink. We shut at twelve, so you can come back with me, and we'll sort out this boyfriend of yours tomorrow.' She hugs me which gives me reassurance.

'Have you got a spare bed?' I ask, thinking of how I ended up in bed with Stevie when I conned him into taking me back to his place and he's only got one bed.

'No, silly.' She grins and kisses me. 'You sleep with me.'

'Of course. Why do I need a boyfriend when I've got a girlfriend?' I reply, taking another taste of my drink.

'That's right. You're getting the idea.' *Oh, I love her so much.*

Chapter Nineteen

I spend the night in bed with Yasmin. When I wake, I'm lying with my back to her but she is right up close, her arms wrapped around me. I lie there awake and in her arms for a few minutes, enjoying the moment, then she stirs and wakes up, too.

It's quite surreal actually sleeping, and I do mean sleeping, with someone. Never really done it before. Now, in the last couple of weeks, I've slept with Phil from work, Stevie, and now Yasmin. Yasmin was the best, though, because she wanted to. We just kissed and cuddled up and, like, went to sleep in each other's arms.

I shower in her massive bathroom but have to put on yesterday's clothes again, then she takes me to work in her sexy Merc. The weather has turned bright and warm again, so we have the top off.

She tries to get me to call a sickie, as she has finished Uni for the summer and has all day to herself, but I insist on going to work. It is a difficult day, though, trying to concentrate while all that's going through my mind is Mum and Stevie.

When Yasmin picks me up again after work, we agree to go together to see Stevie and confront him about my discovery the previous night. I don't know why I have agreed to it – for moral support, I suppose – but I'm apprehensive enough without worrying about what she might say and how she might act. 'Specially how she said, like, 'I'll pull his balls off.'

When she picks me up, she is dressed to kill in near nakedness as usual; it's like she was getting dressed, got halfway, and then gave up. She's wearing a short white flowing pleated skirt that doesn't try to cover her cheeks, and another strappy cropped top just below her boobs. It has three buttons, with only the bottom one done up. No bra, with a lot of breast on show that her top didn't cover, along with her nipples pressed up against the material and very visible. It's just as well it isn't cold. If Stevie overlooks her like this, then he's blind.

We ring the bell, and my heart skips a beat yet again as I see him approach. It happens every time; he has that effect on me. He opens the door. 'Debbie! How lovely to see you. Who's your friend?'

'This is Yasmin. I'm sure you recognise her, she works at BJ's, er, I mean AJ's. She's also my photographer.'

'Hello, Yasmin, yes I do recognise you now.' He holds out his hand and she takes it. 'Nice to meet you.' There's a second's silence. 'Come in, ladies, come in. Door's always open, kettle's always on.'

We go in, and I straight away go to the lounge and sit down like I own the place. He has loud music on again; he likes his music loud does Stevie. Some guy with a stutter ranting on about his g-g-generation. He turns it down.

Yasmin hovers. 'Take a seat, Yasmin,' he says, holding his palm out, gesturing to the chair. 'I'll make us all a cup of tea, yes?'

'Yes please,' I say. This is gonna be difficult, because I can't be angry at him. I'm practically melting in his presence just as it is. And even, like, with Yasmin with me for moral support.

'How do you take yours, Yasmin?' he asks.

'With biscuits, usually,' I answer for her.

'Of course,' he says, smiling at my remark. And then he looks back at Yasmin with a look that asks his question again.

She smiles sweetly at him. He's gotta be melting, hasn't he? She is, like, the epitome of the words 'fucking sexy'. 'No sugar, thanks. Sweet enough.' Her cheery tone again and that sweet smile have got to impress him.

He goes off to the kitchen. 'Wow! Debbie. You didn't tell me he was dish of the day and, like, dessert too.'

She's definitely excited about meeting him, but then she did mention she likes an older man. I nearly say 'he's mine', but then *she's* mine too. I look away, feigning innocence. 'Didn't I mention that? Must have slipped my mind.' I look back at her and we both laugh.

'No wonder your mum likes him,' she says.

'Oh, Yasmin. That was a bit below the belt.' I feel grazed. 'Anyway, I didn't think you were into men.'

'I did say if a boy catches my eye...' she tails off.

Stevie comes back in and we give little throat-clearing coughs. He just stands there in the doorway, leaning against the jamb in his sports shirt and light cotton trousers. He looks delicious. Out of the corner of my eye I can see Yasmin with a glint in her eye, too.

'Do either of you ladies want anything to eat? I'm eating out tonight, so I've nothing planned, but you two are quite welcome.'

We look at each other and I'm sure we're both thinking the same after her line about the main dish and dessert. 'No thanks,' I say.

'Yasmin?'

'No, I'm fine thank you. Watching the figure,' says Yasmin.

'Oh.'

Is that all he can say? Oh? And what with her figure, too. He goes back to the kitchen, and I still don't think he's noticed that she's almost naked. He probably wouldn't even if she actually was.

He comes back with three cups of tea on a tray. Cups and saucers even. He sets them down and passes us each one before taking his own and sitting on the sofa next to me. 'So, Debbie? To what do I owe this pleasure? Double pleasure,' he adds, nodding his head towards Yasmin.

'Yesterday, I like, left college early, end-of-term as you know all too well.' He nods as he drinks his tea; quite the English gentleman. 'I went straight home,' I continue, 'and, like, found you and Mum in her bed in the midst of sex.' Straight in. Even the look on Yasmin's face is one of surprise, but not Stevie's.

'Oh.'

Oh again.

'I met your mum the other day. She's probably a woman I could date,' he begins quite nonchalantly. 'About 1963,' he laughs, and then clears his throat quietly as he realises Yasmin and I are not laughing. 'She came to my house on, er, Tuesday.'

I can picture the scene.

*

Steven pulls his car onto his drive, gets out to close the gate.

'Good afternoon. You must be Stevie,' a middle-aged woman approaches him.

'Steven,' he simply replies, looking up at the woman.

'I'm Mrs Wilson,' says the woman.

'Pleased to meet you, Mrs Wilson. But, um…' He gives a blank look and waves his palm across his head.

'Jackie Wilson, Debbie's mum.'

'Oh, hello,' his voice brightens. 'Wilson. You know, all this time I've known her and that's the first time I've heard what her surname is. And you're her mum? No wonder you called me Stevie; she's always calling me that. I went to school with a Jackie Wilson; you're not her, are you?'

'Wilson is my married name. I was Smith at school.'

'I went to school with a Jackie Smith, too. You seem to have been elusive.' He opens the gate and shakes Jackie's hand.

'I thought the same about you,' says Jackie.

'Well, it's lovely to meet you. Would you like to come in? Kettle's on.' Steven opens the front door, and they go in.

'I've heard a lot about you...' Jackie begins.

'All good, I hope.'

'But I was wondering if you were just a fantasy or something. She talks about you all the time but, you know, we've never been introduced. I dunno, the younger generation, eh?'

Steven invites Jackie into the lounge and asks her to make herself comfortable while he goes to the kitchen to make tea. 'Would you like sugar in your tea?' he asks calmly, popping his head around the doorway. She smiles and just shakes her head.

'I didn't realise you were so old,' she says, as he returns to the kitchen.

A moment later he comes back with the tea. 'Thanks,' he says, handing her the tea.

'Thanks for what?'

'For what you just said about me being old. I know how old you are, and we're the same age, Jackie,' he says, sitting down on the sofa.

'I didn't mean it like that. I just expected you to be Debbie's kind of age. Not mine.'

'So, how did you find me?' asks Steven, changing the subject.

'I followed her last night. She said she was coming to see you and I offered her a lift, but she refused. I wanted to see you, just to see if you were real, you know, not just some fantasy. She don't stop talking about you. I think I now know why she's kept you a secret.'

'Yes. I've mentioned to her that I'm too old for her. No. That she's too young for me.' Steven sips at his tea as he tries to put some perspective to his relationship with this woman's daughter. 'I don't know if you know, but I'm a school teacher. Girls have always had a crush on me, certainly in my early days of teaching. Even some of my colleagues called me a babe magnet, not because of the schoolgirls but the women teachers – even those older than me had eyes for me. Maybe not so much these days, but it's never been a problem.

'In the early days I was too frightened to contemplate any sexual thought, and now that I'm older, even looking at young women I just see a schoolgirl. And that is just how it feels with Debbie. Probably never even been in love before.' He pauses for a moment.

'If you'll excuse me,' Jackie puts a reassuring hand on his knee, 'but I can see why they would have a crush on you and be attracted to you. And why Debbie does. You're an attractive man. Film star looks, even.'

'Thank you,' he replies with a smile.

Jackie can't help but smile back, but she moves her hand away from his knee.

'From someone like you, I take that as a compliment. But from the young girls... Well, I don't need to say any more.' He takes a sip of his tea and Jackie does the same. 'You can see it in the girls with their body language, with too many buttons undone, prolonged eye contact, and always finding excuses to touch, like asking for more individual, one-to-one help, to get me close.' He pauses again. 'I just can't get Debbie out of my head, though. As she so delicately reminds me, she's not a schoolgirl. I want her as a friend; she's lovely and great fun. But that's all. We haven't been to bed, has she told you?'

'She told me that you were hot in bed.'

'Yeah. Apparently, she's told everyone that. So, yeah, I am a fantasy.' He drains his cup and stands up. 'And I bet she's not told you I'm a widower.' He puts on some music, with low volume.

'No. Oh, I'm sorry.' Jackie looks a bit embarrassed. 'No, she didn't.'

'This is where one of my problems comes from.' He sits back down next to Jackie on the sofa. 'I'm a one-woman man. When I was young, I got into a fight with another boy at school, and he kicked me straight between the legs. I began to tell Debbie the story but never finished it.' He starts to tell Jackie but falls short again, and she can sense him becoming a bit emotional. 'It would've made her understand how I feel about her. Why I feel that way.'

'Tell me, Steven,' she says, and puts her hand on his knee again for reassurance. He places his hand over hers.

'He kicked me hard; bloody hard. I just crumbled to the ground in agony. I was in pain for ages, and in the end, I went to the doctor. To cut a long story short, one of my testicles was damaged and I had to have it removed. Cancer risk.

'I was still young, thirteen or fourteen. A virgin, anyway. I was told that it would probably give me problems in the future and that I probably wouldn't be able to have children. It scared me. It was a time when I was just beginning to notice girls, and I was scared stiff... er, sorry. But that was just it,' he continued. 'I didn't think I'd be able to get an erection, and if I did whether it'd hurt. I didn't even masturbate because I was so scared. Yes, of course I masturbated when I was a boy; every boy does, it's only natural. I can remember quite clearly the feeling and luxurious sensations of that very first time. But not after that fight. No way. I was scared that it might hurt, never mind with a girl.'

Jackie gives him a sympathetic look. 'Didn't you get natural erections, you know, without being stimulated? You know, like wet dreams or something,' she asks.

'I did at times, when I was younger. I hated it, tried to stop it, because I was just scared. At the same time, I've been inflicted, if that's what you say, with film star looks. It must be the Italian in me.'

'Italian?'

'I have an Italian mother.' Jackie nods her understanding. 'All the girls fancied me and chased me, and the boys resented it. It's one of the reasons I got into the fight. That's why I took up karate, and when they all knew I was doing karate I became everybody's buddy, but I just kept my distance from the girls. I left school, did my further education and everything, but by that time when everyone around me was sexually active, I'd lost all confidence in myself. I was afraid that if I got together with a girl and things led to the bedroom, I wouldn't be able to perform to her standards, if at all, and then I might get a bad reputation and become a laughing stock. You know what it's like when you're young.

'Then I became a teacher, and at twenty years old I was doing my training and thrown in front of a class full of fourteen/fifteen-year-old girls, all looking up to me with lust in their eyes. None of them were virgins, probably, and there's me, never even been kissed before. Even now, at forty-seven, some still have eyes for me. But it's just water off a duck's back, and it should be the same with Debbie. She's great fun and she has captured my better side to the point that I can't get her out of my head. I'm back on square one, though, when it comes to women. And then I meet a girl,' he clenches his fists just a little, 'and she's twenty-seven years younger than me. She might just as well be one of my pupils. And I've not had sex since my wife…' he chokes off.

Jackie just rubs her hand on his knee. 'You must be ok, though, if you did get married. You must have become sexually active at some point. I'm sure you didn't exist in a sexless marriage.'

'We were childhood sweethearts. Well, kind of. Not quite sweethearts. We met at primary school and were just friends, like kids are at that age, and we just went through school together. Her name was Taylor as well. Debbie Taylor. People thought we were brother and sister 'cause we'd sit together in class. But that's the only time we were together. Outside the classroom, I would go my way, with the boys, playing football or something, and she'd go hers. We'd see each other occasionally outside of school but just as friends. We'd do things together at times, like going to the park or into town and having coffee. We even went to the cinema once. But not as boyfriend and girlfriend, just friends. We then went onto college together.

'But it was when we came into puberty that she started to get closer.' He continues to pour his heart out. 'But just like with all the girls, I kept a distance between us. Fair play to her, she kept coming into my life and she never bothered with any other boys. She was the most beautiful girl in school. Big blue eyes, long blonde hair, and a little kink in her nose. All the boys were after her, yet she seemed not to bother. She just hung about with me. We were just friends, no more.

'As we got a bit older, when I started working in the school, I told her everything. And she told me her story.

She said that it didn't matter to her that I couldn't give her children; she actually had a problem that meant she couldn't have kids herself. So, it was the perfect marriage. It was our destiny. We were friends and became lovers, and we lost our virginity together, aged twenty-one. She made me get an erection and it didn't hurt. She made me ejaculate and it didn't hurt, and together we learned to have sex.

'We're both an only child, so the family chain stopped there. But we were happy together and life was great, and we never really had a problem about being childless. It made us stronger even, that we could live an adult life with no dependants. Unfortunately, the problem she had as a child that prevented her having children got the better of her, and she died…'

Steven stops, clearly emotional but not crying. Concerned, Jackie puts her arm around him and pulls his head onto her shoulder as he blinks back tears.

'Steven, bless you,' she says, and kisses him on the head. 'Do you want to tell me what happened?'

He looks up at her. 'She developed a kidney problem when she was about nine, and when she had some tests, it was realised she'd had MRKH since birth.'

'MRKH?' asks Jackie.

'It means she was born without a womb. I can give you its full name: Mayer Rokitansky Kuster Hauser syndrome. A bit of a tongue twister, but I learned to say it. But it didn't stop us, and we had a good sex life, no problems. But her kidney problem developed into kidney failure, and she needed a transplant. I offered one of mine, but we weren't compatible. She had no siblings to turn to, so we joined the waiting list…' he tails off with emotion.

'The thing is, as I said, I'm back to square one, only it's thirty years later. I'm single again, and then when I meet a girl I like, she's only twenty bloody years old. And all I can think is that it's just a schoolgirl crush. It's a typical situation that often becomes headline news. A teacher and a pupil are having an affair. The pupil is so insistent – a little girl's crush she believes to be love – and eventually the teacher cannot resist anymore and gives in to his lust and desires.

'I haven't given in; I never would. I have different opinions about women, but then along comes Debbie and she's not a little schoolgirl with a pubescent crush, but a fully grown, sexually active woman. And she knows what she wants,' says Steven, slowly bringing his finger round to point at himself. 'You know, she's lovely, beautiful, fun to be with, and everything. But *twenty*.'

Jackie kisses him again, this time on the lips. It is a quick peck, but as they look into each other's eyes, the spark lights the flame and they kiss again. Full on. A passionate kiss as they embrace each other, his tongue gently brushing over her top lip – just as he did with Debbie – their hands behind each other's head, Jackie running her fingers through his hair. Steven brings his hand down and runs it over her breast...

That's it. I can no longer picture the scene.

*

'And then last night, she texted me, asked me to come round... and that's where you found us,' says Stevie, concluding his explanation.

'What makes me laugh is you're dating me but, like, shagging her,' I interrogate him. 'I mean, you know.'

'It's a completely different situation. Now you know why it's been so difficult for me. Jackie, your mum, is my age; she understood,' he says. 'She opened her heart to me too, yesterday. Told me all about herself and how she met your dad.'

*

'I was late in life too, just like you, when I lost my cherry; well, I mean, compared to today's kids,' Jackie tells him. 'It was a confidence thing like you, I suppose. I just didn't have the nerve. The first time I saw an erect penis, I ran a bloody mile. It was at my local pub when I met Debbie's dad. I say my local. It was just the pub round the corner where we lived, and I only ever went in the once. It was a funeral for a neighbour. He was a lovely old boy and it was *his* local, that's why they had the wake there.'

She pauses a second, reminiscing. 'He'd had a good innings – nearly ninety, I think. Anyway, I was in the pub, and on fruit juice, when this lad walked over and began to chat me up, trying to by me a drink. I don't drink. Never have, except on this one occasion. He kept insisting and I kept saying no. It wasn't, like, harassment or anything; he was quite nice and made me laugh. So, I got him to buy me a whisky. God, it burnt my throat, but I drank it all and I swear I was instantly pissed.

'We agreed to meet again. I reckon it was the whisky that made me, but I told him not in a pub. No alcohol. We actually met in the park, and the rest is history. We began courting and dating, and he was the one that I lost my virginity to. Things were great, we got a place together and lived a happy life 'till I fell pregnant with Debbie. We got married soon after, before I began to show – bit of a shotgun wedding, to be honest. But no sooner was she born than I was literally left holding the baby. The only man I'd been with, still a virgin at twenty, just like you. Twenty-two in my case.

'Because I didn't drink, I was his blinking chauffeur, then I had the baby and he couldn't bear staying at home because of her, so he was off out without me and shagging…'

It's her turn to be a little emotional, a tear in her eye.

'I don't think we had much sex after Debbie was born. He was always making excuses but he was going out pubbing and picking up girls. He didn't want sex with me, and I knew why. He was getting his fill elsewhere.

'I don't blame Debbie at all in this. I love my daughter unconditionally, and basically brought her up on my own. It was only when I caught him *in our* bed with some young…' she pauses, thinking for the right word, 'slag. Whore. Bitch!'

All the time Jackie is talking, Steven just sits listening, but at this point he speaks. 'I know. Debbie told me. The day she finished school.'

*

'But you should've told me all this, I would have understood,' I try to reassure him.

'But you're so much younger. I'm perhaps not as virile as you expect and like your other experiences. I bet you've never been with anyone over thirty.'

I think for a little while. Sir Francis, of course. And, er… Alex, Phil. Pauline? 'No, I don't think so.'

'How many partners have you had?'

I think again. 'I've been having regular sex since I was, like, fifteen, so I don't know. Once a week at least, so fifty-two times five…' I try to calculate.

'Two hundred and sixty,' says Stevie, ever the mathematician.

Crikey. Is it that many? No, it can't be. It wasn't a regular thing at first; ok, all the boys I was hanging about with in my schooldays I got round to having sex with, taking a few cherries with me, but nowadays it's probably once a week on average. But it's still probably near two hundred. *Oh my God, I've never looked at it like that.*

'How many of them have been one-offs?' he asks.

'Most of them,' I admit. 'All of them. Probably.' I quote what Pauline told me. 'There's no such thing as a slut. People like to fuck. Get over it.'

Stevie raises his eyebrows at that. 'Well, I've had two. One is your mum, and it's the same for her. And with all the problems I've had, you can't wonder at it.' A deathly silence follows. 'I get into bed with you, it's a disaster, then what?'

'Well, you've proven that you're not incapable. Why will it be a disaster?' Yasmin has been sitting all quiet until now, and then her cheery voice perks us all up.

'I told Debbie I was not impotent, or celibate, or gay. I just, I dunno, it's not straightforward for me to just jump into bed. I'm just not like that,' Stevie tells her.

'You did with Mum,' I say.

'Different situation,' Stevie responds. 'A couple of years of pent-up emotion…'

'But do you still think it's a crush with Debbie?' asks Yasmin. 'I don't. She's told me everything. She has feelings for you, not just wanting to get you into bed.'

'That's right, Yasmin. You're absolutely right,' says Stevie, and she smiles her sweet smile at him, but he doesn't react. 'It's me, probably. But I've explained as much as I can.' Stevie shrugs his shoulders.

'Was it a disaster with Mum?'

'No. It was, er…' he says shyly. 'But we've agreed not to take it any further for your sake.'

'My sake? Why?'

'It would be uncomfortable.'

'So, you're saying that you and Mum don't wanna, like…, and you're, like, gonna keep dating me like nothing's happened?'

He looks sullen. 'We didn't want to upset you.'

'Upset me!' I'm raging. 'I caught you both, like… like, fucking shagging. Upset me? Like, I'm being cheated on by a boyfriend I've never been with…' I tail off, shaking my head. 'With my fucking mother!'

*

Yasmin and I leave Stevie to get ready for his night out. It ended quite happily and, he kisses us both as we leave, Yasmin having to stand on tiptoes in her trainers to reach up to him and put her hands around his neck. She kisses him on the lips and, although not quite a snog, Yasmin prolongs it, raising one leg and lifting her heel. As she does, it raises both her top and her skirt, showing off her gorgeous peach of a bum and her boobs – so much so that I get a glimpse of nipple, they look like small hazelnuts and taste of honey.

Stevie has his hands on her bare waist, and fortunately/ unfortunately he can't see what I can see. I then realise that I am biting my bottom lip; it's an emotional reaction, but who is it for? Stevie or Yasmin? He says he hopes to see Yasmin again soon, and I shall be seeing him tomorrow, maybe to go biking.

Driving back in her car, Yasmin tries to put some perspective on things. 'I can see where he's coming from,' she begins. 'You can see that he's, like, in turmoil about any relationship after he lost his wife. He had relationship probs before they married, and now he's gotta start all over again. Bless him. But he's struggling with you because you're so much younger than him. I can see his point of view. I think he's got the future in mind, as in when he's, like, a pensioner and you'll still only be in your thirties. And there's, like, his reputation, his morals as a schoolteacher nagging at him.'

'Yeah. I suppose you're right. But, like, I dunno. I love him.' *Did I say the right thing to Yasmin?* 'I don't want to give him up, even for my mum.'

'Just give him time. He wants to be friends; he'll come round eventually.'

Yasmin is so lovely. I put a hand on her thigh as she drives me home.

Chapter Twenty

Next morning I've got my jeans on ready for a motorbike ride. I've still got heels, though – boots, which should be ok – when Stevie picks me up. I say goodbye to Mum and give her a kiss. I love her to bits, and I can't be mad at her for going off with Stevie. She deserves a bit of love and affection that she can't get from me. And I can't really be mad at Stevie either. I just accept that what happened was only natural, I suppose; keep it in the family.

Stevie stays in his car as I run out to meet him. He and Mum exchange a wave. I told her last night that I'd spoken to him about catching them in the act.

'Oh my word,' she'd said. 'He's the first man I've seen since your dad. It just happened. We were, like, chatting and one thing led to another and… he's such a sexy hunk. He's got a body to die for.'

'I know, Mum. I've seen it even if I ain't touched it,' I said, perhaps a little too regretfully. 'And don't forget, so have you.'

'I'd forgotten what sex was like till the other night and…'

With another glance out of the window, she urges me to get going. 'He's out there waiting for you. Go, now, before I'm tempted to push you out the way and go with him myself.'

I run off and get into Stevie's car and we kiss. It's a bit strange, me kissing him after he's waved at my mum in that knowing way.

'I went into town last night,' says Stevie as he drives away, 'to see if I could find you after the dinner last night.'

'Yasmin said you were in. Why didn't you text me or something?'

'I didn't take my mobile. I'm the sort of considerate bloke who doesn't have his mobile on the end of my thumb at the dinner table,' he says, putting his thumb in the air. I roll my eyes. 'I'm from a generation from before mobile phones. You were probably born with one in your hand.

'Anyway, I went to BJ's and said hello to Yasmin. I asked if you were in, but she said she hadn't seen you. She gave me my drink on the house, which was nice, and... er...' He goes quiet.

'And what?'

'She kissed me across the bar. All the blokes were looking daggers at me.' He smiles. 'I actually felt quite good about that. And I'm sure she served me out of turn.'

'Yeah. That sounds like Yasmin.' It makes me smile, thinking of her. 'So where did you get to?'

'I was accosted by one of the fat slags...'

'I was out with them,' I say, 'so how come I didn't see you?'

'It was in the corridor up to the toilets. Dressed like a prostitute...'

'Yeah. I was with her when she bought that dress. Didn't think even she would have the nerve to wear that.'

I can picture the scene.

*

Steven comes out of the toilet and there is Hazel in the corridor, waiting for him. She'd obviously seen him go in, and she is wearing the red lurex dress. It is totally see-through, and with her very brief knickers and a bra that's more like a tiny bikini top and just covers her nipples, very little is left to the imagination.

'Hello, lover boy,' says Hazel, cornering Steven in the corridor.

'It's Stevie, er, I mean Steven.' Then he mutters to himself, 'I don't believe I just said that. I don't even know my own bloody name anymore. So, are you Sharon or Tracy?'

'It's Haze,' she says, moving closer so their bodies are pressed against each other. She reaches down and finds his crotch. Rubs it. 'How about giving me some of that electric sex I've heard about? I bet you can't resist me in this dress.'

She quickly pulls down his zip in experienced fashion. Her downward movement has her dropping to her knees, and her fingers are in his trousers in an instant.

Steven grabs hold of her wrist and pulls her back to her feet. 'Get out of it, you stupid fat slag.' It isn't said aggressively, but it is assertive.

A guy comes out of the toilet and sees the confrontation. 'Alright, darlin'? Is this grandad giving you some grief?'

Hazel looks at him with spite in her eyes. 'Why don't you fuck off, arsehole?'

'Don't talk to me like that, bitch. I'm trying to help.' He actually raises his hand; whether to hit her or not, he never gets the chance. Steven's karate skill comes into play quickly as he grabs the guy's arm.

'I think I heard the lady say "fuck off, arsehole".'

The guy then tries to kick out, but Steven is too quick, taking hold of his leg and lifting him up, then ceremoniously dumping him on his back.

'Oh, my hero,' says Hazel in a real damsel-in-distress manner, and she tries to kiss him.

Steven pushes her face away, zips up his trousers, and begins moving back towards the stairs down to the bar room. The stairs are spilt in two flights, with a large window mirror on the back wall, from where you can see back into the bar. Steven notices three doormen coming quickly up the stairs.

'Oh-oh,' he says, and looks up to see a CCTV camera pointing down the corridor. 'Great.'

He looks back down the corridor, where the guy he's dumped on the floor is just getting back to his feet, and spots an emergency escape door. He takes hold of Hazel's hand and leads her to the door. 'Come on, Sharon.' He opens the door, which leads to a small flat roof, and they step out. Shutting the door behind them, they head for the corner where there is a metal staircase leading to a back alley behind the pub.

Steven starts to take the staircase but, still holding hands, Hazel stops him. 'I can't go down there in these shoes,' she says.

Steven rolls his eyes. 'Ok. Hitch up your dress and climb on my back.'

'What?'

'I'll carry you down.' He points at the door they've just exited. 'They'll be after us in a minute.'

Hazel hitches her dress over her hips – it's short enough, so doesn't need much raising – and she climbs onto Steven's back. He runs down the stairs, his athleticism making it quite easy.

'Whoo, whoo,' shouts Hazel.

'Shut up, woman!' Steven calls back.

They get to the bottom, and he puts her down, Hazel readjusting her dress. He takes her hand again, then they hurry out of the alley before they get cut off at the other end.

'It's like a scene from a James Bond movie,' she says. 'No one will believe us.' It makes Hazel smile. 'Oh, James,' she says in a sultry voice.

'Oh, not you as well,' says Steven, rolling his eyes.

Out in the street, they walk away from BJ's entrance, still hand-in-hand. 'Right, Miss Moneypenny. We can't go back in there; they'll recognise you, if not me. Are you with Debbie and Tracy?'

She just nods.

'Text one of them or something, tell them where we are.'

'I can't, I don't have my mobile on me,' she says, holding out her arms in a gesture of innocence, while still keeping hold of Steven.

'What do you mean, you ain't got your mobile? I thought you youngsters had them permanently attached to your thumb, all huddlin' together and taking selfies.'

'I don't have anywhere to put it,' she says, patting herself down with her free hand as if looking for it on her person.

'You not got a handbag?'

'No. I hate handbags.'

'Where do you keep your money?'

'Jules carries it for me. She's, like, got more handbags than the Queen had. Anyway, I don't need money to buy myself drinks dressed like this,' she says, and Steven looks her up and down as if noticing for the first time the sexy dress she is wearing. 'They all get rewarded. One of them might get lucky.'

He inhales and exhales a very heavy sigh. 'Right, come on.' They're still holding hands, so it's easy for him to drag her along. 'We'll go to another bar and hopefully they'll come looking.'

'Anyway, where's *your* mobile phone, hmm?'

'I didn't bring it with me. Me and the others all agreed no mobile phones so that we don't all sit there like people your age looking at their phones all night long instead of talking to each other. I'm from a generation that doesn't have their whole world on the end of their thumb,' he says, holding up his thumb.

'We could just go back to your place...' she begins.

'No, we couldn't,' he retorts.

'You're my hero. I did say someone might get lucky. You saved me from being hit by that guy...'

'Oh, yeah. He wasn't about to buy you a drink, was he?' mocks Steven. 'The only way I'm gonna get lucky is if I can get rid of you. Listen,' he continues, as they walk along to the next bar. 'Why did you and Tracy dump Debbie the other night when we first met?'

'What you on about?'

'That night me and Debbie first met. You left her alone in a gay bar, remember?'

'We were just having a laugh. She's always getting in the way when we're chatting up boys,' she says innocently.

'What do you mean? You don't seem to have a problem. And she's doing alright as far as I can tell. She pulled me.'

'Yeah, you must like fat birds.'

'What?' They're walking side by side, but Steven stops and turns so they're face-to-face. 'Fat? Is that what it's all about? I can't believe that. She's not fat. She's beautiful; she's got curves.' He shakes his head. 'Not like you. Everybody's fat compared to you. You could hide behind a lamppost; or looking at the way you're dressed, you're better off standing *under* a lamppost. You look like a ten-pound whore. Are you sure that dress is meant for wearing out and not just the bedroom?'

SUGAR DADDY?

He starts to walk off, and she has to hurry to keep up with him, but she quickly grabs his hand again. 'Why don't you find out?' she suggests to his bedroom reference.

She walks along with him as if they are a couple, Hazel swinging their arms. As they reach the next bar and walk in, the doormen open the door for them. 'Evening sir, madam,' they say, eyes all over her.

Inside, they go straight to the bar and Steven buys them both a drink. 'Let me reward you like I do the others,' says Hazel, and she puts a hand on his cheek and reaches up and kisses him on the mouth. It lingers, and Steven has to push her away.

'Enough,' he says, and takes a gulp of his beer.

'What do you wanna do? D'you wanna sit down? Dance?' She stands very close to him, her body rubbing against his. He doesn't seem to mind.

'We wait. Wait to see if Debbie or Tracy come in.'

'Why do you keep calling me and Jules Sharon and Tracy?'

'Surely you've read that comic,' says Steven, raising one eyebrow.

'What comic?'

'You're too young,' he says.

'Yes, but I'm amazing in bed.' Again, she rubs up against him, and again he doesn't flinch. 'I said one guy will get lucky. Perhaps it's you, you've pulled.'

'I'd rather pull a muscle.'

'If Debbie can have it, why can't I? Or are you gay or something? Guys can't normally resist me if they get a chance,' she says, emphasising her body with a wave of her hand.

'I'm not interested in you.'

'You bought me a drink.'

251

'So? You've not got the money to buy me one.' She harrumphs at that. 'Come on then. Let's see it. Let me see you get a drink out of someone, Miss Irresistible. And when someone does, tell them you're on pints of lager.' Steven tips his glass to indicate what he's drinking.

Hazel looks around the room; it's packed, but there are plenty of guys without girls. One guy is standing on his own like a wallflower. 'Ok,' she says to Steven, and she goes up to the guy.

'Hello. My name is Haze. Hazel. Saw you standing on your own, thought I would see if you want some company.' She smiles sweetly at him and puts a hand on his arm.

'Er, hello. I'm Danny. Nice to meet you.' He moves the arm that Hazel is touching so that he can shake hands. Then he clearly puts his hand in his pocket so that she can't get at it again, but this gives her the opportunity to link arms with him.

'I like it in here,' she says, getting conversational. Out of the corner of her eye she can see Steven watching her. She turns so that her back is towards him and faces Danny. 'Mm. This music makes me horny,' she pouts at him and rubs her body closer to him with a little movement to the rhythm of the music. 'Do you wanna dance?'

Just then, another guy comes over carrying two drinks – one for Danny. 'Who's your friend, Danny?'

'This is Hazel. She's asked me if I wanna dance.'

Danny's friend looks Hazel up and down. 'Very sexy. For a woman.'

'Thanks,' says Danny, taking his drink, then he puts his arm around his friend, and they kiss, fully on the lips.

Hazel's jaw drops and she turns to see Steven in fits of laughter. She walks away from Danny and his boyfriend and back to Steven. He's still laughing, almost in a fit of giggles.

'It's not funny,' she says, all straight-faced.

Steven nods as he laughs. 'Yes, it is. And you've got a face like a slapped arse.' He carries on laughing, tears starting to appear in his eyes, and looks at her again. He wipes his eyes and tries to put on a straight face, but he can't hold it for more than a couple of seconds before he bursts into laughter again. Eventually, Hazel's face begins to crack, and she laughs along with him.

She moves close to him once again and puts a hand on his backside. 'Looks like you're gonna have to buy me another drink instead.'

'Yeah, I don't mind. I'll buy you one as thanks for the entertainment.' He's managing to keep a straight face, but then bursts out laughing again. Hazel laughs with him once more, pressing her body up against his. 'No one's gonna buy you one now, we've attracted too much attention.'

'It's my dress that's drawn the attention,' she says, and right on cue an admirer comes over to them.

'Hi, my name is Peter,' he addresses Steven. 'I'd like to ask you if I could ask your daughter for a dance and buy her a drink.'

Steven looks at the lad; he's probably twenty, twenty-one. Steven is amazed that someone of his age needs 'her dad's' approval. He looks at Hazel and she looks askance, too.

She looks back at Peter and bites on her bottom lip, but he's not looking.

'Yes,' he says, putting a hand on Peter's shoulder. 'Of course you can, son. This is Hazel.' Peter smiles; Hazel's mouth is open. 'I'd be pleased for you to take her off my hands.'

'Would you like to dance?' the guy asks, looking Hazel directly in the eye.

'Go on, Hazel. Told you *I'd* get lucky. Give the lad a dance. But watch out,' Steven says, turning back to Peter, 'her bite is worse than her bark.' Steven has his hand behind her back and is practically pushing her towards Peter and the dance floor.

She hands Steven her empty glass and takes Peter's offered hand. 'Yes please, I would love to dance. See you later, Dad, don't wait up.' And they make their way to the dance floor.

Steven watches them for a while as they dance, and they seem to be fine. They are dancing close, bodies grinding up against each other; the young lad has his hands around her waist, and she has her arms behind his neck. She looks at Steven over Peter's shoulder and raises a hand to wave him off.

Good, he thinks, *she's pulled, and off my hands*. He leaves the pub, makes his way to the taxi rank, and goes home.

Chapter Twenty-One

'So, what happened to you?' Stevie asks as we go into his house to get ready to go motorbiking. 'Are you not bothered that I spent my night with whatshername?'

'Not really. I believe you when you tell me what happened. It's a strange chain of events, but with her, like, anything is believable. And as I knew you were in town, I expected to see you at some point. I texted and called you, like, half a dozen times. And Haze. I dunno, here we are, the twenty-first century, and neither of you had a mobile phone on you. I was wondering what had happened to you. And Haze for that matter. Now I know.' I put my arm around his waist and pull him close. 'I'm flattered that you came straight from your party to see me.'

'The evening went well with the work gang, but the party started to break up about ten-thirty and I felt like I wanted to see you. The night was still young.' Stevie sits down on the sofa and gestures for me to join him, patting the seat next to him. I don't need any prompting, but just the gesture is enough to lift my heart. That, and the fact that he has admitted he wanted to see me last night after his party. 'It turned into quite an adventure.'

After a moment while he seems to be reflecting on last night's events, he takes my hand. 'What did you get up to then?'

'Well, I stayed at BJ's all night, waiting for you to appear. 'Specially as I received no reply to my texts. It was a bit strange, because I was constantly looking out for you.

Jules was her normal self, though, dancing, getting drunk, eyeing up all the boys. The night went by, the bar closed, and people began going home. Yasmin finished her shift, and she took me home.'

I think about telling him the real truth but decide to leave it at that.

*

I was standing alone in BJ's, having left Jules on the dance floor when a boy approached her to ask for a dance. We had got up to dance together, but, like, the guy came over to us and she was all over him, so I just went back to the bar. I wasn't really interested, still hoping to see Stevie. Then that boy from the other night, the one I handcuffed to the bed and sat on his face, came over to me.

'Hi, Debbie,' he says quite cheerily, 'fancy meeting you here.'

'Yeah. Fancy.' Sorry. No enthusiasm. All systems offline. *What was his name again?*

'I was, like, hoping to see you again. I left in a hurry the other night. Sorry. Didn't get the chance to speak and swap mobile numbers.' He rattles on and went 'Can I see you again?'

I look up at him, my eyes widening. 'You are seeing me again.'

'I mean, like, properly. Go out with you. D'you know what I mean?'

Oh, God. 'I'm, er, already seeing someone,' I begin. Then, she must've seen the confrontation as Yasmin comes over to save me.

'Debbie? Who's your friend?'

'This is, erm…'

'Grant. Nice to meet you,' he says.

'I'm sure it is,' quips Yasmin. That makes me laugh. Good old Yasmin. Then she goes one better. She reaches up and kisses me on the cheek. 'This is my girlfriend. Can I help you at all?'

Whatshisname's face is a picture. His eyes go totally wide, and his mouth drops open. He stays like that for what seems like ages, stunned into silence, till Yasmin puts her finger on his chin and closes his mouth. He swallows but still stays silent.

'If you'll excuse us,' says Yasmin, very diplomatically, and we walk off.

I grin at her. 'Yasmin. You're so funny.'

'You're lost, ain't you? Just 'cause I told you Stevie was in earlier…'

'I was just hoping to see him, that's all. He's not answering his mobile or my texts.' *She said I'm lost. Oh my God, is it that obvious?* I go for a change of tack. 'Shouldn't you be behind the bar?'

'Yep. And? They can't sack me. My dad's the owner.'

'I didn't know that.' I say, surprised. 'You've never said nothing about that.'

She narrows her eyes. 'Are you sure I haven't told you? This place used to be an hotel, if you remember.' I shake my head. 'No. Probably a bit too long ago. Anyway, it was called the Johnson Hotel. And that's my dad, Adam Johnson. AJ.' She just gives me one of her charming smiles that makes me melt.

I smile back at her then change the subject. 'Did it worry you that a boy was chatting me up?'

'No, silly. You've got a boyfriend. Stevie. Remember? I worry about you, though. Like a lost little lamb, bleating for its mum.' Then she adds 'baa', making sheep noises.

'He was just a boy I, like, took home the other night. Handcuffed him to my bed and took his cherry. Now he's chancing it again,' I explain.

After a quick kiss, Yasmin goes back behind the bar, and I look around for a vacant chair. When I find one, I slump down with my drink, which is now empty, and check my mobile again. Nothing. I try ringing Stevie's number again, but there is still no answer.

I get up and make my way to the bar for another bottle, and Yasmin is over in a flash to bring me a drink. 'Cheer up, sweetheart.' Instantly I'm cheered, her voice perking me up and calling me sweetheart. 'That fella over there just got that,' and she points at him.

The fella smiles back, still watching Yasmin strutting round the bar, although he can't possibly hear our conversation. Yasmin actually smiles back and turns her point into a wave. She turns back to me. 'He's a bit of alright, don't you think?'

I look at him again and he's still smiling. 'Yeah, he's ok,' I say without enthusiasm, but she's right. Male crumpet.

'Leave it with me,' says Yasmin. 'We could have some fun.' I am almost expecting her theatrical wink. She goes to walk off then turns back to me. I'm still looking at the crumpet and not Yasmin when she asks me, 'Have you still got them handcuffs?'

I do a double-take at her. 'Yes. Actually. Why?' Then comes the wink. Not quite theatrical, but a wink.

She goes over to the crumpet and speaks to him for a moment or two before going back to serving. The crumpet makes his way round the bar to see me. 'Hello,' he says. 'She told me your name is Debbie.' I nod. Closer up, he's even better looking. Wow! 'My name's Nathan.'

'Hiya, Nathan. Did you buy me the drink?' I say, waving my bottle. 'Or is it one of the many that Yasmin gets bought?' He looks a little lost at that, so I explain, 'Sexy babe like her. Guys are constantly buying her drinks in the hope of getting lucky. Then when I want one, she just goes "he bought that".'

Nathan looks a bit crestfallen but doesn't reply.

'Are you on your own?' I ask.

He nods. 'You?'

'Well, I did come in with two friends. One's disappeared, and the other is her over there trying to swallow that guy whole,' I say, pointing at Jules and a guy who's probably pulled. *Get a room!*

'I don't normally come in here on my own,' says Nathan, 'but I just fancied a drink. Do you come very often?'

'I come as much as I can. 'Pends how good the guy is,' I say, quick as a flash. 'I'm pretty good on the dance floor, too.'

'I don't dance...' begins Nathan.

'What d'you mean, you don't dance? You'll want me on my back later. Or, like, on my knees. But you don't want me on the dance floor. That's not the way to get into a girl's knickers.' He just smiles at that. 'Come on,' I say, practically pushing him to the dance floor. 'It's easy. Just move your legs to the beat and point in the air.'

We do as I say, but I'm dancing while Nathan is all over the place.

'Not like you've just scored a goal. Point in the air like this.' I try to get him to follow my lead. There's an improvement. 'That's better. But you're right. You don't dance.'

We carry on regardless, and he seems to be enjoying being with me, holding hands as we dance. I pull him close and put my arms around the back of his neck; he has his arms around my waist. 'So *how* do you, like, normally get into a girl's knickers if you don't dance?'

He shrugs his shoulders. But as he does, a thought hits me. 'You're not a virgin, are you?'

'No!' He seems a bit insulted by that.

'Just checking. It must be your looks then.' And I gently rub the back of my hand across his cheek. There's a little bit of a beard there; he really is crumpet. I bring my lips up to meet his and we kiss. Mmm. He's a better kisser than a dancer, that's for sure. Bodes well for later.

I try to keep up the conversation. 'What do you do then? You know, for a living.'

'I'm training to be a schoolteacher.' I raise my eyebrows. *That sounds familiar.* 'I've been doing some modelling work to fund my education.'

'A model, eh? Yeah, I can see why with those looks. So, like, how come you can't dance and yet you're a model?'

'I don't have to dance to do modelling, just pose. But I've finished my university whatsit and now I'm learning the ropes in front of real live schoolkids.'

'Look out for all them lusty fifteen-year-olds trying it on,' I say.

'Oh, tell me about it,' he begins, shaking his head to clear some thought. 'All "sir this" and "sir that", undoing another button on their blouse or shortening their skirt. It's so distracting.' *Sounds like someone I know. Me, I mean. Undoing buttons and that.*

'Are you tempted at all?'

'No,' he says quickly. 'No. But it don't stop them trying it on. And some of them are not little girls, you know what I mean? But I wouldn't, you know, with a schoolgirl.'

'Like I said, it must be the looks. And my luck. I'm not like no schoolgirl who's all puppy-eyed at sir, all "hello,

Mr Taylor".' What made me come out with Taylor, heaven only knows, but of course I'm thinking of Stevie.

'My name's not Taylor,' says Nathan.

'No. It was just a name that came into my head.' Inside, I'm chastising myself. 'Go on then. What're you teaching?' I bet it's sport or maths.

'Maths.'

'What's five times fifty-two?' I ask quick as a flash, remembering Stevie's quick calculation to my er...

'Two sixty.' Quick. 'I'm a maths teacher, not a mathematician. But simple arithmetic is standard teaching.'

'Don't you have a girlfriend?' Change of direction.

'I was seeing a girl at Uni. I saw lots of girls, you know how it is at Uni,' he says, but I shake my head.

'I've never been to Uni,' I tell him.

'But when we left,' he continues, 'we went our separate ways...' He tails off but then perks up again. 'It's not, like, it's all over and that. We're still in contact with each other like on Facebook and stuff, and seen each other a couple of times since Uni, but we're not, like, going out as such.'

I just raise my head to him, a kind of backward nod, and smile. 'Oh.' *Is he gonna be one to slip the net? I hope not.*

'What do you do then, if you ain't been to Uni?'

'I work in an office.' *Oops. Done it again. Come on, Debbie, you should know better by now; Stevie taught you that.* 'An accounts office, I mean. I travel the country closing deals for a big construction company and arranging the finances and everything.' *That sounded a bit more professional, I think.*

'You're an accountant but don't know five times fifty-two.'

'I'm an accountant, not a mathematician. But, yeah, I know what five times fifty-two is alright.' I put on a serious expression.

'Travelling the country? You mean staying in hotels and that?'

'Top hotels an' all. It's a hectic lifestyle at times, but, like exciting, meeting some interesting people.' I think back to Glasgow and Pauline.

'Don't your boyfriend mind about you working away?' he asks. I stall a bit, thinking about Stevie. Boyfriend? *I'm not sure.* Does he mind? *I don't know.* 'I can see you pondering, hear the cogs turning. Have I hit a nerve?'

Yes. 'No. I, er, don't have a boyfriend. I'm only twenty. There's a big wide world out there,' I say with a sweep of my hand. 'Undiscovered territory.'

'Hmm. And you like exploring?' he asks, and I smile at that.

'And how old are you, Nathan?' See. I'm remembering his name, not like whatshisname the other night.

'I'm twenty-four.'

'And do you like exploring?'

He nods just as I realise my mobile is going off. My heart skips a beat. It's Stevie, it's Stevie, it's Stevie, it's Stevie! Oh my God. He's not here, is he? Not seen me dancing with another guy? No, it's a text from Yasmin. *Am I disappointed or relieved?* I mentally shrug my shoulders.

<small>Hi babe, when the bar closes soon, I'll be straight off. Bring Nathan to my house but don't tell him, it'll be our secret ;-) x x x</small>

'Who was that?' asks Nathan as I put the mobile away. 'Somebody important? Boyfriend?'

'No, er, I don't have a boyfriend. I told you that.'

'Seemed like someone important the way you scrambled to get it. And it was only a text.'

'No. It was just one of my friends, that's all.' *Caught me out a bit there*. I check the time. The bar will be closing soon. Time flies when you're having fun. 'The bar'll be closing in a minute. Come on, buy me another drink; a nightcap. Maybe a cocktail. I'll have sex, er…'

'On the beach?'

'Yeah. But we're a long way from the seaside,' I point out.

We go to the bar, and Nathan orders our drinks just before the bar closes. I see Yasmin about to leave, and I nonchalantly wave as I sip my drink.

Chapter Twenty-Two

The taxi drops me and Nathan off outside Yasmin's house, and I lead him to the door and quite casually into the house. She's left the door unlocked, and once we are inside, I turn and take Nathan in an embrace. 'Do you wanna go straight upstairs?'

He has his arms around me when Yasmin appears. 'Straight upstairs sounds good to me,' she says. *Wow! Is she dressed for the occasion or what?* Never mind how she dresses in BJ's; she's now in a black baby doll that, like, holds no secrets. It ties at the front at the bust and 'exposes' her beautiful torso. And she's wearing a pair of red silk knickers that have a heart-shaped peep-hole on the bum.

She looks at Nathan and takes his hand, having to break up our embrace.

'Oh, hello, again,' says Nathan, looking her up and down. Maybe he's undressing her with his eyes, but there's not much undressing left to do. 'Do you two both live here?'

'No,' I say exactly at the same time as Yasmin says, 'Yes.'

'Told you tonight was your lucky night,' she says, leading us up the stairs.

We get to the bedroom where there is music playing, and Yasmin pulls him into an embrace. He doesn't hold back. His hands are all over her as they snog. Not forgetting me, he breaks the kiss and pulls me into the embrace. Group hug!

I'm fully dressed, but he still lets his hand go exploring, slipping it under my top and seeking out my boobs, caressing me through the silky material of my bra. Oh! I let out a gasp. He's hit the right button there.

Yasmin is working away at taking off his shirt and, breaking up the huddle, she, like, lifts it over his head to reveal his torso. It's, like, good enough to eat. This man really is crumpet.

'Come on, let's have you on the bed. Got your handbag, Debbie?' asks Yasmin as we all clamber onto the bed, us girls lying him on his back. I know what she means about my handbag, and I take out the cuffs. 'You're in the house of erotica. Let us take you on a thrill ride,' she tells him, then handcuffs him to the bed without a struggle.

He lies there, naked from the waist up, totally at our mercy. What a gorgeous body. Nothing is said, but we look at each other with a knowing glint in our eyes, and together we undo his trousers and take them off. Now just in his tight boxers, we can clearly see his cock bursting at the seams. I climb on the bed alongside him and go down on his nipple, licking it and sucking it whilst I finger his other one. I hear the moans of delight coming from the back of his throat in hoarse breaths.

Then Yasmin turns the volume of the music up and begins to dance. In her sexy lingerie she begins to gyrate to the music, pouting her lips, bringing her hands up her thighs, over her body under her baby doll, tantalisingly over her breasts, round the back of her head and running her fingers through her hair, lifting her hair high. It's her lap dancing skills coming into play, and me and Nathan are her front seat audience.

It is so erotic. Now I know what she meant when she told Nathan he was in the house of erotica.

So, I join in. I climb off the bed and begin to dance alongside Yasmin, trying to mirror her moves, but I'm still fully clothed. Yasmin turns to me and, still dancing, her back to Nathan on the bed to give him full view of her heart peep-hole, she begins to undress me.

She starts by rubbing my boobs over my clothes, then brings her hands up inside my top and lifts it off. Then she takes me around the neck and brings my face to hers and we begin to kiss. Our tongues are darting in and out of each other's mouths, so sensuously, all in view of Nathan. Tongues touching, lips gliding, and gentle nibbling of lower lips.

Yasmin's hands are around my back, and in skilled fashion she unclips my bra. She takes the bra right off as she backs away from me, and I perform the same, revealing her wonderful boobs by pulling the bow that holds her baby doll, leaving it to hang open. She shrugs it off, and there we are, both baring our breasts. There is no prompting needed at all, and we begin to caress each other's boobs, all in full view of our 'prisoner'.

I'm not sure how he's taking it, if he's even saying anything at all, because I'm, like, lost in the passion and lust that is surging through me as Yasmin begins to lick my nipples.

She kisses me over my boobs and moves her lips down my body, then she brings her hands up my skirt, raising it as she takes hold of my knickers, pulling them down as she lowers her body in front of me. She then encourages me onto the bed alongside Nathan, finishing the job of removing all my clothes and dropping my skirt onto the floor.

Instinctively, I open my legs and bring up my knees, and Yasmin is down on me, and… and… oh, her tongue is there, right – there! My breathing is heavy, the sensations tingling, powerfully, from down below. Yasmin is, oh, oh. That's so –good! I'm not sure if I am just thinking that or if I am saying it aloud, I am so lost in the moment. Then Yasmin moves away and begins kissing Nathan.

'See how good she tastes,' she tells him between kisses, giving him time to catch his breath. She then gets back to her feet and takes my hand to carry on dancing. I am behind Yasmin, my groin pressed up against her bum, and we're gyrating our bodies to the rhythm. Poor Nathan must have been, like, screaming inside to be released from his manacles and for his cock – so prominently erect inside his boxers – to be freed.

But he seems to be enjoying the show as I put my arms around Yasmin, bring my hands up, caress and squeeze her boobs, and finger her nipples. Her head tips back as she moans with pleasure, so I kiss her neck and lower my hands over her smooth body until I find the silk of her knickers. I run my hands over the material as she arches her back, presenting me with full access as I caress her pleasure pot through the silk.

But why have silk when you can have gold? I slip my hands into the front of her knickers, feeling the hair that frames the jackpot, and soon I have my finger in the opening to her fanny, wet and inviting. Oh! Yasmin is gasping sighs of pleasure as we continue our dance with my hand inside her saucy knickers.

I then take both hands to the hem of her knickers and slowly pull them down her thighs, just as she did with mine. I drop to my knees as I take them over her feet, and with her delicious bum in my face I begin kissing the silky-smooth skin of her cheeks. Then Yasmin turns around and drops to her knees, and we resume kissing, our tongues actively duelling, as we caress each other's boobs and body.

I make to stand up and bring Yasmin with me, practically pushing her onto the bed beside Nathan. I clamber up over her and, taking both her breasts in my hands, I lean down and put my tongue to her nipple, fingering the other. I can hear Yasmin breathing heavily as I continue my manipulation of her nipples. It is so fantastic, giving pleasure in this way, woman to woman. Yasmin is squirming away as I tease and tantalize her, and all thoughts of a boy on the bed are almost forgotten.

But then I reach out to him and feel his chest, running my hand over him in, like, a figure of eight, gently catching his nipples. Moving my hand lower, over his boxers, I can feel his cock bursting for release. But not just yet. I rub my hand over it again and again, running my fingertips along his full length, before I – and I'm sure he – can resist no more. Then I slip my hand inside. By now I'm concentrating on Nathan and have left Yasmin. I'm not really sure what she is up to as I'm so focussed on the matter in hand. Literally.

Slowly, slowly, oh so slowly, I pull his boxers right off, then take hold of him once again. It feels so big because I'm so worked up, though he's probably no more than average. But there's a rocket ready for take-off, and I go down on him, my lips over his tip, just coaxing him with a little movement of my lips, no more than light kissing. My tongue then brushes over the tip of his penis, and I lower my lips further down, tasting his juices that have obviously been teased out of him by my and Yasmin's performance.

Nathan is making sounds of delight with deep breaths as I suck hard on his cock, running my lips up and down, with my tongue flicking over the head. As I caress his balls with delicate fingers, I feel a hand on my head. It must be Nathan's – it's too big to be Yasmin's – and I realise that she has freed his hands. I look up and can see her dancing again, but the hand on the back of my head pushes me back down and I carry on sucking him. Yasmin then joins me, both of us sucking him together, our lips constantly meeting in a kiss around his shaft and over his bell end. Mmm. We take it in turns to fully have him in our mouths while the other caresses his cock with our lips and tongue. I'd love him to come right now, but no, not yet. I want a lot more of him yet. And Yasmin.

'There are two hot babes here, ready for a good fucking,' I hear Yasmin say as she breaks away. 'Which one do you want?'

'Both,' Nathan says between breaths.

'You've only got one cock, so you can't fuck us both at the same time,' she says. 'Let's do it like this,' and she climbs up the bed. 'Get on your knees, Debbie,' she orders me, and I do as I'm told, facing her, my bum in the air. 'Now fuck her,' she tells Nathan, and he comes up behind me, feeling me from behind with his cock, hands all over my bum.

I'm grinning at Yasmin like the proverbial Cheshire cat. And then he's in, oh, yes, yes, he's in, his cock easing between my outer lips. He pushes further, gently sliding his cock inside me. Deep inside. I have a sudden intake of breath. A real gasp of delight. Oh. Oh, yes, yes! That is, like, fantastic! I thrust my bum back at him to get all of him in, right up to the hilt, and feel him pressing his hard cock against the wall of my fan. All the way in. Oh. My. God!

Nathan begins to shag me, his cock deep inside then withdrawing before plunging back in again, again, and again. It feels glorious. And then Yasmin puts her hands on my head and gently coaxes me towards her, her legs wide open, her pleasure pot inviting me down. I reach out with my tongue through gasps of breath as Nathan continues to shag me. Then one big thrust from Nathan pushes me forward right into Yasmin, my face enveloped by her fanny before I can catch my breath. She is so wet, I'm like, mmmm. And I probe with my tongue, licking away frantically, trying to concentrate on the job whilst taking Nathan's full length as I ride with him on my knees. Oh my God! Two exquisite sensations in one!

Yasmin is moaning and squirming under my tongue, Nathan is grunting as he thrusts into me, and I'm having convulsions of pleasure sweeping through me from all directions. I can feel myself beginning to shudder, feeling the rage of an orgasm pulsing its way right through me, down to my fanny, my clitoris penetrated into submission, and, and, oh yes. Yes. Yes!

And all at the same time I can feel Yasmin's legs trembling and begin to thrash around with my hands on the back of her thighs, straightening her legs then raising her knees before straightening them again, and again.

I move away, forcing Nathan to withdraw as I tell him, 'Go on, Nathan. Fuck her. Fuck her while she's hot.' He moves into position and, like, hits the bullseye as Yasmin cries out in ecstasy, in the throes of an orgasm, Nathan catching her at that precise moment, her legs wildly thrashing around.

'Ah! Ah!' she screams out, her orgasm's release building to a crescendo under Nathan's power. She shifts and makes his cock slip out so that she can squirt out her orgasm. God, I wish I could orgasm like Yasmin. I squirt a little, probably no more than a dribble, but she just explodes.

Then Nathan is back inside her thrusting away, but again she makes his cock slip out, and with another squeal of delight she 'splashes' again. This happens a couple more times before he pulls out again and starts coming, shooting his load all over her belly. Yasmin looks down 'No! Not yet,' she panics, brushing his semen as if trying to push it back into his cock.

I take hold of Nathan's cock, still in the throes of his ejaculation, and prod her clitoris with the tip of his cock, and whoosh! She comes again with another squeal of ecstasy as their juices mingle together, soaking us all. I continue prodding her while Nathan's cock is still hard in my hand, squeezing out the last dregs of his cum, and once again Yasmin squeals her way to another orgasm. It's like shaking the prosecco bottle and this time the cork comes out.

By now, Nathan has stopped coming, and I let go of him as he rolls over onto his back, exhausted, all of us covered in each other's bodily fluids. I sneak in close to Yasmin and whisper, 'An orgasm. With a man. I told you it was all about the cock.'

She turns to me and smiles brightly, a grin right across her face. Then she turns to look at Nathan, puts her hand on his chest, and goes 'Thank you.' She kisses his torso and moves her hand down to take hold of his cock, still fully erect, smothered in the juices of all three of us. Then lowering her head, she kisses the tip of his cock and says, 'Thank you. Thank you.'

She lies there, her head on his torso, his cock in her hand, gently rubbing it with her thumb in appreciation, as I bring my body right up behind hers in a group hug. *Heaven*.

Chapter Twenty-Three

'I really love it that you wanted to see me after your works party,' I say again. 'It's very affectionate.' I hug Stevie's arm and give him my best Debbie smile.

He puts his arm around my shoulders and kisses my head. I don't attempt to advance any further kissing; I'm just happy to be with him like this. My mobile buzzes in my bag and I reluctantly break off the embrace to look at it.

'It's from Haze,' I tell Stevie. 'Says she had a great night.'

'Oh yeah? In what way?'

I hit the call button, shake my head to move my hair back, and put the phone to my ear. Haze answers very quickly. 'Hi, babes,' she says.

'I've heard about some of your adventures last night, you must tell me more.

'Oh, lover boy. What a hero. He rescued me last night from some guy trying to hit me,' she begins.

'I know. I heard.'

'And then he took me to Evolution, and we met this guy. And, like, wow! He thought lover boy was my dad.' She laughs.

'Stevie. His name's Stevie.'

'Steven,' pipes up Stevie. I wave him away. *Whatever.*

'So, this guy you met...' I begin.

'He's a bit of beef ok. He, like, drives a Porsche and has a high-powered job in a bank. Only twenty-four, and I'm seeing him again tonight. Called Peter.'

'A Porsche? Fantastic.' I'm impressed.

'He wined me, dined me, sixty-nined me.' I could feel the excitement in her voice.

'Dined you?'

'Well, I had plenty of that beef,' we laugh together, 'and a very large portion of pork. We went back to my place, and we snogged for ages. He couldn't keep his hands off me. He said it was my dress that was turning him on.'

Oh, yes. That dress. I roll my eyes.

'He kept calling me Hazel all night. That was lover boy's fault,' she continues, telling me all the dirty details.

'Hmm-mm.' I'm nodding on the phone. Stevie has got up and moved away – I'm not sure where – as Haze continues. 'Sounds fantastic,' I say.

And then she adds more, just to put the icing on the cake. 'He tells me he's a semi-professional footballer. And he certainly knows how to, like, use his athleticism.'

I think about Stevie and his athleticism, and how I might get to live out my fantasy. Or is that wishful thinking? Just as I'm daydreaming, she breaks the silence. 'I'm in heaven. I'm in love.'

'I'll have to meet him if you're going out with him again,' I try to sound off-hand, but I'm actually keen to meet him.

Then Haze adds, 'Remember, he's all mine.' She sounds just like me.

'That's what I say about Stevie.'

'Yeah. You've got lover boy. I've got the footballer. I'm a WAG.'

After the conversation finishes and I hang up, Stevie comes back into the lounge with our biker jackets. 'Well, Stevie. I think I need to go out and, like, buy a hat. And you need to get your best suit out so that you can give her away... Daddy.'

'Oh, good. He did me a favour getting her off my back – literally. And she's seeing him again? Not one of the two-hundred-and-sixty one-night stands then?' *I think he is being sarcastic. I think.*

*

We speed through the countryside on Stevie's Harley for another exciting ride, and I have the chance to hang onto him as I ride pillion. We stop at a country park, and after buying some tea and cakes from the cafe, we go and sit on the grass in the lovely warm July sunshine. Stevie has actually brought a blanket.

'How sweet it is,' Stevie basks in the sun as we sit on our jackets. 'This is the life.'

'So, what you gonna be up to through the school holidays?' I ask him.

'Dunno,' he replies, shrugging his shoulders. 'Perhaps tidy up the garden. Bit of bike riding.' He shrugs again. 'It's a long time to have off when you're on your own.'

'But you've got me now. There's no need for you to be on your own. I could book some time off work, you could take me to Italy or somewhere,' I say with a smile. He smiles back, but his smile is a conundrum to what he's thinking, and I can't work it out.

'I love being with you.' I put my arm through his and rest my chin on his shoulder. 'You just make everything so wonderful. My life was in a regular cycle till you came along…'

'I love spending time with you.' At least I think that's what he says, through a mouthful of cake. He drinks some more of his tea and lies back with his hands behind his head. 'Ah,' he exhales, enjoying the moment and soaking up the sunshine.

SUGAR DADDY?

He leaves a small amount of his cake on the paper plate – a piece with a large chunk of chocolate on it. I look at it, then look at him looking at me looking at his cake. He gives me a 'don't you dare' stare, and I grab the piece of cake and quickly put it in my mouth with a grin. He sits up. 'Hey!' He rolls over, grabs hold of me and puts his mouth against mine in a half kiss, half trying to recover his cake, and we roll over in the grass together.

The kissing part becomes a little more intense, And we roll over so that I end up on top. I pin him down, his arms above his head, sitting over him and looking down at him. *Wow, he's so sexy.* 'Now I've got you where I want you.' I lean forward once I've swallowed the cake and we kiss, lingeringly, again.

The kiss lasts a few moments and then we break off, but it was blissful. It was not the sort of kissing I usually do; more of a loving kiss. 'That's better,' I say.

'Yes,' he agrees. 'Totally against my nature, against all my instincts.'

Oh, here we go again. Kill the moment, why don't you? He is so frustrating at times. I sit up straight, still straddling him. I can feel the makings of a hard on under his jeans.

I run my fingers through my hair and look down at him in despair. 'Screw your fucking instincts!' I say in desperation. 'It does my head in. Can't you see I love you?' *There. I've said it now.*

Stevie sits bolt up. I know I just pinned him down, but he's obviously a lot stronger than me. As he sits up, he nearly throws me off him before he takes hold of my shoulders to hold me down. It repositions his semi-hard on, but I can still feel it growing against my bum. Either that or he is a very big boy. No, he is really perking up.

It's maybe got something to do with my strappy red top with my black bra visible over the hem. *God, I'm sexy.* Sitting like this we are at head level, and he looks me straight in the eye.

He sighs and lets his shoulders drop before speaking. 'You know the difficulties I had when I was a teenager, and how I eventually lost my virginity. I loved my Debs, er, my wife. The only woman I've ever loved. And now she's gone, I'm twenty, nearly thirty years older, and gotta start all over again. I'm still young. I'm not after a quick fix. I want friendship, companionship; sex again. Love,' he says.

'You had a quick fix with my mum,' I remind him.

'Yeah. Point taken. But that was probably just an outpouring of pent-up emotion. For both of us. Probably, in my case, partly brought on by you. But it's not easy starting from scratch when it was never easy first time around. And then the girl I meet is only twenty years old, a thousand more times sexually experienced than me, and now she tells me she loves me.

'And what if I tell her that I love her, too, eh? I'm nearly fifty. In just over two years I will be, and you'll still be early twenties. In ten years' time when I'm sixty, you'll still only be just thirty. What then? I won't be able to give you children, and there's boys out there that can. And I don't want any more heartache.'

He goes on, 'I've said before, I love being with you. Why do you think I came looking for you last night? That's my friendship, my companionship. Your mum is lovely, and I admit I went to bed with her probably to satisfy an urge that you've brought on. That's why we agreed to leave it, because it would be too awkward to carry on, stuck in the middle of a love triangle. But if I had sex with you, it'd probably be the tipping point of falling in love with you. And is that what we want?'

He gulps. 'It's too late now. Screw my fucking instincts. I *am* in love with you. You're beautiful, sexy, and most of all, fun to be with. There's only one step left to take. I think it's going to happen. But I'm just scared.'

I look into his eyes and see the pain of a man who looks lost and out of his depth. I put my hands behind his head, entwining my fingers in his hair, pull him to me and kiss him. A real lovers' kiss, long and slow. He falls back on the blanket, and despite his arms being around me, we collapse, breaking the embrace. It's accidental, and we both fall about laughing.

We roll about in the grass, kissing again and again. I could rip his clothes off right here and now and make mad passionate love to him here on the grass. I don't care that there are lots of people about enjoying a summer Saturday afternoon. I said before I can think of better ways of spending my time on a Saturday afternoon than worrying about sport.

I can still feel his erection, and I put my hand on it and rub it through his jeans. 'I think it's going to happen,' I say.

*

The ride back to Stevie's house through the countryside is as thrilling as ever, probably because I am full of excitement and expectation. I think Stevie is, too. As we hit town and slow for the urban roads, it is something of a come down. We pull up outside his house, and I get off the bike to open the gate as he pulls the Harley onto the drive.

'Ok?' he asks through the intercom in our helmets. I take my helmet off and shake my hair down, running my fingers through it.

'Yes. I love it,' I say, unzipping the leather jacket to reveal my sexy body beneath. And I see him looking.

Stevie still has his helmet on, yet I put my face up to it and kiss the visor as if I am kissing him. 'Thank you.'

He doesn't put the Harley in the garage, just leaves it on the drive next to his car. He doesn't take off his helmet or jacket till we are indoors. I think he is in just as much a hurry as I am.

Once we are both free of the warm bike clothing, I go up to him in the hallway and put my arms around his waist. I look into his eyes as he leans down, and we kiss, passionately, his arms around my neck and shoulders.

I lower one hand, momentarily breaking the kiss. 'Where were we?' I keep lowering my hand until I reach his groin and run my hand over his cock. He doesn't have his hard on, but it is stirring once again. 'That's it, I remember.'

He breathes heavier as I do this, and he deepens our kiss, his hand behind my head pulling me closer. His hand runs through my hair, gently pulling it, his other hand on the middle of my back, lowering down to find my bum. Then his hand in my hair comes down and around my front, and he squeezes my breast. I exhale a sigh of pleasure at his touch.

'Let's go upstairs,' he suggests, and I take him by the hand, even though it's his house, leading him up to his bedroom. *This is it.*

This is the moment I've waited for. And not just for Stevie, but for the first time in all the shags I've ever had, this is going to be the first time I have *made love*. It crossed my mind back at the park about making mad, passionate love, and now this is it.

I open the door and go in first, still holding Stevie's hand. He comes in behind me and I let him pass, turn back, and close the door.

Epilogue

Just over twelve years later…

God, I'm sexy.

Me. Debbie Wilson, age thirty-two, size fourteen and, like, dead sexy.

Was Wilson, anyway, and learning karate helped me drop a dress size. I'm a green belt with dash, because I've got a good teacher – sensei.

Just a touch-up of lippy and I'm ready to party. 'Cause, like, tonight is the sixtieth birthday celebration of my stepfather. Stevie.

I leave the ladies loo and go out into the party room where things are in full swing. There's Mum dancing away with some of the guests. She's revelling in the glory of her handsome husband. He may be sixty, but he's still fit, handsome, and drop dead gorgeous… although he's, like, a bit greyer these days.

There's also Yasmin with her husband, Nathan, and their four kids. Yes, Nathan. The schoolteacher that captured Yasmin's heart that night I remember, when we seduced him together. What a night that was.

Her kids are gorgeous: the oldest, Joshua, is nearly eleven; the youngest, Daisy, barely eleven months. And Lilly and Alfie, too. And, of course, I'm the bestest auntie ever. And there's my husband, Jordan, with our daughter, who's just turned three.

But how did we get here? Twelve years ago, I fell in love with the man we are celebrating tonight. It was a time when my whole world got, like, completely turned upside down. I remember that time back in his bedroom…

*

I close the door behind us, even though there is no one else in the house. And as I turn back to Stevie, he is ready with open arms for me to fall into. Without hesitation we are wrapped up in each other and our mouths engage in full lust-led passion. We've kissed before now and snogged on a number of occasions, but nothing as passionate or enticing or erotic as this.

We fall onto the bed, kissing, and Stevie bites my lip and caresses my tongue with his, pulling at my hair as I run my fingers through his, both of us trying to pull off each other's clothes.

My top is buttoned down the front, and in my rush to get it off, I ping a button. Stevie's hands are on my boobs in an instant, and I can feel that hard on once again coming to life. I start to undo his belt and trousers and pull them down, then get my fingers in the elastic of his pants and pull them down, too. And there is my Holy Grail.

Just a gentle touch of my fingers is all that's needed to help finish off his erection. He has pre-cum on it, probably due to the anticipation of what is about to happen, and I can feel the same down in my knickers.

I rub my thumb in the wet and all over the head of his cock. Then I am down on it, my lips gently covering him, the taste of his pre-cum like nectar. I am really working hard, loving every delicious second of it, gripping him with my hand and then onto his balls. (Ball. He really does have only one testicle.) I lick my way down his cock to his single ball and give the lightest, featherlight flicks with my tongue.

Then just as I am going back to sucking him, he puts a hand under my chin and gently lifts my head.

Looking straight into his eyes, I am just about to say something – like, was he enjoying it? – when he totally takes me off guard. 'Stop.'

'What's up, Stevie?' I ask. I can see despair in his expression. 'Did I hurt you holding your balls?'

'No. It was nice. But I can't... I just can't...'

'But you're doing fine, look. Your cock is hard as iron, and wet. Everything is going well. I can't wait to get my knickers off and have you inside me. I'm absolutely dripping down there.' I sit up and start to take down my knickers, but he puts a hand on my arm and stops me.

'No. Don't do that.'

'But...' I'm a little bit speechless. *Is he not gonna go through with it?* 'A small amount of the fluid from inside your body is now inside mine. We can't stop now; I want to have it all.'

'I can't do it, Debbie. I'm sorry, I just can't. I'm forty-eight before the end of the summer, and you're just twenty. Then when summer's over and I'm back at the school, and there's all those schoolgirls, I'm just gonna feel guilty, like I've broken the unwritten code. I can't do it,' he repeats.

I'm stunned. It's like I've been shot with a taser. But rather than fight him, I sit up, straighten my underwear, and look down on him still lying there. 'Ok. Ok, I respect what you're saying. I understand how you feel. I've shagged boys younger than me; I've shagged men older than you. But if you don't wanna do it, I'm fine,' I lie through my back teeth. I'll have spots all over my tongue tomorrow.

'It would be better if you left. Please, put your clothes back on and go. For both our sakes.'

I pick up my bra and put it on. Stevie gets up off the bed, his hard on long gone, and puts his pants back on. I put on my blouse top – bugger, there is a button gone. 'I love you, Stevie,' I say, almost in desperation and with a lump in my throat trying to hold back the tears.

'I love you, too, Debbie. But it's not right. It'll only end in tears.' I can tell he is choking up too.

But I'm not gonna cry in front of him. It's his choice. I don't like it but I have to accept it. I leave.

*

I didn't cry over it. The tears were trying to come but I fought them back. But I did sulk. For, like, a couple of weeks, I stopped going out with Haze and Jules at the weekend. I stopped going to BJ's to see Yasmin, and I even had a couple of days off work. I told Mum all about it, and she was very comforting and sympathetic.

But then right out of the blue, Stevie knocked on our door. It was Mum that answered the door, and she squealed with delight. 'Come here,' she said, and threw her arms around him in a big bear hug.

'Who is it, Mum?' I called from the lounge.

'Come and see,' she invited. So, I went out to the hallway, and there was Stevie. I was stunned. Delighted, I ran up to him and put my arms around his neck then pulled him into a long, lingering kiss.

We all sat in the lounge and Mum made some tea. He told us that he'd missed us but didn't want to bother us or cause any discomfort by opening up some wounds. But he told us that Yasmin had been to see him 'cause she was worried that I hadn't been to AJ's at all, and that my only response to her texts had been short, briefly telling her that Stevie had left me. She had actually persuaded him to go on a date with her.

After he'd initially said no, she'd convinced him by saying, and I quote Stevie, 'How about a nice Italian with a bottle of Pinot Grigio to share? Or there's a Rolling Stones tribute at the local theatre.' But she was doing it for me, to find out what was wrong and, like, see if she could get him to at least see me again.

And it worked.

The conversation between the three of us went on long enough for us to order in pizza and have supper together. I told him that I understood about his emotions, and although I was glad we had made up, I wouldn't be pursuing any sort of relationship with him. Mum had already told me that she missed him too, and regretted their agreement not to make a go of things.

So, I told them that I would 'allow' them to date each other. And they did... and ultimately, he proposed and they got married.

In the meantime, Pauline got in touch with me and, like, took me shopping before going back to a fancy hotel for a gourmet dinner, finished off by another threesome with a guy she'd chatted up in the shoe shop in the retail village with all the designer shops. I hadn't gone that long without having sex since I was a virgin, but that got me back to being the old Debbie again.

And then I met Jordan.

He is of my generation, and he stole my heart just the way Stevie did. And having learned how to actually fall and be in love with one person, I proposed to him on the twenty-ninth of February, after a couple of years' dating. We now have a lovely daughter called Bella, which means beautiful in Italian. Oh, *si. Ora posso parlare Italiano.* I had a good teacher. *Insegnante.*

I wanted to call our daughter Yasmin, but common sense got the better of me.

Yasmin started dating Nathan – they'd kept in touch after that night of lust and passion – and they ultimately fell in love. After they'd had two kids, they got married, before having two more.

I was bridesmaid at Yasmin and Nathan's wedding, but at Mum and Stevie's I gave Mum away. It also meant I had to do a speech. It went something like this:

*

'This is the part in the celebrations where traditionally the bride's father stands up and, like, tells us stories about his little girl and, like, the things she got up to in her childhood and stuff, and how she looks so beautiful today and, like, the groom is a lucky man. Well, that's what I'm gonna do now. My mum *is* beautiful, not just in the way she looks but also what's inside; in that heart of hers.

'I never really had a father, just Mum. Me and Mum were our family. She was my mum *and* dad, and she brought me up on her own. But as I got older, I began to find my own way, and one day I bumped into a man and O.M.G!' I said, waving my hands as if to fan my face. It got a ripple of laughter. 'He was a lot older than me but, like, talk about gorgeous. Like, real male crumpet… and we started to, like, date each other, just going out, sometimes doing my thing like clubbing, and sometimes doing his thing like motorbiking. He was my sugar daddy.

'Then he and Mum met and hit it off straight away. They were the same age, so who was I to stand in their way? Mum and Stevie naturally fell in love, two beautiful people sharing their lives and passions till one day he asked her to marry him. I don't know who was more excited when they told me the news – me or Mum.' A little more laughter. 'Because I was in a win-win situation. A former boyfriend who I loved would be part of my life forever, and I still love him, even more now, because my sugar daddy is now my stepdaddy. Not Stevie anymore, but Daddy. After all this time of not having a proper father, I've now got the best daddy in the world.' A few ahh's from the audience.

'I'm not jealous of Mum for marrying the man who was the man of my dreams, because she has now married the man of *her* dreams. It has taken a long time for her to find him and, like, thanks to me for that. But thanks to my mum for marrying him, 'cause I couldn't be happier: for myself, for Daddy and, like, most importantly, for Mum.

'Please raise your glasses for Jackie and Steven, the bride and groom.'